Alice Oseman was born in 1994 in Kent, England. She completed a degree in English at Durham University in 2016 and is currently a full-time writer and illustrator. Alice can usually be found staring aimlessly at computer screens, questioning the meaninglessness of existence, or doing anything and everything to avoid getting an office job. Alice's first book, *Solitaire*, was published when she was nineteen.

Follow Alice Oseman on Twitter and Instagram:
@AliceOseman

Books by Alice Oseman

SOLITAIRE
RADIO SILENCE
I WAS BORN FOR THIS
LOVELESS
WINNER OF THE YA BOOK PRIZE 2021

Novellas by Alice Oseman

NICK AND CHARLIE
THIS WINTER

Graphic novels by Alice Oseman

HEARTSTOPPER VOLUME 1
HEARTSTOPPER VOLUME 2
HEARTSTOPPER VOLUME 3
HEARTSTOPPER VOLUME 4

Radio Silence

Alice Oseman

HarperCollins *Children's Books*

First published in Great Britain by
HarperCollins *Children's Books* in 2016
Published in this edition in 2018
HarperCollins *Children's Books* is a division of HarperCollins*Publishers* Ltd
1 London Bridge Street
London SE1 9GF

www.harpercollins.co.uk
2 4 6 8 10 9 7 5 3

HarperCollins*Publishers*
1st Floor, Watermarque Building, Ringsend Road
Dublin 4, Ireland

ISBN 978–0–00–755924–4

CHILDREN'S FICTION

Alice Oseman asserts the moral right to be identified as the author of the work.

Typeset in Bembo 11pt by Palimpsest Book Production Limited,
Falkirk, Stirlingshire
Printed and bound in India by Thomson Press India Ltd

School sucks.
Why oh why is there work? I don't— I don't get it.
Mm.
Look at me. Look at my face.
Does it look like I care about school?
No.

'lonely boy goes to a rave', Teen Suicide

UNIVERSE CITY: Ep. 1 – dark blue
UniverseCity

In Distress. Stuck in Universe City. Send Help.

Scroll down for transcript >>>

Hello.

I hope somebody is listening.

I'm sending out this call via radio signal – long out-dated, I know, but perhaps one of the few methods of communication the City has forgotten to monitor – in a dark and *desperate* cry for help.

Things in Universe City are not what they seem.

I cannot tell you who I am. Please call me… please just call me Radio. Radio *Silence*. I am, after all, only a voice on a radio, and there may not be anyone listening.

I wonder – if nobody is listening to my voice, am I making any sound at all?

[…]

FUTURES

"Can you hear that?" said Carys Last, halting in front of me so suddenly that I almost crashed into her. We both stood on the train platform. We were fifteen and we were friends.

"What?" I said, because I couldn't hear anything except the music I was listening to through one earphone. I think it might have been Animal Collective.

Carys laughed, which didn't happen very often. "You're playing your music too loud," she said, hooking a finger around the earphone's wire and pulling it away from me. "Listen."

We stood still and listened and I remember every single thing I heard in that moment. I heard the rumbling of the train we'd just got off leaving the station, heading farther into town. I heard the ticket gate guard explaining to an old man that the high-speed train to St Pancras was cancelled today due to the snow. I heard the distant screech of traffic, the wind above our heads, the flush of the station toilet and "*The train now arriving at – Platform One – is the – 8.02 – to – Ramsgate,*" snow being shovelled and a fire engine and Carys's voice and...

Burning.

We turned round and stared at the town beyond, snowy and dead. We could normally see our school from here, but today there was a cloud of smoke in the way.

"How did we not see the smoke while we were on the train?" Carys asked.

"I was asleep," I said.

"I wasn't."

"You weren't paying attention."

"Well, I guess the school burned down," she said, and walked away to sit on the station bench. "Seven-year-old Carys's wish came true."

I stared for a moment more, and then went to join her.

"D'you think it was those pranksters?" I said, referring to the anonymous bloggers who had been pranking our school for the past month with increasing ferocity.

Carys shrugged. "Doesn't really matter, does it? The end result is the same."

"It does matter." It was at that moment that it all started to sink in. "It's— it looks really serious. We're going to have to change schools. It looks like the whole of C block and D block are… just… gone." I crumpled my skirt in my hands. "My locker was in D block. My GCSE sketchbook was in there. I spent days on some of that stuff."

"Oh, shit."

I shivered. "Why would they do this? They've destroyed so much hard work. They've messed up so many people's GCSEs and A levels, things that seriously affect people's futures. They've literally ruined people's lives."

Carys seemed to think about it, and then opened her mouth to reply, but ended up closing it again, and not saying anything.

1. SUMMER TERM
a)

I WAS CLEVER

"We care about our students' happiness and we *care* about their success," said our head teacher, Dr Afolayan, in front of 400 parents and sixth formers on my Year 12 summer term parents evening. I was seventeen and head girl, and I was sitting backstage because it was my turn to speak on stage in two minutes. I hadn't planned a speech and I wasn't nervous. I was very pleased with myself.

"We consider it our *duty* to give our young people access to the greatest opportunities on offer in the world today."

I'd managed to become head girl last year because my campaign poster was a picture of me with a double chin. Also, I'd used the word 'meme' in my election speech. This expressed the idea that I didn't give a shit about the election, even though the opposite was true, and it made people want to vote for me. You can't say I don't know my audience.

Despite this, I wasn't quite sure what I was going to talk about in my parents evening speech. Afolayan was saying everything I'd scribbled down on the club-night flyer I found in my blazer pocket five minutes ago.

"Our Oxbridge programme has been particularly successful this year—"

I crumpled up the flyer and dropped it on the floor. Improvisation it was.

I'd improvised speeches before so it wasn't a big deal, and nobody could ever tell they were improvised anyway; nobody ever even *wondered* whether they were. I had a reputation for being organised, always doing homework, having consistently high grades and having Cambridge University ambitions. My teachers loved me and my peers envied me.

I was clever.

I was the top student in my year.

I was going to Cambridge, and I was going to get a good job and earn lots of money, and I was going to be happy.

"And I think," said Dr Afolayan, "that the teaching staff deserve a round of applause as well for all the hard work they've put in this year."

The audience clapped, but I saw a few students roll their eyes.

"And now I'd like to introduce our head girl, Frances Janvier."

She pronounced my surname wrong. I could see Daniel Jun, the head boy, watching me from the opposite side of the stage. Daniel hated me because we were both ruthless study machines.

"Frances has been a consistent high achiever since she joined us a few years ago, and it's my absolute honour to have her representing everything we stand for here at the Academy. She'll be talking to you today about her experience as an Academy sixth former this year, and her own plans for the future."

I stood up and walked on stage and I smiled and I felt fine because I was born for this.

THE NARRATOR

"You're not going to improvise again, are you, Frances?" asked Mum, fifteen minutes previously. "Last time you ended your speech by giving everyone a thumbs-up."

She'd been standing with me in the corridor outside the stage entrance.

My mum always loved parents evening, mostly because she loves the brief, confused stares people make when she introduces herself as my mother. These occur because I'm mixed-race and she's white, and for some reason most people think I'm Spanish because I did Spanish GCSE last year with a private tutor.

She also loved listening to teachers telling her over and over again what an excellent person I was.

I waved the club flyer at her. "Excuse me. I'm extremely prepared."

Mum plucked it out of my hand and scanned it. "There are literally three bullet points on this. One of them says 'mention the Internet'."

"That's all I need. I'm well-practised in the art of bullshitting."

"Oh, I know you are." Mum handed me back the flyer and

leaned against the wall. "We could just do without another incident where you spend three minutes talking about *Game of Thrones*."

"You're never going to let me live that down, are you?"

"No."

I shrugged. "I've got all the main points covered. I'm clever, I'm going to university, blah blah blah grades success happiness. I'm fine."

Sometimes I felt like that was all I ever talked about. Being clever was, after all, my primary source of self-esteem. I'm a very sad person, in all senses of the word, but at least I was going to get into university.

Mum raised an eyebrow at me. "You're making me nervous."

I tried to stop thinking about it and instead thought about my evening plans.

That evening I was going to get home and I was going to make a coffee and have a slice of cake and then I was going to go upstairs and sit on my bed and listen to the latest episode of *Universe City*. *Universe City* was a YouTube podcast show about a suit-wearing student detective looking for a way to escape a sci-fi, monster-infested university. Nobody knew who made the podcast, but it was the voice of the narrator that got me addicted to the show – it has a kind of softness. It makes you want to fall asleep. In the least weird way possible, it's a bit like someone stroking your hair.

That was what I was going to do when I got home.

"You sure you're going to be okay?" Mum asked, looking down at me. She always asked me that before I had to do public speaking, which was frequently.

"I'm going to be okay."

She untwisted my blazer collar and tapped my silver head girl badge with one finger.

She asked me, "Remind me why you wanted to be head girl?"

And I said, "Because I'm great at it," but I was thinking, *because universities love it.*

DYING, BUT IN A GOOD WAY

I said my piece and got off stage and checked my phone, because I hadn't checked it all afternoon. And that's when I saw it. I saw the Twitter message that was about to change my life, possibly forever.

I made a startled coughing noise, sank into a plastic chair, and grabbed Head Boy Daniel Jun's arm so hard that he hissed, "Ow! What?"

"Something monumental has happened to me on Twitter."

Daniel, who had seemed vaguely interested until I said the word 'Twitter', frowned and wrenched his arm back. He wrinkled his nose and looked away like I'd done something extremely embarrassing.

The main thing that you need to know about Daniel Jun is that he probably would have killed himself if he thought it'd get him better grades. To most people, we were exactly the same person. We were both smart and we were both going for Cambridge and that was all anybody saw: two shining gods of academia flying high above the school building.

The difference between us was that I found our 'rivalry' absolutely hilarious, whereas Daniel acted as if we were engaged in a war of who could be the biggest nerd.

Anyway.

Two monumental things had happened, actually. The first was this:

@UniverseCity is now following you

And the second was a direct message addressed to 'Toulouse', my online alias:

Direct Messages > **with Radio**

hi toulouse! this might sound really weird but i've seen some of the Universe City fan art you've posted and i love them so much

i wondered whether you'd be interested in working with the show to create visuals for the Universe City episodes?

i've been trying to find someone with the right style for the show and i really love yours.

Universe City is non-profit so i can't exactly pay you so i totally understand if you want to say no, but you seem like you really love

the show and i wondered if you'd be interested. you'd get full credit obviously. i honestly wish i could pay you but i don't have any money

(i'm a student). yeah. let me know if you're interested at all. if not, i still love your drawings. like, a lot. ok.

radio x

"Go on then," said Daniel, with an eye-roll. "What's happened?"

"Something monumental," I whispered.

"Yes, I got that."

It struck me suddenly that there was absolutely no way I could tell anybody about this. They probably didn't even know what *Universe City* was and fan art was a weird hobby anyway and they might think that I was secretly drawing porn or something and they'd all hunt down my Tumblr and read all my personal posts on there and everything would be awful. School Brainiac and Head Girl Frances Janvier Exposed as Fandom Freak.

I cleared my throat. "Erm… you wouldn't be interested. Don't worry."

"Fine then." Daniel shook his head and turned away.

Universe City. Had chosen. Me. To be. Their artist.

I felt like dying, but in a good way.

"Frances?" said a very quiet voice. "Are you okay?"

I looked up to find myself face to face with Aled Last, Daniel's best friend.

Aled Last always looked a little like a child who'd lost their mum in a supermarket. This was possibly something to do with how young he looked, how round his eyes were, and how his hair was soft like baby hair. He never seemed to be comfortable in any of the clothes that he wore.

He didn't go to our school – he went to an all-boys' grammar school on the other side of town, and though he was only three months older than me, he was in the school year above. Most people knew who he was because of Daniel. I knew who he was because he lived opposite me and I used to be friends with his twin sister and we took the same train to school, even though we sat in different carriages and didn't talk to each other.

Aled Last was standing next to Daniel, gazing down at where

I was still sitting, hyperventilating, in the chair. He cringed a little and followed up with, "Er, sorry, erm, I mean, you just looked like you were about to be sick or something."

I attempted to say a sentence without bursting into hysterical laughter.

"I am fine," I said, but I was grinning and probably looked like I was about to murder someone. "Why are you here? Daniel Support?"

According to rumour, Aled and Daniel had been inseparable their whole lives, despite the fact that Daniel was an uppity, opinionated dickhead and Aled spoke maybe fifty words per day.

"Er, no," he said, his voice almost too quiet to hear, as usual. He looked terrified. "Dr Afolayan wanted me to give a speech. About university."

I stared at him. "But you don't even go to our school."

"Er, no."

"So what's up with that?"

"It was Mr Shannon's idea." Mr Shannon was the head teacher of Aled's school. "Something about camaraderie between our schools. One of my friends was supposed to be doing this actually... he was head boy last year... but he's busy so... he asked if I'd do it... yeah."

Aled's voice got gradually quieter as he was speaking, almost like he didn't think I was listening to him, despite the fact that I was looking right at him.

"And you said yes?" I said.

"Yes."

"*Why?*"

Aled just laughed.

He was visibly quaking.

"Because he's a turnip," said Daniel, folding his arms.

"Yes," Aled murmured, but he was smiling.

"You don't have to do it," I said. "I could just tell them you're sick and everything will be fine."

"I sort of have to do it," he said.

"You don't really have to do anything you don't want to," I said, but I knew that wasn't true, and so did Aled, because he just laughed at me and shook his head.

We didn't say anything else.

Afolayan was on stage again. "And now I'd like to welcome Aled Last, one of the boys' school's *wonderful* Year 13s, who will be setting off to one of the UK's most prestigious universities in September. Well, if his A levels go to plan, anyway!"

All the parents laughed at this. Daniel and Aled and I did not.

Afolayan and the parents started to clap as Aled walked on to the stage. He approached the microphone. I'd done it a thousand times and I always got that little stomach flip beforehand, but watching Aled do it then was somehow three billion times worse.

I hadn't really spoken to Aled properly before. He caught the same train to school as me, but he sat in a different carriage. I knew next to nothing about him.

"Er, hi, yeah," he said. His voice sounded like he'd just stopped crying.

"I didn't realise he was this shy," I whispered at Daniel, but Daniel didn't say anything.

"So, last year I, er, had an interview…"

Daniel and I watched him struggle through his speech. Daniel, a practised public speaker like myself, occasionally shook his head. At one point he said, "He should have said no, for fuck's sake." I didn't really like watching so I sat back in the chair for the second half of it and read the Twitter message fifty times over. I tried to switch my mind off and focus on *Universe City* and the messages.

Radio had liked my art. Stupid little sketches of the characters, weird line drawings, 3am doodles in my 99p sketchbook instead of finishing my history essay. Nothing like this had happened to me, ever.

When Aled walked off stage and joined us again I said, "Well done, that was really good!" even though we both knew I was lying again.

He met my eyes. His had dark blue circles under them. Maybe he was a night owl like me.

"Thanks," he said, and then he walked away, and I thought that'd probably be the last time I ever saw him.

DO WHAT YOU WANT

Mum barely had time to say "nice speech" once I met her at our car, before I was telling her all about *Universe City*. I once tried to get Mum into *Universe City* by forcing her to listen to the first five episodes on our way to a Cornwall holiday, but Mum's conclusion was, "I don't really get it. Is it supposed to be funny or scary? Wait, is Radio Silence a girl or a boy or neither? Why do they never go to their university lectures?" I thought that was fair enough. At least she still watched *Glee* with me.

"Are you sure this isn't some sort of giant scam?" said Mum with a frown as we drove away from the Academy. I lifted my feet up on to the seat. "It sounds a bit like they're trying to steal your art if they're not even going to pay you."

"It was their official Twitter. They're verified," I said, but this didn't quite have the same effect on Mum as it did on me. "They liked my art so much that they're actually asking me to join their team!"

Mum said nothing. She raised her eyebrows.

"Please be happy for me," I said, rolling my head towards her.

"It's really good! It's brilliant! I just don't want people to steal your sketches. You love that stuff."

"I don't think it's stealing! They'd give me all the credit."

"Have you signed a contract?"

"*Mum!*" I groaned exasperatedly. There wasn't much point trying to explain this to her. "It doesn't matter, I'm gonna have to say no anyway."

"Wait, what? What d'you mean?"

I shrugged. "I'm just not gonna have time. I'll be in Year 13 in a few months, like, I've got so much work *all the time*, and Cambridge interview prep on top of that... there's no way I'd have time to draw something for every single weekly episode."

Mum frowned. "I don't understand. I thought you were really excited about this."

"I *am,* like, it's so amazing that they messaged me and thought my art was good, but... I have to be realistic—"

"You know, opportunities like this don't come around very often," Mum said. "And you clearly want to do it."

"Well, yeah, but... I get so much homework every day, and coursework and revision will only get more intense—"

"I think you should do it." Mum stared straight ahead and spun the steering wheel. "I think you work yourself too hard for school anyway and you should take an opportunity for once and do what you want."

And what I wanted to do was this:

Direct Messages > with Radio

> Hey!! Wow... thank you so much, I can't believe you liked my art! I'd be absolutely honoured to get involved!

My email is touloser@gmail.com if it's easier to talk there. Can't wait to hear more about what you're thinking in terms of design!

Honestly, Universe City is my favourite series of all time. I can't thank you enough for thinking of me!!

Hope I don't sound too much like a crazy fan haha! xx

I ALWAYS WISHED I
HAD A HOBBY

I had work to do when I got home. I almost always had work to do when I got home. I almost always *did* work when I got home because whenever I wasn't doing schoolwork I felt like I was wasting my time. I know this is kind of sad, and I always wished I had a hobby like football or playing the piano or ice-skating, but the fact of the matter was that the only thing I was good at was passing exams. Which was fine. I wasn't ungrateful. It'd be worse if it were the other way around.

That day, the day I got a Twitter message from the creator of *Universe City*, I didn't do any work when I got home.

I collapsed on to my bed and turned my laptop on and went straight on to my Tumblr, where I posted all of my art. I scrolled down the page. What exactly had the Creator seen in these? They were all crap. Doodles I did to turn my brain off, so I could fall asleep and forget about history essays and art coursework and head girl speeches for five minutes.

I switched over to Twitter to see if the Creator had replied, but they hadn't. I checked my email to see if they'd emailed me, but they hadn't.

I loved *Universe City*.

Maybe that was my hobby. Drawing *Universe City*.

It didn't feel like a hobby. It felt like a dirty secret.

And my drawings were all pointless anyway. It wasn't like I could sell them. It wasn't like I could share them with my friends. It wasn't like they'd get me into Cambridge.

I continued scrolling down the page, back months and months and into last year and the year before, scrolling through time. I'd drawn everything. I'd drawn the characters – the narrator Radio Silence, and Radio's various sidekicks. I'd drawn the setting – the dark and dusty sci-fi university, Universe City. I'd drawn the villains and the weapons and the monsters, Radio's lunar bike and Radio's suits, I'd drawn the Dark Blue Building and the Lonely Road and even February Friday. I'd drawn everything, really.

Why did I do this?

Why am I like this?

It was the only thing I enjoyed, really. The only thing I had apart from my grades.

No – wait. That would be really sad. And weird.

It just helped me sleep.

Maybe.

I don't know.

I shut my laptop and went downstairs to get some food and tried to stop thinking about it.

A NORMAL TEENAGE GIRL

"Right then," I said, as the car drew up outside Wetherspoon's at 9pm several days later. "I'm off to drink the alcohols, do lots of the drugs and have lots of the sex."

"Oh," Mum said, with her half-smile. "Well, then. My daughter's gone wild."

"Actually this is my one hundred per cent real personality." I opened the car door and skipped out on to the pavement with a cry of, "Don't worry about me dying!"

"Don't miss the last train!"

It was the last day of school before study leave and I was supposed to be going to this club in town, Johnny Richard's, with my friends. It was the first time I'd ever been to a club and I was essentially terrified, but I was on the verge of being so uninvolved with our friendship group that if I hadn't gone, I thought they might stop considering me a 'main friend', and things would get too awkward for me to deal with on a daily basis. I couldn't imagine what awaited me besides drunk guys in pastel-coloured shirts, and Maya and Raine trying to make me awkwardly dance to Skrillex.

Mum drove away.

I crossed the street and peered through the door into Spoons. I could see my friends sitting in the far corner, drinking and laughing. They were all lovely people, but they made me nervous. They weren't mean to me or anything, they just saw me in a very particular way – School Frances, head girl, boring, nerdy, study machine. It's not like they were completely wrong, I guess.

I went to the bar and asked for a double vodka and lemonade. The bartender didn't ask for ID, even though I had a fake one just in case, which was surprising because most of the time I look approximately thirteen years old.

Then I walked towards my friends, barging through the packs of lads and pre-drinkers – more things that make me nervous.

Honestly, I need to stop being scared of being a normal teenage girl.

"What? Blowjobs?" Lorraine Sengupta, known to all as Raine, was sitting next to me. "Not even worth it, mate. Boys are weak. They don't even want to kiss you afterwards."

Maya, the loudest person of the group and therefore the leader, had her elbows on the table and three empty glasses in front of her. "Oh, come *on,* they're not all gonna be like that."

"But a lot of them are, so I literally can't be arsed. Not even worth the effort, tbh."

Raine literally said the letters 'tbh'. She didn't seem to do it ironically and I wasn't sure how I felt about it.

This conversation was so irrelevant to my life that I had been pretending to text for the past ten minutes.

Radio hadn't yet replied to my Twitter message or emailed me. It had been four days.

"Nah, I don't believe in couples falling asleep in each other's arms," said Raine. They were talking about something else now. "I think it's a mass-media lie."

"Oh, hey, Daniel!"

Maya's voice drew my attention away from my phone. Daniel Jun and Aled Last were walking past our table. Daniel was wearing a plain grey T-shirt and plain blue jeans. I'd never seen him wear anything patterned in the year I'd known him. Aled looked just as plain, like Daniel had picked out his clothes.

Daniel glanced down and saw us and momentarily caught my eye before replying to Maya, "Hi, you all right?"

They struck up a conversation. Aled was silent, standing behind Daniel, and was hunched over, as if he were trying to make himself less visible. I caught his eye too, but he quickly looked away.

Raine leaned towards me while Daniel and the others were talking. "Who's that white boy?" she murmured.

"Aled Last? He goes to the boys' school."

"Oh, Carys Last's twin brother?"

"Yeah."

"Weren't you friends with her back in the day?"

"Er…"

I tried to figure out what to say.

"Sort of," I said. "We chatted on the train. Sometimes."

Raine was probably the person I talked to the most out of the group. She didn't tease me for being a massive nerd like everyone else did. If I'd acted more like myself, I think we'd have been pretty good friends, since we had a similar sense of humour. But she could pull off being cool and weird because she wasn't head girl, and she had the right side of her hair shaved so no one was very surprised when she did something unusual.

Raine nodded. "Fair enough."

I watched as Aled took a sip of the drink he was holding and

25

looked shiftily round the pub. He appeared to be deeply uncomfortable.

"Frances, are you ready for Johnny R's?" one of my friends was leaning over the table and looking at me with a shark-like grin.

As I said, my friends weren't horrible to me, but they did treat me like I'd had next to no major life experiences and was generally a massive study nerd.

Which was true, so fair enough.

"Er, yeah, I guess so," I said.

A pair of guys walked up to Aled and started talking to him. They were both tall and had an air of power about them, and I realised then that it was because the guy on the right – olive-skinned and a checked shirt – had been head boy for most of last year at the boys' school, and the guy on the left – stocky physique and an undercut – used to be the boys' school rugby captain. I'd seen them both give presentations when I attended a sixth-form open day at their school.

Aled smiled at them both – I hoped Aled had other friends apart from Daniel. I tried to catch threads of their conversation: Aled said, "Yeah, Dan managed to persuade me this time!" and the head boy said, "Don't feel like you have to stick around for Johnny's if you don't want to. I think we're going home before then," and he looked at the rugby captain who nodded in agreement and said, "Yeah, let us know if you need a lift, mate! I've got my car," and to be honest I wished I could do the same, just go home when I wanted to, but I couldn't, because I'm too scared to do what I want.

"It's pretty grim," said another of my friends, dragging my attention away.

"I feel bad!" said another. "Frances is so innocent! I feel like we're corrupting you by dragging you to clubs and making you drink."

"She deserves a night off studying though!"

"I want to see drunk Frances."

"D'you think you'll be a crier?"

"No, I think she'll be a funny drunk. I think she's got some secret personality we don't know about."

I didn't know what to say.

Raine nudged me. "Don't worry. If any disgusting guys come up to you, I'll just accidentally spill my drink on them."

Someone laughed. "She actually will. She's done it before."

I laughed too and wished I had the guts to say something funny, but I didn't because I wasn't a funny person when I was around them. I was just boring.

I downed what was left of my drink and looked around and wondered where Daniel and Aled had gone.

I felt a bit weird because Raine had brought up Carys and I always felt weird when people brought up Carys because I didn't like thinking about her.

Carys Last ran away from home when she was in Year 11 and I was in Year 10. Nobody knew why and nobody cared because she didn't have many friends. She didn't have any friends, really. Apart from me.

DIFFERENT CARRIAGES

I met Carys Last on the train to school when we were fifteen.

It was 7.14am and I was sitting in her seat.

She glanced down at me like a librarian looking down at someone over a tall desk. Her hair was platinum blonde and she had a full fringe so thick and long that you couldn't quite see her eyes. The sun silhouetted her like she was a heavenly apparition.

"Oh," she said. "All right, my little train-compadre? You're sitting in my seat."

That might sound like she was trying to be mean, but she genuinely wasn't.

It was weird. Like, we'd both seen each other loads of times. We both sat at the village station every morning, plus Aled, and were the last people to leave the train every evening. We'd done this since I started secondary school. But we'd never spoken. That's what people are like, I suppose.

Her voice was different to how I'd imagined. She had one of those posh London *Made in Chelsea* accents, but it was more charming than irritating, and she spoke slowly and softly as if she were slightly high. It's also worth noting that I was significantly smaller than her at this point. She looked like a majestic elf and I looked like a gremlin.

And I suddenly realised it was true. I was sitting in her seat. I had no idea why. I normally sat in an entirely different carriage.

"Oh, God, sorry, I'll move…"

"What? Oh, no, I didn't mean *move*, wow, sorry. I must have sounded really rude." She sat down in the seat opposite me.

Carys Last didn't seem to smile, or feel the need to smile uncomfortably like I was doing. I was extremely impressed by this.

Aled wasn't with her. This didn't strike me as odd at the time. After this incident, I noticed that they sat in different carriages. That didn't strike me as odd either. I didn't know him, so I didn't care.

"Don't you normally sit in the back carriage?" she asked me in the tone of a middle-aged businessman.

"Erm, yeah."

She raised her eyebrows at me.

"You live in the village, don't you?" she said.

"Yeah."

"Opposite me?"

"I think so."

Carys nodded. She kept an unnaturally straight face, which was weird because everyone I knew always tried so hard to smile at you all the time. Her composure made her look significantly older than she was and admirably classy.

She rested her hands on the table and I noticed that they had tiny burn scars all over them.

"I like your jumper," she said.

I was wearing a jumper that had a computer with a sad face on it underneath my school blazer.

I looked down because I'd forgotten what I was wearing. It was early January and it was freezing, which was why I was wearing an extra jumper over my school jumper. This particular jumper was one of the many items of clothing that I bought but never wore around my friends because I thought they'd laugh at me. My personal fashion choices remained at home.

"D-do you?" I stammered, wondering if I'd misheard.

Carys chuckled. "Yes?"

"Thanks," I said, shaking my head slightly. I looked down at my hands, and then out the window. The train moved suddenly and we set off out of the village station.

"So why'd you sit in this carriage today?" she said.

I looked at her again, properly this time. Until this point she'd only ever been a girl with dyed blonde hair who sat at the other end of the village train station every morning. But now we were talking and here she was – she was wearing makeup even though she was still in lower school so it was against the Code of Conduct, she was large and soft and somehow powerful, how did she manage to be this nice but not smile at all? She looked like she could probably murder someone if she had to; she looked like she always knew exactly what she was doing. Somehow I knew this wouldn't be the only time we would ever talk. God, I didn't have a *clue* what was going to happen.

"I don't know," I said.

SOMEBODY IS LISTENING

Another hour passed before it was the acceptable time to move to Johnny R's, and I was trying to stay calm and trying not to Facebook message my mum and tell her to come pick me up because that would be lame. I knew I was lame, but no one else was supposed to know that.

We all stood up to head over to Johnny R's. I was feeling a bit light-headed and like I wasn't really controlling my legs, but I still heard Raine say, "This is nice," and point at my top, which was just a very plain chiffon shirt that I picked out because it looked like something Maya would wear.

I almost completely forgot about Aled, but then as we were walking down the street, my phone started to ring. I took it out of my pocket and looked at the screen. Daniel Jun was calling me.

Daniel Jun had my number only because, being head boy and girl, we ran a lot of school events together. He'd never called me, and only texted me four or five times with mundane school-event-related things such as 'are you setting up the cake stand or am I' and 'you collect tickets at the door and I'll direct people in from the school gate'. This, added to the fact that Daniel disliked me, meant that I had no idea why he was calling me.

But I was drunk. So I answered the phone.

F: Hello?
Daniel: (muffled voices and loud dubstep)
F: Hello? Daniel?
D: Hello? (laughter) shut up shut up— *hello?*
F: Daniel? Why are you calling me?
D: (laughter) (more dubstep)
F: Daniel?
D: (hangs up)

I looked at my phone.

"Okay," I said, out loud, but nobody heard me.

A group of lads barged past me, and my foot slid off the kerb and I was walking in the road. I didn't want to be here. I needed to be doing work, revising essay questions, writing up some maths notes, rereading my message from Radio, drawing some sketch ideas for the videos – I had a mountain of stuff to do and being here was, to be honest, a complete waste of my time.

My phone rang again.

F: Daniel, I swear to god—
Aled: Frances? Is this Frances?
F: Aled?
A: Franceeeeees! (dubstep)

I barely knew Aled. I'd barely spoken to him before this week. Why…
What?

F: Er, why are you calling me?

A: Oh... Dan— Dan tried to prank call you, I think... I don't think it worked...

F: ... Okay.

A: ...

F: Where are you? Is Daniel with you?

A: Oh, we're at Johnny's... that's so weird I don't even know who Johnny is... Dan's... (laughter, muffled voices)

F: ... Are you okay?

A: I'm fine... sorry... Daniel called you again and then he gave me the phone... I don't really know what happened. I don't know why I'm talking to you! Haha...

I walked a bit faster so I didn't lose my friends completely.

F: Aled, if Daniel's with you then I'm just gonna go...

A: Yeah, sorry... erm... yeah.

I felt pretty bad for him. I didn't get why he was friends with Daniel – I wondered whether Daniel bossed him around at all. Daniel bossed a lot of people around.

F: It's okay.

A: I don't really like it here.

I frowned.

A: Frances?

F: Yeah?

A: I don't really like it here.

F: ... Where?

A: Do you like it here?

F: *Where?*

There was silence for a moment – well, silence except for the tinny dance music and the voices and laughter.

F: Aled, please just tell me whether Daniel is there so I can continue with my evening and not worry about you.

A: I don't know where Daniel is...

F: D'you want me to come and take you home or something?

A: Hey... you know... it sounds like you're on the radio...

My mind went instantly to *Universe City* and Radio Silence.

F: God, you're so drunk.

A: (laughs) Hello. I hope somebody is listening...

He hung up. I felt my stomach drop at his final words.

"Hello. I hope somebody is listening," I said, under my breath.

Words I'd spent the last two years listening to over and over, words I'd sketched again and again inside speech bubbles and on my bedroom wall. Words I'd heard in a male voice and a female voice, changing every few weeks, always in that classic World-War-II old-time radio accent.

The opening line of every *Universe City* episode:

"Hello. I hope somebody is listening."

MADE IT

The bouncer at the door didn't question the driver's licence I presented to him, which belonged to Raine's older sister Rita, despite the fact that Rita is Indian and has cropped, straight hair. I wasn't sure how anyone could mistake an Indian girl for a British-Ethiopian girl, but there it is.

Johnny's entry was free as it was before 11pm, which was good news for me, because I hate spending money on things I don't actually want to do.

I followed my friends inside.

It was exactly what I expected.

Drunk people. Flashing lights. Loud music. Clichés.

"Mate, you coming for more drinks?" Raine shouted at me from fifteen centimetres away.

I shook my head. "Feeling a bit sick."

Maya heard me and laughed. "Aw, Frances! Bless your heart. Come on, just one more little shot!"

"I think I'm gonna go to the loo, actually."

But Maya had already started talking to someone else.

"D'you want me to come with you?" asked Raine.

I shook my head. "It's fine. I'm fine."

"Okay." Raine grabbed my arm and pointed at somewhere indiscernible on the other side of the room. "The loo's over there! Come meet us at the bar, yeah?"

I nodded.

I had absolutely no intention of going to the loo.

Raine waved at me and wandered away.

I was going to find Aled Last.

As soon as I was sure that my friends were sufficiently distracted by the bar, I headed upstairs. They were playing indie rock on this floor, and it was a lot quieter too, which I was glad of, because the dubstep was starting to make me feel a bit panicked, like it was the theme music for an action film and I had ten seconds to save myself from an explosion.

And then Aled Last was literally right next to me.

I hadn't planned to go and find him before he'd quoted *Universe City*. But that— that couldn't have been a coincidence, could it? He'd quoted it *exactly*. Word for word. With the exact enunciation, the hiss of the 's' in 'somebody' and the slight gap between 'list' and 'ening' and the smile after the second full stop...

Did he listen to it too?

I'd never met anyone else who'd even heard of it.

It was quite amazing that Aled hadn't been chucked out of the club, because he'd passed out. Or he was asleep. He was sat on the floor anyway, leaning against the wall in a way that made it obvious that someone had put him there. Probably Daniel. Which was surprising, since Daniel was usually kind of protective of Aled. Or so I'd heard. Maybe it was the other way round.

I crouched down in front of him. The wall he was leaning

against was all wet from the condensation in the room. I shook him by the arm and shouted over the music:

"Aled?"

I shook him again. He looked nice asleep, the club lights flashing red and orange over his face. He looked like a child.

"Don't be dead. That would really ruin my day."

He jerked awake, flying forwards off the wall and headbutting me square in the forehead.

It hurt so much that I couldn't even say anything except a soft "Mother*fuck*," a single tear emerging from the corner of my left eye.

While I was curling myself into a ball to try to minimise the pain, Aled shouted:

"Frances Janvier!"

And he pronounced my surname correctly.

He continued, "Did I just hit you in the face?"

"Hit is an understatement," I shouted back, uncurling myself.

I thought he would laugh, but his eyes were all wide and he was quite clearly still drunk, and he just said, "Oh my God, I'm so sorry." And then, because he was drunk, he just brought his hand up to my forehead and gave it a little pat, like he was trying to magic the pain away.

"I'm so sorry," he said again, his expression genuinely concerned. "Are you crying? Oh, wow, I sound like Wendy from *Peter Pan*." His eyes unfocused momentarily before looking at me again. "Girl, why are you crying?"

"I'm not..." I said. "Well, on the inside, maybe."

That's when he started to laugh. There was something about it that made me want to laugh as well, so that's what I did. He rolled his head back against the wall and brought his hand up to cover his mouth while he laughed. He was so drunk and my head was pulsating and the place was disgusting, but just for a few seconds everything was absolutely hilarious.

Once he'd finished, he grabbed my denim jacket and used my shoulder to push himself off the ground. He instantly slapped a hand against the wall to stop himself falling over. I stood up too, not quite sure what I was supposed to do now. I didn't even know Aled got like this. Then again, it's not like I knew much about him anyway. It's not like I had a reason to care.

"Have you seen Dan?" he asked me, his hand flopping back on to my shoulder and leaning in, squinting.

"Who's— oh, Daniel." Everybody I knew called him Daniel. "No, sorry."

"Oh…" He looked down at his shoes, and he seemed very much like a child again, his longish hair more appropriate for a fourteen-year-old, his jeans and his jumper just looking kind of odd on him. He just looked so… I didn't know what it was.

And I wanted to ask him about *Universe City*.

"Let's go outside for a sec," I said, but I don't think Aled heard me. I put my arm round his shoulder and started pulling him through the crowds, through the low bass and the sweat, through the people and towards the stairs.

"Aled!"

I halted in my tracks, Aled resting most of his weight against me, and turned to face the voice. Daniel was barging through the dancers to get to us, a full cup of water in one hand.

"Oh," he said, looking at me like I was a pile of dirty plates. "I didn't know you were out tonight."

What was his *damage*? "You literally called me on the phone, Daniel."

"I called you because Aled said he wanted to talk to you."

"Aled said you were trying to prank call me."

"Why would I do that? I'm not twelve."

"Well, why would Aled want to talk to me? I don't even know him."

"Why the hell would *I* know?"

"Because you're his best friend and you've been hanging out with him tonight?"

Daniel didn't say anything to that.

"Or I guess you haven't," I continued. "Yes, I was just rescuing Aled from the floor."

"What?"

I laughed a little. "Did you just leave your best friend passed out on the floor in a club, Daniel?"

"No!" He held up the cup of water. "I was getting him water. I'm not a complete dick."

This was news to me, but it felt a step too far to tell him that. Instead, I turned to Aled, who was swaying slightly against me. "Why did you call me?"

He frowned at me, and then bopped me gently on the nose with one finger and said, "I like you."

I started to laugh, thinking he was joking, but Aled didn't join in. He let go of me and slung his other arm round Daniel, who staggered backwards a little in surprise, bringing up his other hand to steady the water.

"Isn't it weird," said Aled, his face literally millimetres from Daniel's, "that I was the taller one for, like, sixteen years, but now you're suddenly taller?"

"Yeah, that's so weird," replied Daniel, with the closest thing to a smile I'd seen from him in several months. Aled rested his head on Daniel's shoulder and closed his eyes, and Daniel patted Aled gently on the chest. He murmured something to Aled I couldn't quite hear, and then handed him the water. Aled took it without saying anything and started drinking.

I glanced between the pair, and then Daniel seemed to remember I was there.

"Are you going home now?" he said. "Can you take him home?"

I put my hands in my pockets. I didn't really want to be here anyway. "Yeah, sure."

"I didn't just leave him on the floor," he said. "I was getting him water."

"You already said that."

"Yeah, I just didn't think you believed me."

I just shrugged.

Daniel moved Aled over to me, where he immediately clung round my shoulders again and spilt a bit of water on my sleeve.

"Shouldn't really have brought him here anyway," said Daniel, but he was saying it to himself, I think, and I could honestly see a bit of regret or something in his eyes as he gazed at Aled, who was on the verge of falling asleep in my arms, the club lights flashing on his skin.

"What…" Aled mumbled as we stepped into the street. "Where's Dan?"

"He said I had to take you home," I said. I wondered how exactly I was going to explain this to my friends. I made a mental note to text Raine once we got to the train station.

"Okay."

I glanced at him, because he'd suddenly sounded so much like the shy Aled I'd spoken to on parents evening – the Aled with the whispery voice and the shifty eyes.

"You get my train," he continued, as we started walking down the empty high street.

"Yep," I said.

"You and Carys sit— sat together."

My heart did a little jump at Carys's name.

"Yes," I said.

"She liked you," said Aled, "more than... erm..."

He seemed to lose his train of thought. I didn't want to talk about Carys so I didn't press him.

"Aled, do you listen to *Universe City*?" I said.

He stopped walking instantly, and my arm fell from his shoulder.

"What?" he said, the streetlamps bronzing him and the Johnny R's neon sign flashing softly behind him.

I blinked. Why did I ask that?

"*Universe City?*" he said, his eyes droopy and his voice loud like we were still inside the club. "Why?"

I looked away. Obviously he didn't then. At least he wouldn't remember this conversation. "Doesn't matter."

"*No,*" he said, stumbling off the kerb and almost falling on to me again. His eyes were wide. "Why did you ask me that?"

I stared. "Er..."

He waited.

"You just... I thought I heard you quote it. I might have been wrong..."

"*You* listen to *Universe City*?"

"Er, yeah," I said.

"That's so... unlikely. I haven't even got 50,000 subscribers yet."

Wait.

"What?"

Aled stepped forward. "How did you know? Dan said no one would work it out."

"*What?*" I said, this time with more force. "Work what out?"

41

Aled said nothing; he just started to grin.

"Do you listen to *Universe City*?" I said, though by this point I'd forgotten why I was asking, whether it was because the idea that someone else loved it as much as I did made me feel less completely weird, or whether I just wanted Aled to say what he was seemingly refusing to say.

"I *am Universe City*," he said. And I stood there.

"What?" I said.

"I'm Radio," he said. "I'm Radio Silence. I make *Universe City*."

And I just stood there.

And we said nothing.

A gust of wind whipped round us. A group of girls laughed from a nearby pub. A car alarm was going off.

Aled looked away, as if there were someone standing next to us that he could see but I couldn't.

Then he looked back, put a hand on my shoulder, leaned in, and asked, quite genuinely, "Are you all right?"

"It's... er..." But I didn't quite know how to say that I'd been obsessed for two years with a podcast show on YouTube about the adventures of an agender science fiction university student who always wears gloves and uses special powers and detective skills to solve mysteries around a city, the name of which is the stupidest pun I'd ever heard in my life, and I had thirty-seven sketchbooks in my room with drawings that I'd done of this specific show, and I'd never met anyone else in real life who'd even heard of it, and I'd never told any of my friends, and just now, outside Johnny R's on the last school day before study leave, I'd found out that a person whose twin sister had been my temporary best friend and who'd lived opposite me my entire life, a person who never said anything when he was sober, was the person who had made it.

This tiny blond seventeen-year-old who never said anything, standing on a high street.

"I'll listen," said Aled, with a blurry smile. He was *so* drunk – did he know what he was talking about?

"It'd take hours to explain," I said.

"I'd listen to you for hours," he said.

1. SUMMER TERM
b)

ALED LAST IN MY BED

I don't like other people inside my room because I'm terrified they're going to uncover one of my secrets, like my fan art habits or my Internet history or the fact that I one hundred per cent still sleep with a teddy bear.

I particularly do not like other people in my bed, not since I was twelve and I had that nightmare about a Tamagotchi that spoke in a really deep voice while a friend was sleeping over. I punched her in the face and she got a nosebleed and cried. An accurate metaphor for most of my past friendships.

Despite this, that night, I ended up with Aled Last in my bed.

Haha.

No. Not like that.

When Aled and I got off the train – or in Aled's case, fell off the train – and walked down the stone steps that joined the station to our countryside village, Aled announced that Daniel Jun had his keys, because Daniel was wearing his jacket, which had his keys inside them, and he couldn't wake his mum up because she would "literally chop his head off". The way he said it was pretty convincing, and his mum's one of the Academy's parent governors, so for a few seconds I actually believed him. I've always found Aled's mum intimidating, like with one word she could probably shatter my self-esteem and feed it to her dog. Not that that's very hard.

Anyway, yeah. So I was like, "What, d'you wanna sleep at mine or something?" obviously joking, but then he leaned all his weight on my shoulder and was like, "*Well...*" and I let out this laugh like I'd seen this coming from the moment Aled had crouched down in the middle of the road.

So I just said, "Fine. Fine." He'd fall asleep straight away anyway, and I wasn't one of those weird forty-year-olds who thought that boys and girls couldn't platonically share a bed.

Aled came into my house and fell on to my bed without saying anything and when I came back from the bathroom where I'd changed into pyjamas, he was asleep, facing away from me, his chest moving slowly up and down. I turned off the light.

I wished I was a bit more drunk too, because it took me a good two hours to fall asleep, like it always does, and for the whole two hours, when I wasn't playing games on my phone or scrolling through Tumblr, I had to stare at the back of his head in the soft blue light of my bedroom. The last time somebody had slept in my big double bed with me was Carys, when I was fifteen, a few nights before she ran away, and if I squinted a little, I could almost pretend that it was her, with the same blonde hair and elf ears. But when I opened my eyes again, it was quite clearly Aled, and not Carys, who was in my bed. For some reason I found that kind of reassuring. I don't know.

Aled needed to cut his hair, and his jumper, I suddenly realised, belonged to Daniel.

I KNOW, RIGHT

I woke up first, at eleven-ish. Aled didn't seem to have moved for the entire night, so I checked quickly to see whether he'd died (he hadn't) before getting out of bed. I briefly went over last night's decisions. They all seemed to match up to my expectations of myself – pushover, will put self in awkward positions to guarantee the safety of people I barely know, will ask awkward questions and deeply regret them later… Aled Last being in my bed really was a classic Frances thing to happen. What exactly was I going to say to him when he woke up?

Hey there, Aled. You're in my bed. You probably don't remember why. I promise I didn't bring you here by force. By the way, you know that weird podcast thing you make for YouTube? Yeah, basically I've been obsessed with it for years.

I immediately went downstairs. Better break the news to my mum before she found him and assumed that her daughter had gained a small, blond, apologetic boyfriend without telling her about it first.

Mum was in the lounge in her unicorn onesie watching *Game*

of Thrones. She looked up as I entered the room and slumped down next to her on the sofa.

"Hello there," she said. She had a packet of dry Shreddies in one hand. She popped one into her mouth. "You look a bit sleepy."

"Well," I said, but wasn't quite sure where to go from there.

"Did you have fun at the disco?" she asked, but she was grinning. Mum pretended to be clueless about anything twenty-first-century teenagers did. Along with being sarcastic to teachers, this was another thing she enjoyed. "Did you *get down*? Did you turn up?"

"Oh, yeah, we were jiving and everything," I said, and did a little rendition of a jive.

"Good, good. That'll get you laid."

I laughed loudly, mostly at the idea of me ever 'getting laid' in any situation ever, but then with exaggerated slowness she pressed pause on the TV remote, cast aside the pack of Shreddies and stared into my eyes, linking her fingers together on her lap as a head teacher might do over their desk.

"Speaking of which," she continued, "I was just wondering who exactly the lovely young chap sleeping in your bed is."

Oh. Okay.

"Yeah," I said with a laugh. "Yes. That lovely young chap."

"I came into your room to get some washing and there he was." Mum spread out her hands as if reliving the scene. "At first I thought he was some sort of giant teddy bear. Or one of those Japanese cartoon pillows that you were showing me on the Internet."

"Yeah… no. He's real. A real boy."

"He was wearing clothes so I'm assuming there wasn't any hanky-panky."

"Mum, even when you use the phrase 'hanky-panky' ironically, it still makes me want to plug my ears with superglue."

Mum didn't say anything for a moment, and neither did I, and then we both heard a loud crash come from upstairs.

"It's Aled Last," I said. "Carys's twin brother?"

"Your friend's *brother*?" Mum cackled. "Oh, wow, we're turning into a bit of a romantic comedy here, aren't we?"

It was funny, but I didn't laugh, and Mum's expression turned serious.

"What's going on, Frances? I thought you were going to stay out later with your friends. God knows you deserve some kind of end-of-term celebration before you get stuck into your exam revision."

She looked at me sympathetically. Mum had always thought I cared too much about schoolwork. Mum was generally the opposite of what you'd expect any normal parent to be, but somehow she managed to be amazing anyway.

"Aled was drunk so I had to take him home. He forgot his keys and his mum's a bit of a dickhead, apparently."

"Oh, yes, *Carol Last*." Mum pursed her lips. She gazed off, reliving a memory. "She always tries to talk to me at the post office."

Another thump sounded from my room. Mum frowned and looked up. "You haven't seriously wounded him, have you?"

"I think I'd better go check on him."

"Yes, go and check on your man. He's probably clambering out the window."

"Come on now, Mother, my romantic partners wouldn't ever want to clamber out of the window."

She smiled that warm smile of hers that always made me think she knew something I didn't. I stood up to leave.

"Don't let him escape!" said Mum. "This could be your only chance at securing a spouse!"

Then I remembered the other thing that Mum should probably know about.

"Oh, by the way," I said, turning in the doorway, "you know *Universe City*?"

Mum's laugh dropped into an expression of confusion. "Er, yes?"

"Yeah, so, Aled made it."

I realised then that Aled probably wasn't going to remember having told me that he was the creator of *Universe City*. Great. Another awkward situation I was going to have to deal with.

"What?" said Mum. "What d'you mean?"

"He sent me that Twitter message. He's the creator of *Universe City*. I found out yesterday."

Mum just stared.

"Yeah," I said. "I know, right."

WEIRD

I walked back into my room to find Aled crouching next to the bed, holding a coat hanger like it was a machete. As I entered he spun round to face me, his eyes all wild and his hair – too long – sticking out in all directions from where he'd slept. I guess he looked sort of... well... petrified. Fair enough.

It took me a few seconds to decide what to say.

"Were you... planning to decapitate me with a coat hanger?"

He blinked once, and then lowered his weapon and stood up straight, his terror subsiding a little. I gave him a once-over – of course, he was still in the same outfit as last night, Daniel's burgundy jumper, and dark jeans, but for the first time I noticed that he was wearing these really excellent lime green plimsolls with fluorescent purple laces and I really wanted to ask him where he'd got them.

"Oh. Frances Janvier," he said. And he still pronounced my surname correctly.

Then he let a long breath out and sat down on my bed.

It was like I was seeing an entirely different person. Now that I knew he was the Creator, the voice of Radio Silence, he didn't

53

even look like Aled Last any more – not the Aled Last I knew. Not Daniel Jun's silent shadow, not the boy who didn't even seem to have a personality at all. Not the boy who just smiled and agreed with you whatever you said to him and generally, to be honest, seemed to be the most boring, basic individual in the known universe.

He was *Radio Silence*. He'd been making a YouTube show for over *two years*. A beautiful, limitless, explosion of a story.

I was on the verge of having a fangirl meltdown, for Christ's sake. How embarrassing is that?

"Jesus Christ," he said. His voice was so quiet now he was sober, it was like he wasn't quite used to normal conversation or something, like he had to force himself to speak out loud. "I thought I'd been kidnapped." Then he put his face in his hands, elbows on his knees.

He stayed like that for quite a while. I stayed standing awkwardly in the doorway.

"Er... sorry," I said, though I wasn't sure what I was apologising for. "You, like, you did ask. I didn't just lure you into my house. I didn't have any ulterior motives." He looked up at me, eyes wide again, and I groaned. "Oh, yeah, sounds like something someone with ulterior motives would say."

"This is really awkward," he said, his mouth twisting into a sort of half-smile. "I'm the one who should be apologising."

"Yeah, this is really awkward."

"Do you want me to just leave?"

"Er..." I paused. "Well, I'm not gonna, like, stop you from leaving. I'm seriously not a kidnapper."

Aled gave me a long look.

"Wait," he said. "We didn't... did we, like, hook up?"

The idea sounded so completely idiotic that I actually let

out a laugh. In hindsight, I think that might have been a bit rude.

"Oh, no. No. You're good."

"Okay," he said. He looked down and I couldn't really tell what he was thinking. "Yeah. That'd be really weird."

There was a pause again. I needed to say something about *Universe City* before he went. He clearly didn't remember anything about that. I'm a rubbish liar, and I can't keep secrets either.

He finally put down the coat hanger that he'd been clutching in one hand.

"You have a really cool room, by the way," he said shyly. He nodded towards my *Welcome to Night Vale* poster. "I love *Welcome to Night Vale*."

Of course he did. *Welcome to Night Vale* was another Internet podcast show that I adored, just like I did *Universe City*. I preferred *Universe City* though – I liked the characters more.

"I didn't know you were into stuff like that," he continued.

"Oh." I wasn't sure where he was going with this. "Well, yeah."

"I just thought you… you know… liked studying and… erm… being head girl, and… yeah."

"Oh, right." I let out an awkward laugh. School was my life and soul and everything about me. So I guess he was right. "Well, yeah… my grades are pretty important, and being head girl and stuff… like, I'm applying to Cambridge, so I need to— I have to study quite a lot, so… yeah."

He watched me as I spoke, nodding slowly, and said, "Ah, yeah, fair enough," but it didn't sound like he cared half as much about that as he had about my *Welcome to Night Vale* poster. He then realised he was staring, so he looked down and said, "Sorry, I'm making this even weirder." He stood up, flattening his hair with one hand. "I'll just leave. It's not like we're gonna see each other much any more."

"What?"

"Because I've left school and stuff."

"Oh."

"Haha."

We stared at each other. It was so awkward. My pyjama bottoms had Teenage Mutant Ninja Turtles on them.

"You told me you make *Universe City*," I said so quickly that I was immediately scared he hadn't heard me. My reasoning was that since there was no easy way to bring this up, I might as well just blurt it out. This is how I get through most of my life.

Aled said nothing, but his face dropped and he actually stepped backwards a little.

"I told you…" he said, but his voice drifted into silence.

"I don't know how much you remember, but, like, I'm literally…" I stopped myself before I said something that made me sound truly insane. "I really, really love your show. I've been listening to it since it started."

"What?" he said, and he sounded genuinely surprised. "But that's, like, over two years…"

"Yeah." I laughed. "How weird is that?"

"That's really…" His voice got a little louder. "That's really cool."

"Yeah, I seriously love it, like, I don't know, the characters are all just so well-rounded and relatable. Especially Radio, the whole agender thing is literal genius, like, when the girl voice first appeared I listened to the episode, like, twenty times. But it's so good when you're not sure whether it's a boy voice or a girl voice, those are amazing. I mean… none of the voices are girl or boy voices, are they? Radio doesn't have a gender. Anyway, yeah, the sidekicks are all so brilliant as well, but there's not all the *Doctor Who* sexual tension, they're just their own people, and it's so good how they're not always BFFs with Radio, sometimes they're enemies. And every single story is so hilarious but you really can't guess what's going to happen, but all the ongoing plots are good too, like, I still have no idea why Radio can't take their gloves off or what's being kept in the Dark Blue Building or whether Radio's ever going to meet Vulpes, and I'm not even gonna bother asking you about the February Friday conspiracy because, like, that would ruin the whole thing. Yeah, it's just… it's so good, I can't explain how much I love it. Seriously."

Throughout this, Aled's eyes got wider and wider. Halfway through, he sat back down on to my bed. Near the end, he covered his hands with his sleeves. When I'd finished, I instantly regretted everything.

"I've never met a fan of the show before," he said, his voice quiet again, almost inaudible. And then he laughed. He brought his hand up to cover his mouth like he had last night, and I wondered, not for the first time, why he did that.

I glanced to one side.

"Also…" I continued, thinking that was when I was going to tell him that I was Toulouse, the fan artist that he contacted on Twitter. It flashed through my head, me telling him, him freaking out, me showing him my thirty-seven sketchbooks, him freaking out even more, him calling me weird, him running away, me never seeing him ever again.

I shook my head. "Erm, I forgot what I was about to say."

Aled lowered his hand. "Okay."

"You should have seen my face yesterday when you told me," I said, with a forced laugh.

He smiled, but he looked nervous.

I looked down. "So… yeah. Anyway. Erm. You can go home now, if you want. Sorry."

"Don't apologise," he said, in that whispery voice.

It took quite a lot of effort not to say sorry for saying sorry.

He stood up, but didn't go to walk out of the door. He looked like he wanted to say something, but didn't know which words to choose.

"Or… I could get you some breakfast? If you want? No pressure, you don't have to…"

"Ah… I'd feel bad," he said, but he was smiling faintly and for the first time I felt like I knew what he was thinking.

"It's fine. People don't come round my house very often, so, erm… it's nice!" I realised how sad I sounded as soon as I said it.

"Okay," he said. "If you don't mind."

"Cool."

He glanced around my room one last time. I saw him spot my desk and the messy worksheets and revision notes scattered everywhere, including on the floor. He looked at my bookshelves, which had a mix of classic literature I was planning to read for my Cambridge interview and some DVDs on them, including the entire Studio Ghibli collection Mum got me for my sixteenth birthday. He looked outside my window towards his house. I didn't know which window of his house belonged to him.

"I never told anyone about *Universe City*," he said, glancing back at me. "I thought they'd think I was weird."

There were a hundred things I could have said in reply to that, but I just said:

"Same."

And then we were silent again. I think we were just trying to absorb what was happening. To this day I have no idea whether he was particularly happy about this revelation. Sometimes I think maybe everything would have been better if I'd never told him that I knew. Other times I think it's the best thing I'd ever said in my whole life.

"So… breakfast?" I said, because there was no way this conversation, this meeting, this stupidly extreme coincidence was ending here.

"Yeah, okay," he said, and though his voice was still all quiet and shy, he really sounded like he did want to stay, just so he could talk to me for a bit longer.

WE'D MAKE MILLIONS

He actually didn't stay for very long. I think he was aware that I was having an internal breakdown at this entire situation, but I made him some toast anyway and tried not to bombard him with questions even though I wanted to. After I'd asked who knew about *Universe City* (only Daniel) and why he'd started making it (he was bored) and how he did all the voice effects (editing software), I thought I'd better try to calm down, so I just got myself some cereal and sat opposite him at the breakfast bar. It was May, not quite summer, but the morning sun was burning into my eyes through the kitchen window.

We talked about the classic stuff like school and study leave and how much revision we'd each done. We'd both done our art exams, but he still had English lit, history and maths, and I still had English lit, history and politics. He was predicted all A⋆s, which was unsurprising for someone who'd got into one of the top universities in the country, and he said that for some reason he wasn't really very stressed about his exams. I did not mention that I was so stressed that I was losing more hair in the shower than I probably should have been.

At one point he asked if I had any painkillers, and I suddenly noticed that his eyes were pretty bloodshot and watery and he hadn't really eaten much of the toast. I've always been able to remember what he looked like on that first day at my breakfast bar. In the sunlight, his hair and his skin looked almost the same colour.

"Do you go out a lot?" I asked, handing over some paracetamol and a glass of water.

"No," he said. Then he laughed a little. "I don't really like going out, to be honest. I'm a bit of a loser."

"I don't either," I said. "Last night was my first time at Johnny R's. It was a lot sweatier than I expected."

He laughed again, hand over his mouth. "Yeah, it's disgusting."

"The walls were, like, *wet*."

"Yeah!"

"You probs could have set up a waterslide. I would have enjoyed it more if there was a waterslide, not gonna lie." I made a weird waterslide gesture with my hands. "Drunk watersliding. I'd pay for that."

That was a strange thing to say. Why had I said that? I waited for him to give me that 'Frances, what are you talking about?' look.

But it didn't come.

"I'd pay for a drunk bouncy castle," he said. "Like, there could be a room where the whole floor is a bouncy castle."

"Or a room that's basically a children's play centre."

"Did you ever go to Monkey Bizz?"

"Yeah!"

"You know they had that bit at the back with the tyre swings over a ball pit? I'd want that."

"Oh my God, yes. We should make this, we'd make millions."

"We really would."

There was a pause while we were both eating. It wasn't awkward.

Just before he left, as we were standing in the doorway, I said:

"Where did you get your shoes? They're so nice."

He looked at me like I'd told him he'd won the lottery.

"ASOS," he said.

"Ah, cool."

"They're…" He almost didn't say it. "I know they're weird. They were in the women's section."

"Oh. They don't look like women's shoes." I looked at his feet. "They don't look like men's shoes either. They're just shoes." I looked back at him and smiled, not quite sure where I was going with this. He was staring at me, his expression now completely unreadable.

"I have a coat from Topman," I continued. "And I tell you what, the men's section of Primark is the best for Christmas jumpers."

Aled Last pulled his sleeves over his hands.

"Thank you for what you said about *Universe City*," he said, not quite looking me in the eye. "I just… that really, erm, means a lot to me."

This was the perfect opportunity to say it to him.

That I was the artist he contacted via Twitter.

But I didn't know him. I didn't know how he would react. I thought he was the coolest person I'd ever met, but that didn't mean I trusted him.

"It's fine!" I said.

Once he'd waved goodbye and walked off down our drive, the thought hit me that this was probably the longest conversation I'd had with someone my age for at least a few weeks. I thought maybe we could be friends now, but then again, maybe that was a bit weird.

I went back up to my room and I could see my sketchbooks peeking out from underneath my bed and I thought, *If only he knew*. I thought about Carys, and whether she was something I should bring up – Aled knew we'd been friends. God, he'd been there on the train all that time, hadn't he?

I thought that I needed to tell him about me being the artist because if I left it too long he might start to hate me and I didn't want that to happen. Nothing good comes out of lying to people. I should know that by now.

POWER

Carys never lied about anything. She also never told the full truth, which felt worse, somehow. Not that I realised that until she was long gone.

She dominated our train conversations with stories about her life. About arguments with her mum and her school friends and teachers. About terrible essays she'd written and exams she'd failed. About sneaking out to parties and getting drunk and all the gossip in her year group. She was everything I wasn't – she was drama, emotion, intrigue, power. I was nothing. Nothing happened to me.

But she never did tell the full truth and I didn't notice. I was so dazed by the way she shone so brightly, her incredible stories and her platinum hair, that I didn't find it weird that she and Aled arrived at the train station separately in the mornings and he walked twenty metres behind us in the afternoons. I didn't find it weird that they never spoke nor sat together. I didn't question anything. I wasn't paying attention.

I was blinded, and I failed, and I'm never letting that happen again.

UNIVERSE CITY: Ep. 2 – skater boy

I'll be taking on allies from now on. Until I hear from you, survival will be my priority.

Scroll down for transcript >>>

[…]

He has a brilliant bike, I can tell you that. Three wheels and glow-in-the-dark. And of course, it's useful to have someone around who has the use of his bare hands. I can't tell you what a pain it is to have to keep these gloves on all the time.

I'm still not sure why I asked for his help. I've survived for this long by myself. But since talking to you, I suppose… I suppose I've had a slight change of heart.

If I'm to get out of here, I'm going to have to team up with some city folk every now and then. There are things in Universe City that you cannot possibly imagine out there in the real world, creeping around in the metallic dust. Monsters and demons and synthetic abominations.

Every day you hear of the latest fatality – some poor loner wandering back from a lecture, a tired geek in the back corner of the library, a miserable young girl alone in her bed.

And this is what I'm getting at, old sport:

I've come to the conclusion that it's impossible to survive alone in Universe City.

[…]

ONLINE

Mum and I were watching *The Fifth Element* while eating pizza when my phone buzzed, signifying I had a Facebook message. I picked it up, expecting it to be my friends, but nearly choked on pizza crust when I read the name on the screen.

(19:31) Aled Last
hey frances just wanted to say thanks again for taking me home last night, i realise i probably ruined your night... i'm so so sorry xx

(19:34) Frances Janvier
Hey it's fine!! Don't worry!! <3
To tell you the truth I didn't reeeeally want to be there...
And I kiiiinda used you as an excuse to go home not gonna lie

(19:36) Aled Last
ah that's good then!
i thought it'd be a good idea to get drunk because i was

nervous about going to johnny's but i think i overestimated how much i needed to drink haha
i've never been that drunk before

(19:37) **Frances Janvier**
Don't worry!! You had Daniel with you as well so it's all good! he was getting you water when I found you ☺

(19:38) **Aled Last**
yeah that's true ☺

(19:38) **Frances Janvier**
:D

Both of us stayed online for a few minutes after that and I wanted to say something else and I felt like he did too, but neither of us knew what, so I clicked my phone screen off and tried to focus on the film, but all I could think about was him.

STOP-MOTION

The day after that was a Sunday and it was the day I'd decided to start study leave revision and it was the day I got an email from Radio Silence – Aled – while I was midway through a maths question on differentiation.

Radio Silence <universecitypodcast@gmail.com>
to me
Hi Toulouse,
Thanks so much for getting back to me on Twitter! I'm so glad you want to work with the show; I've been wanting to implement some sort of visual aspect for a while.

The email went on for a few paragraphs and Aled talked about all his ideas for the show – repeating pixel gifs like the ones he'd seen on my blog, or stop-motion drawings on a whiteboard, maybe an update to the *Universe City* logo if it wasn't too much responsibility. He asked me whether I was definitely sure I could commit, because he couldn't let his subscribers down – if I was doing this, I was *doing this*, I couldn't back out without a very good reason.

It made me feel sick.

I put my phone down on top of the maths answers I'd been writing in a notebook. The letters of the email and the numbers on the paper all fuzzed together for a moment.

I needed to tell him it was me.

Before I messed up another friendship.

#SPECIALSNOWFLAKE

It took until Monday evening for me to come up with a plan.

I was going to ask him about his shoes. That was how I was going to start another conversation with him.

Somehow that was going to turn into me telling him that I was Toulouse, the fan artist that he had emailed about the podcast that I'd already told him I was obsessed with.

Somehow. I didn't know how.

It'd be fine.

I'm well-practised in the art of bullshitting.

(16:33) Frances Janvier
Aled!! This is really random but I was just wondering where you said you got your shoes from?? I'm kinda obsessed with them and have been scrolling through websites for the past hour lmao

(17:45) Aled Last
hi! oh errr they were from ASOS but they're a really old pair of Vans, i don't think you can buy them any more?

(17.49) Frances Janvier

Ah mannn that's too bad

(17:50) Aled Last

sorry!! ☹

if it's any consolation Dan always says they look like shoes for 12-year-olds and makes a really disgusted face every time i wear them

(17:52) Frances Janvier

Well, that must be why I like them, most of the things in my wardrobe look like they belong to a 12-year-old. I am 12 years old on the inside

(17:53) Aled Last

whaaat you always dress so professionally for school tho!!

(17:53) Frances Janvier

Oh, yeah… well… gotta keep up my head girl study machine reputation

At home I am all about the burger jumpers and Simpsons shirts

(17:55) Aled Last

burger jumpers?? i need to see these

(17:57) Frances Janvier

[webcam photo of Frances's jumper that she is currently wearing – it has burgers all over it]

(17:58) Aled Last
DUDE
that is amazing
Also
i have a jumper from the same website?? i'm literally wearing
it right now?

(17:58) Frances Janvier
WHAT!!
Show me now

(18:00) Aled Last
[webcam photo of Aled's jumper that he is currently wearing
– it has UFOs on the sleeves]

(18:00) Frances Janvier
Omfg
I love it
I didn't know you wore stuff like that?? You're always in
plain stuff when I see you out of uniform

(18:01) Aled Last
yeah i'm always scared people will laugh at me... idk it's
probably silly haha

(18:02) Frances Janvier
No it's not I'm exactly the same
All of my friends look so cool and beautiful and classy all
the time... if I turned up wearing a burger jumper they'd
probably just send me home

(18:03) **Aled Last**
omg your friends sound mean

(18:03) **Frances Janvier**
Nah they're cool they're just... idk I feel a bit different from
them sometimes. #specialsnowflake am I right!!!!

(18:04) **Aled Last**
no it's all right i know the feeling! haha

In the end we chatted on Facebook until gone 10pm and I
completely forgot about telling him I was the artist until 3am
when I remembered, and started to panic, and couldn't fall asleep
for another two hours after that.

AWKWARD

"You're an idiot," said Mum, when I relayed to her the entire situation on Wednesday. "Not an unintelligent idiot, but a sort of naïve idiot who manages to fall into a difficult situation and then can't get out of it because she's too awkward."

"You just described my life." I was lying down on the lounge carpet working my way through a maths past paper while Mum was watching a *How I Met Your Mother* rerun, cross-legged on the sofa with a cup of tea in her hands.

She sighed. "You know you just need to say it, don't you?"

"It feels too major to say over Facebook."

"Then go to his house. He literally lives across the road."

"That's weird, no one knocks unexpectedly on other people's doors any more."

"Okay – message him and say you need to go to his house to tell him something important."

"Mum, that literally sounds like I want to declare my love to him."

She sighed again. "Well, I don't know what to say then. You

74

were the one complaining that this is stopping you focusing on your revision. I thought that was important to you."

"It *is*!"

"You barely know him! Why is this bothering you so much?"

"We've had a long conversation on Monday; it feels awkward to bring it up now."

"Well that's life, isn't it?"

I rolled over so I was facing Mum.

"I feel like we could be friends," I said. "But I don't want to mess it up."

"Oh, sweetheart." Mum gave me a sympathetic look. "You've got lots of other friends."

"They only like School Frances though. Not Real Frances."

LOGARITHMS

Despite doing well in all of the exams I have ever taken, I always panic about them. I know that sounds like normal behaviour, but it doesn't feel normal when you're reduced to tears because of exponentials and logarithms – a completely useless topic from one of my maths exams. I couldn't find any notes on it in my folder, and the textbook was useless at explaining anything. I remember absolutely nothing from my maths AS level nowadays.

It was 10.24pm the night before my exam and I was sitting on the lounge floor with my mum, most of my maths notes and textbooks spread out on the floor around us. Mum had her laptop on her lap and was clicking through various websites to see if she could find any decent explanations of what logs were. I was trying not to start crying for the third time that evening.

The idea that I might go down a grade because I physically could not find an explanation of a particular topic made me feel like stabbing myself.

"Do you have anyone you could talk to about this?" Mum asked, still scrolling through Google. "Are any of your friends in your class?"

Maya was in my maths class, but she was terrible at maths and would have no better idea than I did. And even if she did, I wasn't sure whether I'd be able to message her. I'd never messaged her before, discounting group chats.

"No," I said.

Mum frowned and closed the laptop. "Maybe you should just go to bed, love," she said in a soft voice. "Being tired for the exam will make everything worse."

I didn't know what to say, because I didn't want to go to bed.

"I don't think there's anything you can do. It's not your fault."

"I know," I said.

So I went to bed.

And I just cried.

Which is pretty pathetic, to be honest. Which is what I am. I shouldn't be surprised at myself.

It would explain why I did what I did that night.

I messaged Aled again.

(00:13) Frances Janvier
Are you awake?

(00:17) Aled Last
hello yes i am? are you ok??

(00:18) Frances Janvier
Ah sorry for just messaging you randomly again...
Just had a bit of a rough evening lol

(00:19) Aled Last
it's honestly fine!!!! what's up??
if you're feeling crap it's always better to talk about it

(00:21) Frances Janvier
Okay well I've got my C2 maths exam tomorrow
And I realised today I missed an entire topic in my revision
And it's like one of the hardest topics – logarithms?
And I was just wondering (if you're not doing anything else right now!!) if you knew any decent websites or anything that explained it properly?? I just can't get my head around it and I feel like shit

(00:21) Aled Last
oh god that's so horrible

(00:23) Frances Janvier
Like... if I get a B in maths... I don't even know if Cambridge will want to interview me
Idk
This sounds really dumb I know I really shouldn't be so upset about this haha

(00:23) Aled Last
no i totally get it... there's nothing more stressful than going into an exam knowing you're underprepared
let me see if i can find my notes, hang on

(00:24) Frances Janvier
Only if you're not busy!! I feel really bad asking you but like... you're the only person I can ask

(00:25) Aled Last
hey maybe this is a crazy idea but
i could come round if you like?
like, right now?
to help?

(00:25) Frances Janvier
Seriously!??? That would be literally amazing

(00:26) Aled Last
yeah! i mean i'm only over the road and i don't have to get
up early tomorrow

(00:27) Frances Janvier
I feel awful, are you sure about this? It's gone midnight

(00:27) Aled Last
i want to help! you helped me home from johnny's last week
and i feel awful about that so... this makes us even? Haha

(00:27) Frances Janvier
Okay!! Oh wow you are a lifesaver

(00:28) Aled Last
on my way

When I opened the door at half past twelve the night before my
C2 maths exam, I immediately gave Aled a hug.

It wasn't awkward, even though I initiated it and he sort of
went, "Oh," and stepped backwards a little because he wasn't
expecting it.

"Hello," I said after letting him go.

"Hi," he said, almost a whisper, and then cleared his throat. He was wearing a Ravenclaw hoodie with grey pyjama shorts, bed socks and his lime green plimsolls, and he was holding a purple ring-binder. "Er, sorry I'm wearing pyjamas."

I gestured to myself because I was wearing a dressing gown, a stripy T-shirt and Avengers leggings. "No judgement here. I actually live in pyjamas."

I stepped aside to let him in and then shut the door. He wandered a little way into the hallway before turning to face me.

"Was your mum okay with this?" I asked.

"I may possibly have climbed out of the window."

"That's extremely clichéd."

He smiled. "Okay. So... logs?" He held up the folder. "I brought my notes from last year."

"I thought you would have burned them or something."

"I put way too much effort into these to *burn* them."

We sat in the lounge for over an hour and Mum made us hot chocolate and, with his tiny voice, Aled explained to me what exponentials and logarithms were and what sorts of questions could come up and how you solved them.

For someone who was so quiet, he was shockingly good at explaining things. He explained everything step by step and made sure we did an example question for each subtopic. For someone like me, who could probably ramble nonstop until I died, it was quite an amazing thing to listen to.

And when we'd finished, I felt like things were going to be okay.

"You've literally saved my life," I said, as I led him to the door again.

Aled looked a little more tired now, a little watery-eyed, and he'd tucked his hair behind his ears.

"Not literally," he said with a chuckle. "But hopefully I helped."

I wanted to say he'd done more than that, but it sounded embarrassing.

Because it hit me then what he'd done for me. He'd got up in the middle of the night, in his pyjamas, climbed out of the window of his bedroom to come and help me with one topic of a maths exam. We'd only had a long conversation in person one time before this. Why would anyone do something like that for someone else? For *me*?

"I have something to tell you," I said, "but I've been too scared to say it."

Aled's expression dropped. "You have something to tell me?" he said, instantly nervous.

I took a breath.

"I'm Toulouse," I said. "Touloser on Twitter and Tumblr. The fan artist you messaged."

And there was a long pause.

And then he said:

"Is this a lie? Is this... are you just having a joke? Was this Dan's— Daniel's idea or something?"

"No, I— it's... I know it sounds like a joke... but I just didn't know how to say it. When you told me you were the Creator I, like... I freaked out internally, and, like, I was about to tell you, but I had no idea how you would react and I didn't want you to hate me."

"Because I'm the Creator," he interrupted. "The creator of your favourite YouTube channel."

"Yeah."

"So... okay." He looked down at his shoes.

He almost looked sad.

"So… have you just… were you just pretending to be nice all this time?" he said, his voice so quiet and soft. "Like… erm… you know, taking me home, and… I don't know… were you lying about your clothes and stuff? And asking me for help with maths? Just so you could be friends with the creator of your favourite YouTube channel and like… get secret spoiler access or…?"

"What? No! None of this has been a lie, I swear."

"So why have you been talking to me then?" he said.

At the exact moment he said, "I'm so unimpressive," I said, "Because you're cool."

We looked at each other.

Then he laughed softly and shook his head. "This is so weird."

"Yeah…"

"I mean, like, this coincidence is *insane*. This shouldn't be happening right now. We live opposite each other. We have the same taste in clothes."

I just nodded.

"You're head girl and you do fan art secretly?" he said.

I nodded again and resisted the urge to apologise.

"Am I the only person who knows?" he said.

I nodded a third time and we both had a moment of understanding.

"Okay," he said, and then bent down to put his shoes on.

I watched him tie his laces, and then he stood up.

"You— I don't have to do it, if you don't want," I said. "If it's too awkward."

He pulled his sleeves over his hands. "What d'you mean?"

"I mean, if it's weird to let me do the *Universe City* art… I mean, I could just never see you again, you can ask someone else, someone you don't know. I don't mind."

His eyes widened. "I don't want to never see you again." Then he shook his head slightly. "I want you to do the art."

And I believed him. I really did.

He wanted to see me again and he wanted me to do the art.

"Are you sure? I don't mind if you don't want me to..."

"I do!"

I tried and failed to contain a grin. "Okay."

He nodded, and we looked at each other for a moment, and though I think he might have wanted to say something else, he turned around and opened the door. He looked back one more time before he left. "I'll message you tomorrow."

"Okay!"

"Good luck with your exam." He waved slightly and then left. I shut the door and turned around.

Mum was standing behind me, looking at me.

"Well done," she said, with a small smile.

"What?" I said, dazed, trying to replay everything that had just happened before I forgot it all.

"You told him."

"Yes."

"He didn't hate you."

"No."

I stood very still.

"Are you okay?" said Mum.

"I just... have no idea what he's thinking. Like ninety-nine per cent of the time."

"Yeah, he's that sort of person."

"What sort of person?"

"The sort of person who doesn't speak spontaneously." She folded her arms. "Who won't say anything if you don't ask."

"Hm."

"D'you like him?" she said.

I blinked, not quite understanding the question. "Erm, yes, obviously?"

"No, I mean *like him.*"

I blinked again. "Oh. Er, I haven't thought about it."

And then I did think about it.

And realised that I didn't like him in that way at all.

And it didn't matter.

"No, I don't think so," I said. "That's a bit irrelevant, isn't it?"

Mum frowned a little. "Irrelevant to what?"

"I don't know, just irrelevant." I stepped past her and started trudging upstairs, saying, "What a random question."

SOMETHING BEFORE
WE CONTINUE

We didn't see each other in person for a while after that, but we carried on messaging each other on Facebook. Tentative 'how are you's became angry rants about TV shows and even though we had really only hung out with each other twice, it felt like we were friends. Friends who barely knew anything about each other except the other's most private secret.

I just sort of want to say something before we continue.

You probably think that Aled Last and I are going to fall in love or something. Since he is a boy and I am a girl.

I just wanted to say –

We don't.

That's all.

WE ARE OUT THERE

The only person I've had an actual crush on in my life is Carys Last. Well, unless you count people I didn't know in real life, such as Sebastian Stan, Natalie Dormer, Alfie Enoch, Kristen Stewart, etc. Not that Carys was particularly more attainable than any of those.

I think the main reason I had a crush on her was because she was pretty, and I think the secondary reason I had a crush on her was because she was the only queer girl I knew.

Which is a bit silly, the more I think about it.

"So I was chatting to this girl from the Academy, *super* pretty, and— *wait*." Carys paused and stared at me. This was probably two months after we started sitting together on the train. I felt very stressed about it every single morning and afternoon because she was very intimidating and I was scared about saying something stupid in front of her. "You know I'm gay, don't you?"

I did not know.

She raised her eyebrows, probably at my expression of absolute shock. "Ah, I thought everyone knew that!" She rested her chin in her hand, her elbow on the table between us, and gazed at me. "That's funny."

"I've never met any gay people before," I said, "or bisexual people."

I almost added 'apart from me', but stopped myself at the last minute.

"You probably have," she said, "you just didn't know that they were gay."

The way she said it was like she'd met every person in the entire world.

She fluffed up her fringe with one hand and said in a spooky voice, "*We are out there.*"

I laughed, not knowing what to say.

She continued her story about the girl from the Academy and how she thought people were generally more homophobic at the Academy because it was a mixed school rather than an all-girls' school like ours, but I found it difficult to concentrate because I was trying to process what she had told me. It took me a moment to realise that my primary feeling about it was actually jealousy. She was living the teenage experience and I was doing homework every evening until midnight.

I hated her for having everything sorted and I admired her for being perfect.

I had a crush on her and I couldn't help it, but I didn't have to kiss her.

I didn't have to and I shouldn't have.

But that didn't stop me kissing Carys Last, one day in the summer two years ago, and ruining everything.

DANIEL JUN

On the morning of my first history exam, something pretty surprising happened.

Daniel Jun came to talk to me.

I was in the biggest room in the sixth form area, pretentiously named the 'Independent Learning Centre', or ILC, instead of what it actually was – a common room. I was reading some mind maps I'd made the week before, trying to memorise all the effects of the Truman Doctrine and the Marshall Plan (not an easy task at 8.20am), when he strode over to me, winding his body through the tables of last-minute-panic revisers.

Daniel really did think he was the ruler of the school even though we were head boy *and* girl, and he frequently went on long rants about capitalism on Facebook.

I found it bizarre that someone as mellow and kind as Aled Last could be best friends with someone as horrendous as Daniel Jun.

"Frances," he said, as he reached my table, and I looked up from my mind maps.

"Daniel," I said, with obvious suspicion.

He leaned on my table with one hand, but not before moving my mind maps swiftly away to make room.

"Have you spoken to Aled recently?" he said, running a hand through his hair.

That was completely not the question that I was expecting.

"Have I spoken to Aled recently?" I repeated.

Daniel raised his eyebrows.

"Well, we talk to each other on Facebook sometimes," I said, "and he helped me with some revision last week."

This was true, even though 'sometimes' meant every day, and 'helped me with some revision' meant literally came to my house for two hours in the middle of the night in his pyjamas even though we'd only spoken properly in person once before.

"Right," said Daniel. He nodded and looked down, but didn't move. I stared at him. His gaze moved towards my mind maps. "What's that?"

"This is a mind map, Daniel," I said, trying not to get too annoyed. I didn't want to be in a bad mood in my history exam. Writing about the division of Germany for two hours was sad enough.

"*Oh*," he said, looking at it as if it were a pile of vomit. "Okay."

I sighed. "Daniel, I really need to revise. It would be really great if you could go away."

He stood up straight again. "Fine, fine." But he didn't move. He just kept staring at me.

"*What?*" I said.

"Did…"

He paused. I stared. A new expression appeared on his face, and it took a moment for me to realise that it was *worry*.

"I just haven't seen much of him for a while," he said, and as he said it, his voice sounded different, softer, not like himself.

"Okay?"

"Has he said anything about me to you?"

Daniel stood, without moving, for a second more.

"Nope," I said. "Did you have an argument or something?"

"No," he said, but I wasn't sure whether he was telling the truth. He turned to walk away.

But then he stopped and turned back.

"What grades do you need to get? For Cambridge?"

"A★AA," I said. "How about you?"

"A★A★A."

"Oh, is it more for science?"

"I don't know."

We stared at each other for a moment, and then he shrugged and said, "Okay, bye," and walked off.

Maybe if I'd known what I know now, I would have said something to Aled. Would have asked him more about Daniel, about their relationship. Or maybe I wouldn't. I don't know. It's done now.

BORING

"Frances? Hello?"

I glanced up. Maya was looking at me from across our lunch table.

Our exams had come to an end and I was back at school. This meant we were starting our new A2 classes and I didn't want to let my concentration slip and miss out on any important information so I didn't think I'd get much time to see Aled before the summer holidays, but we'd agreed to meet up at the weekend anyway, and to be honest, I was pretty excited about it.

"Did you hear any of that?" continued Maya.

I had been doing some maths questions from the textbook. Homework that most people didn't do, but I always did.

"Er, no," I said, embarrassed.

My friends laughed.

"We were just thinking about going to the cinema on Saturday," said someone else. "You in?"

I glanced around for Raine, but she wasn't there.

"I think…" I paused. "Er, I've got too much work to do. I'll have to let you know."

My friends laughed again.

"Classic Frances," said one, just in a teasing way, but it still hurt a bit. "Don't worry."

The irony was that I actually didn't have any work to do at the weekend. We'd just finished our AS exams and we'd only just started our A2 courses.

But I was seeing Aled on Saturday and, to be honest, even though I'd only been speaking to him for a month, mostly on Facebook, I'd rather have hung out with him.

I was boring when I was with my school friends. I was quiet, work-obsessed, boring School Frances.

I wasn't like that when I was with Aled.

BABAR

The next time we saw each other in person after the midnight logarithms session was at his house, the Saturday of the week I went back to school. I didn't even feel nervous, which I found a bit weird because, as previously mentioned, I was usually nervous when seeing my school friends, let alone a guy I'd known properly for about four weeks.

I stood in front of his door and checked I wasn't wearing anything ridiculous by accident and then rang the doorbell.

He opened it within two seconds.

"Hi!" he said, with a smile.

His appearance was markedly different to the last time I'd seen him. His hair was longer, covering his ears and eyebrows completely now, and gone were the mismatched hoodie and shorts – he was back in plain jeans and a T-shirt. They didn't seem to suit him.

"Hi," I said. I sort of wanted to give him a hug, but I sensed that might be a bit awkward.

Despite being friends with Aled's twin sister for a year, I'd never been inside their house. Aled gave me a tour. There was a to-do list blackboard and a chores rota in the kitchen, fake flowers in vases covering the windowsills and surfaces, and a greying Labrador named Brian who loped after us until we went upstairs. Aled's mum wasn't home.

His room, on the other hand, was a treasure cavern. Every other room in his house was cream and brown, but his room had no visible wall due to all the posters, fairy lights covering the ceiling and the bed, several houseplants, a whiteboard with scribbles all over it, and no less than four different beanbags. He had a blanket on his bed that had the pattern of a city at night on it.

He seemed pretty nervous about letting me in his room. The floor, desk and bedside table were bare, like he'd tidied up and hidden things before I'd arrived. I tried not to stare too long at any particular part of the room and sat down on his desk chair – a safer option than the bed. Bedrooms are windows to the soul.

Aled sat down on his bed and crossed his legs. His bed was a single, less than half the size of my bed, but Aled wasn't very tall – we were the same height – so it was probably okay.

"So!" I said. "*Universe City!* Art! Planning! Stuff!"

I clapped my hands in between each word and Aled grinned and looked down. "Yes…"

We'd agreed to meet on that day to have a 'meeting' about *Universe City*. I specifically used the word 'meeting' when I suggested meeting up. It felt a bit weird to just ask him to hang out with me because I wanted to see him. Even though that was true.

Aled opened his laptop. "I was just looking at your blog because there's a few particular drawings that I thought would be really good for the videos… like, a good style…" He tapped away on the keyboard, but I couldn't see the screen. I spun from side to side on his desk chair.

Then he paused and looked up. He gestured for me to come towards him. "Come and look."

So I went and sat with him on the bed.

We went through my blog and chatted for a while about what sort of style would work for twenty-minute-long videos without me having to make a twenty-minute-long animation once a week (impossible). I did most of the talking at first, but he got more confident as we went on and by the end we were both rambling.

"But the thing with drawing the characters is that I think everyone's idea of what they look like is slightly different and there'd always be some people who were disappointed," he was saying, typing out notes on Evernote. We were both farther up the bed, leaning against the wall. "Like especially Radio – if you tried to draw Radio we'd face all sorts of questions like does their appearance change with their voice, or are they completely androgynous, and then what does total androgyny look like when gender isn't even anything to do with appearance or voice?"

"Yeah, exactly, you can't just have Radio in, like, masculine clothes with a skinny feminine body... that's such a stereotypical view of androgyny."

He nodded. "People can still be agender if they wear skirts and have beards and stuff."

"Exactly."

Aled typed 'Radio – no physical appearance' after a new bullet point, then nodded to himself, and then looked at me. "D'you want a drink or anything?"

"Yeah, sure! What've you got?"

He ran through the options and I picked lemonade and then he left to get us drinks. He made sure to shut his laptop, as if scared that I might immediately start searching his Internet history. I didn't blame him. I didn't trust me either.

I sat still for a moment.

And then I couldn't resist my curiosity any longer.

I went first to the bookshelf above his bed. On one side was a collection of aged CDs, including every Kendrick Lamar album, which surprised me, and five different Radiohead albums, which surprised me again. On another side was a pile of well-used notebooks and it felt too invasive to see what was inside them.

There wasn't anything on the desk, but after looking closer I noticed there were small splatters of dried paint and PVA glue. I didn't dare open any of the drawers.

I read some of the scribbles on his whiteboard. Not much of it made sense, but it seemed to be a mix of to-do lists and notes about upcoming *Universe City* episodes. 'Dark Blue' was circled. On the right he'd written 'stars – beaming down something, metaphor?' In one corner were the words 'JOAN OF ARC'.

I wandered over to his wardrobe, which was covered in film posters, and opened it.

This was extremely invasive, but I did it anyway.

I guess I wanted to know whether there was someone like me out there in the world.

There were T-shirts. A lot of T-shirts. T-shirts with patterned breast pockets, T-shirts with animals on them, T-shirts with all-over patterns of skateboarders and chips and stars. There were jumpers, huge woollen ones with wide necks, turtle-necks and ripped ones, cardigans with elbow patches, oversized sweatshirts, a boat pattern or a computer on the back or one that sported the word 'NO' in black Helvetica. There was a pair of trousers, pale blue, with embroidered ladybirds all over them and there was a five-panel cap with the NASA logo on it. There was a large denim jacket with Babar the Elephant on the back.

"Are you... inspecting my clothes?"

I turned, slowly, to find Aled standing in the doorway, a glass of lemonade in one hand. He looked a little surprised, but not angry.

"Why do you not wear any of this?" I said, feeling almost dazed, because this wardrobe might as well have been mine.

He chuckled and looked down at what he was wearing. Blue jeans and a grey T-shirt. "Er, I don't know. Dan— Daniel thinks I'm really weird."

I took his Babar jacket out of the cupboard and put it on, and then checked myself out in his mirror. "This is literally the best item of clothing I have ever seen. This is it. You have done it. You own the best item of clothing in the entire universe." I turned to him and struck a pose. "I'm probably going to steal this. Just so you know." I started rifling through his wardrobe. "This just... it looks like my wardrobe. I didn't know whether you were joking when you told me on Facebook, I would have worn something better today, but I didn't know. I have some leggings with *Monsters, Inc.* characters on them... I thought about wearing them but, like, I don't know... You need to tell me where you got these trousers because they're literally... I've never seen anything like them..."

I just kept talking and talking and I couldn't remember the last time I'd rambled like this to someone other than my mum. Aled looked at me. The sun was shining through the window on to his face so I couldn't really see what he was thinking.

"I honestly thought," he said, as I finally stopped talking, "you were, like... just some quiet, work-obsessed study machine person. Not that there's, like, anything *wrong* with being like that, but, er, I don't know. I just... thought you were really boring. And you're not."

The way he said it was so frank that I almost blushed. Almost.

He shook his head and laughed at himself. "Sorry, that sounded way less mean in my head."

I shrugged and sat back down on his bed. "I thought you were boring too, to be fair. And then I found out that you make my favourite thing in the entire world."

He smiled, embarrassed. "*Universe City* is your favourite thing in the world?"

I paused, wondering why I'd just said that. I wondered whether it was actually true. Too late to take it back now.

I laughed. "Er, yeah."

"That's... a really nice thing to say."

We got back to *Universe City* stuff, but very quickly got distracted when I was looking through his iTunes and we discovered we both liked M.I.A. and started watching her concerts on YouTube, sitting on his bed with the blanket over us and drinking our lemonade. I ended up reciting the full rap from 'Bring The Noize' as he watched in moderate amazement. I felt embarrassed about it until about halfway through when he started nodding along. After that we wondered whether we should get back to *Universe City* stuff, but Aled admitted he was kind of tired and I suggested watching a film, so we watched *Lost In Translation* because I hadn't seen it before and Aled accidentally fell asleep.

We met up again the next day. We got the train into town to go to Creams, a milkshake café, with the pretence of talking about *Universe City*, but instead we spent an hour talking about all the

TV shows we watched when we were children. We were both obsessed with Digimon and decided to watch the movie when we got home. I was wearing my *Monsters, Inc.* leggings and he was wearing his Babar jacket.

2. SUMMER HOLIDAY
a)

YOUR ART IS SO BEAUTIFUL

"Do you talk to yourself?" Aled said. "Out loud?"

It was the end of July and school was over and we were in my bedroom. I was on the floor, sketching ideas for my first *Universe City* episode on my laptop. I always brought my laptop with me to his house because Aled had a weird thing about other people using his laptop. He joked that he thought his mum checked it secretly while he was at school, and this had made him paranoid. I thought it was fair enough – I wouldn't want anyone accidentally stumbling across my Internet history, even Aled. Some things you really should just keep to yourself.

He was sitting on my bed, writing the script. The radio was on and the sun shone a strip of light across the carpet.

"Erm, sometimes," I said. "Yeah. If there's nobody around. It just happens by accident."

He didn't say anything, so I asked, "Why?"

He stopped typing and looked up, leaning his chin on one hand. "I was just thinking the other day… about the fact that I never speak to myself out loud. And I thought maybe that was normal, but then I wondered whether that was actually really strange."

"I thought talking to yourself was strange," I said. Mum had caught me doing it several times and laughed at me.

We both looked at each other.

"So who's the strange one?" I grinned.

"I don't know," he said, and then shrugged. "Sometimes I think if nobody spoke to me, I'd never speak again."

"That sounds sad."

He blinked. "Oh, yeah."

Everything with Aled was fun or good. Usually both. We started to realise that it didn't even matter what we did together, because we knew that if we were both there, we would have a good time.

I started to feel less embarrassed about all the weird things I did, like suddenly singing songs with absolutely no context, and my bottomless database of random encyclopaedic facts and that one time I started a four-hour-long text conversation about why cheese was a food.

I kept teasing him for having such long hair until he said one day, quite decisively, that he actually wanted it to be long, so I stopped teasing him after that.

We played video games or board games or watched YouTube videos or films or TV shows, we baked cakes and biscuits and ordered takeaway. We could only do stuff at his house when his mum wasn't in, so we were at my house most of the time. He'd sit through me screaming along to *Moulin Rouge* and I'd sit through him reciting every line from *Back To The Future*. I tried to learn the guitar using his guitar, but gave up because I was shit. He helped me paint a night-time cityscape mural on my bedroom wall. We watched four seasons of *The Office*. We sat in each other's rooms with our laptops on our legs; he kept falling asleep at random times of the day; I kept persuading him that *Just Dance* sessions were a good idea; we discovered that we were both very passionate about *Monopoly*. I didn't do any homework when I was with him. He didn't do any uni reading when he was with me.

But at the heart of it was *Universe City*.

We started sketching things for the video art and sticking all our ideas on my bedroom wall, but there were so many ideas that it took us ages to decide on anything. Aled had started asking me for advice while he was plotting future episodes and giving me spoilers and I felt so undeserving I almost told him to stop. Almost.

"I don't think this is working," I said, after we'd sat in silence for a while, sketching and typing. Aled glanced up, and I moved to show him what I was drawing on Photoshop — it was a city-scape of Universe City, with its flashing lights and dark alleyways. "I think the shapes are wrong. Everything's too pointy and square, it feels really flat."

"Hm," he said. I wondered whether he knew what I was talking about. I often found myself suddenly saying things that didn't really make sense in front of Aled and I think sometimes he just pretended to understand what I was saying. "Yeah. Maybe."

"I'm just not sure…" My voice trailed away.

I made my decision.

I leaned forward, reached underneath my bed and grabbed my current sketchbook. I opened it, flicked through, and found what I was looking for — another sketch of the city, but in this one the city looked completely different. It was more of an aerial view, and the buildings were curved and soft, like they were swaying in the breeze.

I'd never shown anyone my sketchbooks before.

"How about something like that?" I said, showing Aled the drawing.

Aled slowly took the sketchbook out of my hands. He gazed at it for a moment, and then said, "Your art is so beautiful."

I made a vague coughing noise.

"Thanks," I said.

"Something like this would be really good," he said.

"Yeah?"

"Yeah."

"Okay."

Aled continued to stare at the sketchbook. He ran his thumbs over the edges, and then turned to me. "Is this all *Universe City* stuff?"

I hesitated, and then nodded.

He looked back at the sketchbook. "Can I look through this?"

I knew he was going to ask, and I felt stupidly nervous about letting him, but I still ended up saying, "Yeah, sure!"

ANGEL

Aled caught the flu a few days later, but we were still aiming for my first episode to come out on August 10th, so I continued to visit him while he was sick. Also, I was starting to get used to seeing him every day, and felt a bit lonely when I didn't. None of my school friends had talked to me for a while.

Aled's mum never seemed to be home. I asked him why, and he said that she worked long hours. All I knew of her was that she enforced strict curfews – Aled had to be home by 8pm every evening – but that was it.

One afternoon while he was curled up in bed under his cityscape blanket, shivering, he said, "I don't understand why you keep coming here."

I wasn't sure whether he meant just while he was ill, or generally.

"We're friends," I said, "and I know I'm hilarious, but also I'm a worrier."

"But this isn't fun for you," he said, with a weak laugh. "I'm ill." His hair was greasy and stuck up in tufts. I was sitting on the floor, fully involved in the process of making him a sandwich with various items I'd brought from my house in a giant cool box.

"I don't know, I'd just be sitting by myself if I was at home. And that's even less fun."

He made a grumbling noise and said, "I just don't understand."

I laughed. "Isn't this what friends do?" But then I realised that I wasn't actually sure. No one had ever done something like this for me before. Was this really weird? Was I overstepping a boundary, invading his personal space, was I being really clingy…

"I… don't know," he mumbled.

"Well, you're the one who has a best friend." I regretted saying it as soon as it came out, but neither of us could deny it was true.

"Dan? He wouldn't visit while I was sick," Aled said. "There's no point. It'd just be boring."

"I'm not bored," I said, because it was the truth. "I have you to chat with. And sandwiches to make."

He laughed again and hid his face under the blanket. "Why are you so nice to me?"

"Because I'm an angel."

"You are." He stretched out his arm and patted me on the head. "And I'm platonically in love with you."

"That was literally the boy-girl version of 'no homo', but I appreciate the sentiment."

"Can I have my sandwich now?"

"Not yet. I don't think I've perfected the crisps to cheese ratio."

After his sandwich, Aled fell asleep, so I left a message on his whiteboard ('GET WELL SOON') along with a drawing (me driving an ambulance), and then walked back home, realising that the fact of the matter was that I didn't really know how to behave around friends at all.

REALLY DUMB

I didn't understand why Carys ever hung out with me until I realised that nobody else wanted to be friends with her, and essentially, I was the only option. This made me feel a bit sad because I knew that if she'd had the choice, she probably would have chosen someone else. She only liked me because I listened to her.

Once we'd moved from the grammar school to the Academy after the grammar school burned down, she started talking less about her school friends, and though she never told me why, I figured it was because there was nothing to tell, and nobody to talk about.

"Why d'you talk to me every day?" she asked me, one day in the spring on the way to school.

I didn't know whether to say it was because *she* talked to *me* every day, or because I didn't have anyone else to talk to, or because I had a crush on her.

"Why not?" I said, and grinned.

She shrugged. "Lots of reasons, really."

"Like what?"

"I'm just a bit annoying, aren't I?" she said. "And really dumb compared to you."

Her school grades were awful, I knew that. But I never felt like it made her inferior to me. In many ways, it felt like she transcended school – she didn't care, she didn't feel the need to care.

"You're not annoying or dumb," I said.

I really did feel like the whole thing would turn into some kind of brilliant romance. I thought she'd wake up one day and realise that I'd been there for her all along. I thought I'd kiss her and she'd realise that I cared about her more than anyone else in the entire world.

Delusional. I was delusional. I wasn't there for her at all.

"I think you'd get on with my brother," she said.

"Why?"

"You're both too nice." She looked down, and then out the window, and the sun shone in her eyes.

On the Importance of the Magic in the Pipes Below Us
Scroll down for transcript >>>

[…]

A spot of computer magic. That's really all it needs, friends. When you live in a city as big as this, how else are you to communicate, but by computer magic? The Governors recently repaired all the pipes – one of the few good things they've done for us recently. I swear I can feel something evil about them, but ignorance is bliss, I suppose.

I've got contacts all over the place. More useful than friends, really. I have eyes and ears everywhere, I see and hear everything. I'm ready for whatever they're going to throw at me. I know they're going to throw something at me. I've seen it in my dreams and in my fortune mirror. I can see it from a mile away, from ten miles away. It's coming.

But I have computer magic on my side. I have my friends— no, *contacts*. Way more valuable, old sport, I really am telling you. There's magic under our feet, not just in our eyes.

[…]

A TRUE FACT

"Frances, my darling, what's going on?"

Mum linked her fingers together and leaned towards me over the breakfast bar.

"Wha?" I said, because I had a mouthful of cereal.

"You haven't done a single piece of summer work or Cambridge prep all week." Mum raised her eyebrows and attempted to look serious. This didn't work because she was wearing her unicorn onesie. "And you've been hanging out with Aled about 500 per cent more than your normal friends."

I swallowed. "That is... a true fact."

"You've been wearing your hair down more often. I thought you didn't like it down."

"I can't be bothered to put it up all the time."

"But I thought you preferred it like that."

I shrugged.

Mum looked at me.

I looked at her.

"What's the prob?" I asked.

She shrugged. "It's not a problem. I was just intrigued."

"Why?"

"It's just different and unusual."

"So?"

Mum shrugged again. "I don't know."

I hadn't thought about it, but Mum did have a point. Most of my summer holidays were taken up with me doing summer homework, revision, work experience, or the occasional terrible job at one of the town restaurants or clothes shops.

I hadn't thought about any of those things.

"You're not stressed out or anything, are you?" Mum asked.

"No," I said. "No, I'm really not."

"And that's a true fact, is it?"

"A true fact."

Mum nodded slowly and said, "Okay. Just wanted to check. I haven't seen School Frances for a while."

"School Frances? What d'you mean?"

She smiled. "Something you said a while ago. Don't worry."

LAUGH AND RUN

It took me until a week into August to realise that Aled was actively blocking me from talking to his mum.

I knew only a few things about Carol Last. She was a parent governor. She was a strict single parent. She always made conversation with my mum when they saw each other in the village post office. If she was in, Aled said we had to be at my house or go out somewhere, because apparently she didn't like visitors.

Which sounded like a fair excuse until I actually met her.

That particular day I was planning to go round to his, and both Aled and I were late sleepers so we usually met up at around two. Since our trip to Creams, we'd both been wearing our weird clothes – me in my vast collection of bizarrely patterned leggings and oversized jackets and jumpers, him in his stripy shorts and giant cardigans and baggy T-shirts and those lime green plimsolls. That day he was wearing black shorts and an oversized black sweatshirt which had '1995' on it in bold white letters. His hair had just about grown long enough to have a parting.

I always thought he looked cooler than me, but he always thought I looked cooler than him.

Normally I'd have to knock on his door, but today he was sitting outside, waiting for me. Brian, Aled's ageing Labrador, was sat patiently on the kerb, but as soon as I stepped out of my house, he trotted up to me. Brian was in love with me already, which was doing good things for my self-esteem.

"Hello there," I said to Aled as I crossed the road.

Aled smiled and stood up. "All right?"

We only hugged now when we were saying goodbye. I think that made it more special.

The first thing I noticed was that his mum's car was in the drive. I already knew what Aled was about to say.

"I thought we could take Brian for a walk," he said, pulling his sleeves over his hands.

We were halfway down the road when I broached the topic.

"It's weird that I've never even, like, spoken to your mum."

There was a significant pause.

"Is it?" he said, keeping his head down.

"Yeah, like, I haven't even seen her. You've spoken to my mum loads of times." I figured we were close enough now for me to just ask the awkward question. I'd been doing this quite a lot for the past week. "Does your mum not like me?"

"What d'you mean?"

"I've been to your house, like, twenty times and I haven't seen her even once." I put my hands in my pockets. Aled didn't say anything, but he kept shifting from one foot to the other. "Let's be real. Is she racist or something?"

"No, oh my God, no…"

"Okay," I said, and waited for him to go on.

He stopped walking, mouth half open as if he were about to say something. But he honestly couldn't tell me what it was.

"Does she— does she hate me or something then?" I said, and then added a laugh, thinking it might lighten the tone.

And he said, "No! It's not you, I swear!" so quickly, with his eyes so wide, that I knew he wasn't lying. Then I realised how awkward I was being.

"It's fine, it's fine." I stepped back a little, shaking my head in what I hoped was a sort of nonchalant dismissal. "You don't have to tell me anything if you don't want to. It's fine. I'm just being weird." I looked down. Brian was gazing up at me, so I bent down and ruffled his fur.

"Allie?"

Aled whipped his head around and I looked up too, and there she was. Carol Last, leaning out of her car window. I hadn't even heard her car pull up behind us.

She looked terrifying, in that classic white, middle-class mum sort of way. Dyed cropped hair, slightly round physique, a smile that said 'Can I get you a cup of tea?' and eyes that said 'I will burn everything you love'.

"You heading out, sweetheart?" she said, eyebrows raised.

Aled was facing her so I couldn't see his expression.

"Yep, just taking Brian for a walk."

Then her eyes found me.

"All right, Frances, love?" She raised a hand and smiled. "Haven't seen you for a while."

I knew we were both thinking about Carys.

"Ah, yeah, I'm really good, thanks, yeah," I said.

"How were your exams? Everything go to plan?"

"I hope so!" I said, with a very forced laugh.

"Yes, don't we all!" She chuckled. "Aled's got some pretty high grades to get if he wants to get into this university of his, hasn't he?" She directed this at Aled. "But he revised like an absolute champ so I'm *sure* it'll all work out."

Aled said nothing.

Carol looked back at me with a half-smile. "He's worked so hard. The whole family's so proud. We knew he'd be a smart boy right from when he was a toddler." She chuckled again, looking up as if reliving a memory. "He could read books before he even started primary school. He had real natural ability, our Allie. Always destined to be an academic." She sighed and faced Aled. "But we all know that you don't get anything unless you *work hard*, don't we?"

"Mmm," said Aled.

"Can't get too distracted, can we?"

"Nope."

Carol paused and took a long look at her son. Her voice lowered slightly and then she said, "You won't be too long, will you, Allie? Nan's coming over at four and you said you'd be around."

"We'll be back by four," said Aled. His voice had gone weirdly monotonous.

"All right then," said Carol. She laughed a small laugh. "Don't let Brian eat any slugs!"

And then she drove off.

Aled started walking away down the road immediately. I jogged to catch up.

We walked in silence for a minute.

When we reached the end of the road, I said, "So... does she hate me or doesn't she?"

Aled kicked a stone. "She doesn't hate you."

We turned left and climbed over the stile separating the village from the fields and woods beyond. Brian, knowing our route, had already clambered over it and was sniffing the grass a little way ahead.

"Well, that's a relief!" I said, laughing, but there was still something.

We walked on and into the path through the cornfield. The corn had grown so tall that we couldn't see over it.

After a few more minutes, Aled said, "I just... really didn't want you to meet her."

I waited, but he didn't explain. He didn't, he couldn't. "Why? She seems fine..."

"Oh, yeah, she *seems* fine," Aled said, his voice dripping with a bitterness I hadn't heard from him before.

"Is she... not fine?" I asked.

He wasn't looking at me. "It's *fine*."

"Okay."

"Okay."

"*Aled*." I stopped walking. After a few more steps, he did too, and turned round. Brian was off somewhere ahead of us, snuffling in the corn.

"If you're feeling crap," I said, quoting exactly what he'd said to me the night he taught me an entire maths topic in one hour, "it's always better to talk about it."

He blinked, and then he grinned too, like he couldn't really stop himself. "I don't even know. I'm sorry."

He took a breath.

"I just really don't like my mum. That's all."

And I realised suddenly why he'd had so much difficulty telling me. Because it seems like such a juvenile thing to say. A teenage thing. *Ugh, I hate my parents*, kind of thing.

"She's just horrible to me all the time," he said. "I know she sounded really nice back there. She's just— she's— she doesn't usually act like that." He laughed. "It sounds really stupid."

"It's not," I said. "It sounds shitty."

"I just sort of wanted to keep you and her separate." The sun passed behind a cloud, and I could see him properly again. His hair lifted away from his forehead in the breeze. "Like... when we hang out, I don't have to think about her or any family stuff or... work stuff. I can just have fun. But if she gets to know you, then... the two worlds will, like, cross over." He made a gesture with his hands, and then he laughed again, but it was a sad laugh. "This is really stupid."

"It's *not*."

"I just..." He met my eyes, finally. "I just really like hanging out with you and I don't want anything to ruin it."

I didn't know what to say.

So I just hugged him.

And he went, "Oh," like he did the first time.

"I would literally cut off my leg before I let anything ruin this," I said, my chin on his shoulder. "Not even joking. I'd give up the Internet for a year. I'd burn my *Parks and Recreation* DVDs."

He snorted, "Shut up." But he brought his arms up to circle my waist.

"Not joking though," I said, and squeezed him tighter. I wasn't going to let anything ruin this. Not horrible parents, not school, not distance, not anything. It sounds kind of silly and stupid, this whole conversation. But I... I don't know what it was. I don't know why I felt this way when I'd only known him for two months. Was it because we liked the same music? Was it because our fashion tastes were the same? Was it because there were no awkward silences, there were no arguments, he helped me when no one else would, and I helped him when his own best friend was busy? Was it because I worshipped the story he wrote? I worshipped *him*?

I don't know. I don't care.

Being friends with Aled made me feel like I'd never had a real friend before, ever.

Half an hour later and we were chatting about the upcoming *Universe City* episode. Aled wasn't sure whether Radio should kill the latest sidekick, Atlas, or whether Atlas should sacrifice himself for Radio. Aled liked the sacrificing idea, but I said that Radio killing him would be sadder and therefore better, since Atlas had been the sidekick for over three months. I was kind of attached to Atlas and thought he deserved a good death.

"It could be a zombie situation," I said. "Like, Radio has to kill him before he turns into a raging flesh-eater. That never fails to bring out all the feels."

"That's *so* clichéd though," said Aled. He ran a hand through his hair. "It's got to be something original, or what's the point?"

"Okay, not zombies. Dragons. Dragons instead of zombies."

"Radio has to kill him before he turns into a *dragon*."

"To be honest, it's a bit shocking you haven't put any dragons in there yet."

Aled put his hand on his heart. "Wow. Rude."

"Dragons over zombies any day. Come on."

"Dragons aren't as sad as zombies though. Atlas could easily live a happy dragon life."

"Maybe he *should* live a happy dragon life!"

"What, so he *doesn't* die?"

"No, he just turns into a dragon and flies away. Still sad, but also hopeful. Everyone loves a sad but hopeful ending."

Aled frowned. "Hopeful… for a happy dragon life."

"Yeah. Guarding a princess or something. Burning some middle-aged knights."

"*Universe City* is set in the 2500s. We're straying into AU territory."

We crossed into a sheep field without noticing that the sky had clouded over, and when it started to rain, I lifted up my hand to check that it was really happening – it was summer, it was like twenty-two degrees, and it had been sunny five minutes ago.

"Noooooo." I turned to Aled.

Aled was squinting at the sky. "Wow."

I looked around us. A couple of hundred metres ahead was a patch of woodland – shelter.

I pointed towards it and looked at Aled. "Fancy a jog?"

"Haha, what?"

But I'd already started running – no, sprinting towards the trees across the grass, the rain already heavy enough that it kept stinging my eyes, Brian galloping along beside me. After a moment I could hear Aled running too, and I glanced behind me and stretched out my arm to him and cried, "Come along!" and he did; he reached out and took my hand and we ran like that through the countryside in the rain, and then he laughed, and it reminded me of a child's laugh, and I wished people could always laugh and run like that.

RADIO

My first *Universe City* episode came out on Saturday 10th August.

We'd settled on me making a small animation for each episode, not very long, just one that repeats throughout the twenty minutes. A four-second gif, repeating over and over and over again. The one I made for this episode was of the city – Universe City – growing out of the ground, and stars flashing in the sky. Looking back now, I guess it was pretty crap, but we both loved it at the time, which is what matters, I think.

I listened to Aled record the episode the night before. I was astounded that he let me. I knew Aled was a more private and quiet person than I was, even though we'd played *High School Musical Just Dance* that week, and 'performing', if that's what this was, didn't seem like something he would be okay with. Aled performing an episode of *Universe City* felt more personal than anything I'd seen or heard of him before, including the time we had a 2am discussion about bowel movements.

But he was okay with it.

He turned his bedroom light off. The fairy lights above our heads looked like tiny stars and the tips of his hair were lit up all different colours. He slumped into his desk chair and fiddled for a few minutes with this beautiful microphone, which must have cost a shitload of money. I was on a beanbag, his city blanket wrapped around me because it was always freezing in his house, tired, the room was dark blue and hazy, I could have fallen asleep –

"Hello. I hope somebody is listening..."

He'd written the script out on his laptop. He repeated lines if he got them wrong. As he recorded, the sound waves bounced up and down on his computer screen. It was like I was listening to a completely different person – no, not different, just *more* of Aled. Aled at 100 per cent. Aled being himself. I was listening to Aled's brain.

I zoned out, like I always did. I got lost in the story, I forgot about things.

Every episode of *Universe City* ends with a performance of a song. The same song, every time – a thirty-second rock song Aled had written called 'Nothing Left For Us' – but a new performance.

I didn't realise Aled was going to perform it right then and there until he picked up his electric guitar and plugged it into his amp. Some pre-recorded drums and bass guitar started playing out of his speakers, and when he played his guitar it was so loud that I clapped my hands over my ears. It was like it always was, but so much better in person, like a thousand guitars and chain-saws and lightning all at once, the bass making the wall shake behind my head, and then he started to sing in that shouty way that I could have sung along with, I wanted to sing along with, but I didn't, because I didn't want to ruin it. I already knew both the tune and the lyrics.

There's nothing left for us any more
Why aren't you listening?

Why aren't you listening to me?

There's nothing left.

When he'd finished, he turned round again in his desk chair and said, back in his quiet voice, like I'd snapped out of a dream, "So, what voice? High, low or medium?"

It was 10pm. His bedroom ceiling looked like a galaxy. He told me he'd painted it when he was fourteen.

"You choose," I said.

He pulled his sleeves over his hands. I was starting to figure out what that meant.

I said, "This is the best day of my whole life."

He grinned. "Shut up." He turned back to his laptop, his body silhouetted against the brightness of the screen, and said, "I think medium voice. I like androgynous Radio the best."

FEBRUARY FRIDAY

My Tumblr got over 1,000 new followers in one day. I was flooded with asks telling me how much they loved my art and congratulations for getting to work with the show that I'd been obsessed about, along with a few asks telling me how much they hated it, and me, obviously.

I was everywhere in the *Universe City* Tumblr tag – my art, my blog, my Twitter, *me*. They still didn't know anything about me, really, which I was actually grateful for. Internet anonymity can be a good thing sometimes.

Aled knowing I was Toulouse, the *Universe City* artist, was fine, but the idea of anyone else finding out still terrified me.

And of course, once my involvement with *Universe City* was revealed, I was bombarded with tweets and questions on Tumblr asking who the Creator was. I had expected it, but that didn't mean it failed to stress me out. I couldn't. post anything online for several days after the episode without a fresh wave of questions about who I was and who the Creator was.

As soon as I showed Aled the messages, he panicked.

We were sitting in my lounge on the sofa watching *Spirited*

Away. He read the messages in my Tumblr inbox. As he scrolled, he put a hand on his forehead. Then he started saying, "Oh, no, oh, no, oh, God," under his breath.

"It's okay, it's not like I'm gonna tell them…"

"We can't let them find out."

I didn't really know why Aled wanted to keep *Universe City* a secret. I assumed it was just because he liked his privacy; he didn't want his face on the Internet. It felt a bit invasive to ask.

"Okay," I said.

"I've got an idea," said Aled.

He opened Twitter on his laptop and typed out a tweet.

RADIO @UniverseCity
February Friday – i still believe, i still listen.

"February Friday," I said. "Yes. Good idea."

February Friday, or the 'Letters to February' segment, produces probably the biggest conspiracy theories within the *Universe City* fandom.

The fandom wiki explained it quite well.

February Friday and Fandom Theories
It is commonly believed within the Universe City fandom *that the entire series is a gift from* the Anonymous Creator *to a person they are/were in love with.*

The large majority of the early episodes (2011) *and around half of the later episodes* (2012-*onwards*) *contain a passage, usually towards the end of the episode, directed towards a character who never makes any appearance or has any story arc,* February Friday. *In these segments,*

Radio Silence typically laments their inability to communicate with February Friday, muddled in with abstract imagery and indeterminable metaphors.

Usually the segment is largely nonsensical, leading the fandom to believe that they are mostly comprised of personal jokes which the Anonymous Creator shares with the person IRL represented by February Friday. As these segments contribute nothing to Universe City's plot, and have no sequential plot of their own, the fandom argues that they must contain some significance to the Creator.

Many attempts have been made to determine the meaning of what has become known as the Letters to February, but all attempts are merely guesswork and objective analyses.

So Radio tweeting about February Friday obviously caused a fandom shitstorm. A brief, inconclusive one, but an undeniable *shitstorm*.

And everyone was completely distracted from sending me messages demanding to know who I am and who Radio is.

Since getting to know Aled, I'd thought a lot about the February Friday conspiracy – about who February might be, if they were a representation of somebody he knew. My immediate thoughts went to Carys, but I rejected that idea, since the Letters to February were so romantic. I even considered me at one point, before realising that Aled hadn't even known me when he started making *Universe City*.

Of course, being friends with Aled now meant that I had the opportunity to ask about February Friday.

Which I did.

"So… just putting this out there…" I rolled over on the sofa so I was facing him. "Am I allowed to know the secret of February Friday?"

Aled bit his lip and genuinely thought about it.

"Hmm…" He rolled over so he was facing me too. "Okay, don't be offended, but I think it needs to stay an ultimate secret."

And I thought that was fair enough.

UNIVERSE CITY: Ep. 32 – cosmic noise
<u>UniverseCity</u>

Have you been listening so far?

Scroll down for transcript >>>

[…]

I think by now, February, we've, as they say, 'lost touch'. Not that we ever touched in the first place. In the end I'm still only ever looking where you've looked, I'm only ever walking where you've walked, I'm in your dark blue shadow and you never seem to turn around to find me there.

I wonder sometimes whether you've exploded already, like a star, and what I'm seeing is you three million years into the past, and you're not here any more. How can we be together here, now, when you are so far away? When you are so far ago? I'm shouting so loudly, but you never turn around to see me. Perhaps it is I who have already exploded.

Either way, we are going to bring beautiful things into the universe.

[…]

THE BIG SCHEME OF THINGS

Thursday 15th August was results day. It was also Aled's 18th birthday.

Our friendship had become this:

(00:00) **Frances Janvier**
HAPPY BIRTHDAY HOPE YOU'RE FEELING PARTY AF
LOVE U LOADS U BEAUTIFUL MAN
CAN'T BELIEVE MY SMALL BUDDY IS A MAN NOW
I'M CRYING

(00:02) **Aled Last**
why are you tormenting me with cringe messages like this

(00:03) **Frances Janvier**
¯_(ツ)_/¯

(00: 03) **Aled Last**
Wow
thank u tho luv u (✿♥‿♥)

(00:04) Frances Janvier
THAT was cringe m8

(00:04) Aled Last
that was payback

I was stressing out quite a lot about results day, because that's what I always do. I was also stressing out because I hadn't seen or talked to my school friends in almost three weeks. With any luck, I could just walk in, grab my results and scarper before anyone could ask me the dreaded 'How were your results?' question.

"I'm sure you've done fine, France," said Mum, shutting the car door. We'd just arrived at school and I was boiling in my school suit. "Oh, God, sorry, that's literally the least helpful thing I could possibly say."

"Pretty much," I said.

We walked through the car park, into the sixth-form block and up the stairs to the ILC. Mum kept glancing at me. I think she wanted to say something, but honestly, there really isn't anything to say when you're about to read four letters that shape the rest of your life.

The room was packed because Mum and I were a bit late. There were teachers at desks handing out brown envelopes. There were wine glasses on a table at the back for the parents. A girl from my history class was crying only five metres away and I tried not to look at her.

"I'll get you some wine," said Mum. I turned to her. She looked at me and said, "It's just school, isn't it?"

"*It's just school.*" I shook my head. "It's never *just school.*"

Mum sighed. "It doesn't matter though. In the Big Scheme of Things."

"If you say so," I said, rolling my eyes.

I got four A grades. That's the highest you can get at AS level.

I expected to be happy about it. I expected to be jumping up and down and crying from joy.

But I didn't feel any of that. It just wasn't disappointment.

My Year 10 results day was the day before Carys ran away. It was her Year 11 results day, which was obviously important, because that's when you get most of your GCSE results. I knew she never got very good grades, but that was the only day I ever saw her get upset about it.

I'd just got my results for the science GCSE I'd taken a year early, for which I'd received an A★, and I was walking out of this same room, the ILC, with Mum, staring at the tiny Times New Roman 'a★', the first of many to come. We walked down the stairs and were about to exit the building when Carys and Carol Last walked right past the open door, heading towards the car park.

I heard the words "Really quite pathetic," and I guess it was Carol who said them, but to this day I can't be sure.

Carys had tears streaming down her face and her mum was holding on to her arm so tight that it must have hurt.

I drank the wine mum stole for me in pretty much one go, facing the wall so none of the teachers saw me. Then we passed Dr Afolayan, who tried to catch my eye, and we walked out of the room and down the stairs and out of the building and into the sunlight. My grip on my results envelope had crumpled it and smudged my name.

"Are you okay?" said Mum. "You don't seem very happy."

She was right, but I didn't know why.

"Frances!"

I spun round, praying it wasn't any of my friends, but of course it was. It was Raine Sengupta. She'd been leaning on a railing outside the building, talking to someone I didn't know. She walked up to me. She'd had the right side of her hair freshly shaved.

"All good, mate?" she said, nodding at my envelope.

I smiled. "Yeah! Yep. Four A's."

"Holy shit, well done!"

"Thanks, yeah, I'm really pleased."

"So you're all good for Cambridge, yeah?"

"Yeah, I should be."

"Sweet."

There was a pause.

"How about you?" I asked.

Raine shrugged. "Two C's, a D and an E. Not great, but I think Afolayan'll let me back in. If I do some retakes."

"Ah…" I had no idea what to say, and Raine could obviously tell.

She laughed. "It's fine. I don't do any work and my art course-work was proper *shit*."

We said some awkward goodbyes and me and Mum walked off again.

"Who was that?" said Mum, once we got to the car.

"Raine Sengupta?"

"I don't think you've mentioned her before."

"She's just in our friendship group. We're not that close."

My phone buzzed and it was a text from Aled and he said:

Aled Last
4 A★s! i'm in.

Mum flipped the sun visor down in front of her and said, "Ready to go home?" and I said, "Yeah."

THE CIRCLE OF EVILS

There was a huge Facebook event for the post-exams night happening at Johnny R's on the same day, which everyone in sixth form had been invited to, but I didn't really want to go. Firstly, everyone was just gonna get drunk, which I could do perfectly well by myself in my lounge while watching YouTube videos instead of having to worry about catching the last train home or avoiding sexual assault. Secondly, I hadn't really spoken to any of my school friends apart from Raine very recently, and I think if we were in *The Sims*, our friendship bar would almost be back to nothing.

I knew Aled was busy celebrating his birthday with Daniel, which was a bit weird since I didn't think they'd actually spent a lot of time together recently, but Daniel was actually his lifelong best friend, so fair enough. Mum had bought champagne and said we could order pizza and play *Trivial Pursuit*. I'd be able to give Aled his present tomorrow.

What I was not expecting was Daniel Jun knocking on my door at 9.43pm.

I was pretty tipsy, but even if I'd been sober I still would have laughed my arse off. He was wearing his old grammar school uniform – the one he'd worn until sixth form when he moved to the Academy. In theory it was completely normal – a black blazer and trousers and a plain navy tie and a crest with a gold 'T' on it – but since Daniel's Year 12 growth spurt, the trousers ended just above his ankles and the blazer was so tight and short in the arms that he looked absolutely ridiculous.

He just stood there, eyebrows raised, while I laughed and laughed.

"Oh my God, you look like Bruno Mars!" There were small tears forming in my eyes.

Daniel frowned. "Bruno Mars is of Puerto Rican and Filipino heritage, not Korean, so that's incredibly offensive."

"I was referring to the shortness of your trousers. Are you auditioning for *Jersey Boys*?"

He blinked. "Yes. Yes, that's actually my life goal. I wrote it on my careers survey."

"Your Bruno Mars trivia is impressive, by the way." I leaned against the doorway. "You don't fancy a game of *Trivial Pursuit*, do you? I'm right in the middle of one."

"Well, why else would I possibly be here, Frances?"

We looked at each other.

There was a pause.

"Why *are* you here?" I said. "Aren't you supposed to be with Aled?"

He raised his eyebrows again. "Basically, we were going to go to the post-exams thing at Johnny R's, but Aled doesn't really want to, and he was saying that it'd be nice to see you on his birthday."

"I thought you two were hanging out."

"We are, actually."

"Without me."

"We have been so far."

"So I'd be the ultimate third wheel."

He laughed. "Yeah, I know, right!"

I considered shutting the door in his face.

"Are you coming or not?" he said.

"Are you going to be a dick to me for the entire evening if I do?"

"Probably."

At least he was honest.

"Okay, fine," I said, "but I have two questions. Firstly, why are you wearing your old grammar school uniform?"

"That was the theme of the post-exams Johnny R's thing." He put his hands in his pockets. "Did you even read the Facebook event?"

"I skimmed it."

"Right."

"Secondly, why isn't Aled here?"

"I told him I was going to take a piss."

"He thinks you're in the loo right now?"

"Yup."

I stared at Daniel. This was entirely his idea. He was actually doing something *nice* for someone. Sure, if he was going to do anything nice for anyone ever it was probably going to be Aled, but *still*. This was... something.

"All right then," I said. "Cool. It's gonna be awkward though, since you literally despise me."

"I don't *literally despise you*," he said. "That's so dramatic."

I put on his posh accent. "Oh, sorry, I mean we *don't particularly get on*."

"Only because you give me evils all the time."

"Excuse me, *you're* the one who gives *me* evils all the time!"

We stared at each other.

"An evils paradox," I continued. "The circle of evils. Evils-ception."

"Are you wearing that?" he said.

I looked down. I was wearing my Batman onesie.

"Yes," I said. "Problem?"

"So many," he said, turning round. "So many problems."

So I went inside and told my mum I was going to Aled's, and she said that was fine because she still needed to catch up on *The Great British Bake Off* and could I please not be too loud when I came in, and then I grabbed my keys from the bowl near the door and Aled's birthday card and present from the kitchen table and put some shoes on and I took one last look at myself in the landing mirror. My makeup was pretty crap and my hair had started to fall out of its topknot, but I didn't really care that much. What were we gonna do, get more drunk in Aled's lounge? That's all there was to do, apparently. I don't know. So, yeah, drinking, cool, I don't know.

POWER STATION

"I don't know whether you're aware," I said, as we walked down the road in the complete opposite direction to Aled's house, "but this is not the way to Aled's house."

"You're so amazingly intelligent," Daniel said. "Did you get your four A's?"

"Yep. Did you?"

"Yup."

"Nice." Then I shook my head. "So where are we going? I'm not exactly dressed to go out."

Daniel was walking a couple of steps ahead. He spun round and started walking backwards, looking at me, his face brought out of the dark by the streetlamps.

"We thought we'd camp in the field," he said.

"Is that legal?"

"Probably not."

"Aw, you're breaking a rule! I'm so proud."

He just turned away from me. Hilarious.

"I haven't seen you and Aled hanging out much this summer," I said.

He didn't look at me. "So?"

"I don't know. Have you been on holiday?"

He laughed. "I wish."

"You said you hadn't seen much of him."

"When did I say that?"

"Erm." I was getting the sense that I was venturing into awkward territory. "You know, before my history exam, you came to talk to me…"

"Oh. No, we've just been busy. I work, like, five days a week at Frankie & Benny's in town. And you know he's not very good at replying to texts."

He always replied to my texts, but I didn't say that to Daniel.

"How'd you two get so close anyway?" he said with a frown.

"I rescued him from a club," I said, and Daniel didn't say anything. He looked away and stuffed his hands into his pockets.

The sky wasn't quite black yet, it was still sort of dark blue and hazy, but you could see the moon and a few stars, which was nice, I guess. We climbed over the stile and into the empty field next to the village and I was struck by how quiet it was. There wasn't any wind, any cars, any *anything*. I felt like I hadn't been anywhere so quiet my whole life, even though I've lived here, in the countryside, since I was born.

In a patch of dry earth in the middle of the field was a small campfire and next to that was a large tent, and next to that was Aled Last, his whole body glowing gold from the fire. He was wearing his actual school uniform, which fitted him, because he'd worn it within the past two months, but it still looked sort of odd on him, probably because I was used to seeing him dressed in interestingly-coloured shorts and oversized knitwear.

How was he eighteen? How could anyone I knew possibly be eighteen years old?

I ran past Daniel and his ankle swingers, ran through the grass, and fell on top of Aled.

An hour later and we were three quarters of the way through a bottle of vodka, which did not bode well for me because alcohol just makes me fall asleep.

Aled had opened his present – it was a radio shaped like a skyscraper. The windows lit up in time with the audio that was playing. He told me that it was the best thing he'd ever seen in his whole life, which was probably a lie, but I was glad he liked it. It was battery-operated so we put Radio 1 on in the background and there was some kind of electronic-themed show going on, lots of mellow synth and low bass. The lights of the town and the power station flickered in the distance.

Daniel took one look at it and then said, "Jesus fucking Christ. You know about *Universe City*, don't you."

Drunk Daniel was only more sarcastic and more sweary and more patronising than Sober Daniel, but somehow that made it easier to laugh at him rather than punch him in the face.

"Er," I said.

"Er," Aled said.

"Don't *er* me, I can see right through you both." Daniel threw his head back and laughed. "Well, it was only a matter of time before someone worked it out." He leaned towards me. "How long've you been listening? Were you there when I used to play bass in the theme tune?"

I laughed. "You play bass?"

"Not any more."

Aled interrupted before I could say anything else. For the last half an hour he'd been setting a stick alight and making shapes with the fire in the air like a sparkler. "She's the new artist."

Daniel frowned. "Artist?"

"Yeah, she made the gif for last week's episode."

"Oh." Daniel's voice quietened a little. "I haven't listened to last week's yet."

Aled grinned. "You're such a fake fan."

"Shut up, I'm obviously a fan."

"Fake fan."

"I was the first person to even *subscribe*."

"Fake fan."

Daniel chucked a handful of dirt at Aled and Aled laughed and rolled over to avoid it.

This whole evening was silly. I didn't really understand why we were hanging out. Aled wasn't in my year group; he didn't go to my school. Daniel didn't even like me. What sort of a friendship group is two boys and one girl?

Daniel and Aled started talking about their results.

"I'm just… really relieved," Daniel was saying. "Like, getting into a good uni to do biology… I've wanted it for, like, six years. I'd hate myself if I messed it up now."

"I'm really pleased for you," said Aled, who was lying on his side, still poking a stick into the fire.

"You must be really pleased for *you* though."

"Haha, yeah, I don't know," said Aled, which I didn't really get. Why wouldn't he be pleased about his results? "It's good. I just don't think I care about anything *that* much."

"You care about *Universe City*," I said.

Aled glanced at me. "Ah, yeah. Okay. That's true."

I could feel myself getting tired and my eyes shutting. Carys popped into my head – we'd got drunk like this on the same day two years ago, results night, at that house party. That had been a bad night.

When exactly was I going to bring Carys up with Aled?

"Well, I saw *a lot* of people crying about their grades this morning, so I think you should be celebrating," said Daniel. He passed the vodka and Coke bottles to Aled. "Drink up, birthday boy."

I knew I'd reach the next level of drunk soon where I'd say stuff I'd regret later. Maybe I'd fall asleep before then, but maybe I wouldn't. I ripped some grass out of the ground and started scattering it into the fire.

KANYE WOULDN'T
HAVE LIKED IT

We were in a field and then we weren't and then we were again – somehow I'd acquired a blanket and Aled and I were singing along to Kanye West. Aled knew the full rap but I didn't, so he gave a dramatic performance in front of the stars. It was warm and the sky was lovely. Kanye wouldn't have liked it.

We were in the tent and Daniel had fallen asleep after throwing up in the brambles and staggering back to us with a giant scratch all up one arm and Aled was saying, Aled is saying, "On the one hand I'm thinking yeah this work is important, like, it's really important that I get the grades and get accepted, but on the other hand my brain is just like, I don't know, I just don't care, it'll all be all right in the end or something, like, so it's getting to the point where I just don't do any work if I don't have to, I only do the things I have to do, but I just don't care? I don't know, this doesn't make any sense…" For some reason I keep nodding and smiling and saying, "Yeah."

I'm asking Aled, "Who's February Friday?"

But he's saying, "I can't tell you!"

And I'm saying, "But we're friends!"

And he's saying, "That's irrelevant!"

"Are you in love with them? Like the fandom says?"

He laughs and doesn't answer.

We're standing in the middle of the field seeing who can scream the loudest.

We're taking blurry night-time photos and tweeting them to each other, and I'm wondering whether this is a good idea, even though I know no one would be able to make out our faces, but somehow struggling to do anything about it.

RADIO @UniverseCity

@touloser toulouse candid [blurry photo of her with a double-chin]

toulouse @touloser

@UniverseCity Radio revealed [blurry photo of Aled's shoes]

We're lying in the grass.

I say, "I think I can hear a fox."

Aled says, "The voice inside my head is Radio's voice."

I say, "How are you not cold?"

Aled says, "I stopped feeling anything ages ago."

We're lying in the tent.

I say, "I used to get these really bad nightmares called night terrors where you wake up and you still think you're in the nightmare."

Aled says, "Every night I get chest pains and I'm convinced I'm gonna die."

I say, "You're not supposed to get them once you're a teenager."

Aled says, "Chest pains or night terrors?"

★

We've been trying to record an episode of *Universe City* for the past ten minutes, but all that's happened so far is Aled and I have played a game of tag, resulting in me falling on him again (by accident this time). I spent a good few minutes pretending to be a character I made up on the spot and called 'Toulouse', like my Internet identity, and now all three of us are playing Never Have I Ever.

"Never have I ever..." Aled taps his chin. "Never have I ever farted and blamed it on someone else."

Daniel groans and I laugh and both of us take a swig of our drinks.

"You haven't done that?" I ask Aled.

"No, I'm not that shameless. I take responsibility for my actions."

"Fine. Never have I ever..." I look between the pair. "Broken curfew."

Daniel laughs and says, "You are *lame*," and takes a drink, but Aled shoots him a look and says, "I'm lame as well then," and Daniel immediately looks guilty.

"Never have I ever..." Daniel taps his bottle. "...said 'I love you' and didn't mean it."

I make a long 'Oooooh' sound. Aled raises his cup as if to take a drink, but then seemingly changes his mind and rubs his eye instead, or maybe he'd just needed to rub his eye in the first place. Neither of us drink.

"Okay, never have I ever..." Aled pauses then, and his eyes glaze over. "Never have I ever wanted to go to university."

Daniel and I don't say anything for a moment, and then Daniel laughs like Aled's probably joking, and then Aled laughs like he's probably joking too, but I don't know what to do, because it doesn't feel like Aled is joking at all.

★

I doze off not long after that in the tent and then wake up to find Daniel sleeping next to me but Aled nowhere, and I stumble out of the tent to see him walking in circles in the grass, his phone close to his mouth, mumbling things I can't quite hear properly. I wander over to him and ask, "What are you saying?" and he looks up and his whole body flinches and he says, "Jesus Christ, I didn't hear you coming," and then both of us forget what we were talking about.

Daniel wakes up to sing 'Nothing Left For Us' with us. The visuals are just blurry shapes – us running across the landscape in the dark, flashes of eyes, flashes of skin. We post the episode to YouTube before we change our minds.

Daniel and I lie next to each other and he says, "One day, when I was five, some girl made fun of my real name, like, *all day*. She was just running round the playground screaming "DAE-SUNG, DAE-SUNG, DAE-SUNG, DAE-SUNG'S GOT A STUPID NAME," in a really silly voice and it made me *so* upset, like, I was *crying* and my teacher had to call my mum. And I was still crying when my mum came to pick me up. My mum's honestly the sweetest lady in the world, and she took me home and said to me, "How about we give you a real *English* name, huh? We live in England now and you're an English boy." Which made me really happy at the time. And she told my school to change my name in the register to Daniel and that was that."

I nod at him. "Do you wish people called you Dae-Sung?"

"Yeah. I know my mum had good intentions but 'Daniel' feels like a lie. I might change it back once I get to university…"

"I wish I had an Ethiopian name sometimes," I say. "Or just

148

an East African name... I wish I was closer to my ethnicity in general, really."

Daniel rolls his head towards me. "What about your parents? Aren't they...?"

"My mum's white. My dad's Ethiopian but he and my mum got divorced when I was four and he lives in Scotland now with his own family. We still talk on the phone fairly often but I only see him a few times a year, and I hardly ever see my grandparents and aunts and uncles and cousins from that side of the family. I just wish I felt closer to them... sometimes I feel like I'm the only black person I know. Like, my dad's surname is Mengesha. I wish I was Frances Mengesha."

"Frances Mengesha. That sounds good."

"I know, right."

"Your initials would be FM. Like FM radio."

We can still hear the fox. It sounds like someone being brutally murdered.

Aled lies down next to the fire and closes his eyes and Daniel rolls over and kneels up and puts his hands flat on the grass on each side of Aled's face and leans over him. Aled opens his eyes but can't keep eye contact. His eyes scrunch up as he laughs and rolls over, pushing Daniel away.

I go to investigate the fox, I head towards the sound, towards the National Trust footpath through the woods, and you think I'd be scared or something, in the dark in the woods in the night, but I'm not.

I almost make it there when a person starts walking towards me, and that's when I get scared, *shit* scared, I nearly fall over or turn and run, but then I shine my phone light on the person, and it's legitimately Carys Last, wandering around in the dark in the middle of the night, and I'm like:

"Jesus Christ."

No – wait. It's not her. It's just a dream.

Wait, am I asleep now?

"Not him," Carys says. "It's me." But I wouldn't be surprised if it was Jesus because she looks like she's walking out of heaven itself, or maybe it's just my phone torch shining on her skin and her platinum hair.

I wasn't dreaming. This did happen, two years ago, on results night.

We'd been at a house party. She'd wandered off into the woods.

Why am I remembering this now?

"Are you, like… a were-fox?" I asked her.

"No, I just like wildlife," she said. "At night."

"You shouldn't walk around in the dark at night."

"Neither should you."

"Well, shit. You got me there."

Maybe nothing was happening.

We'd been drinking. Me especially. And we'd been to a lot of house parties before this. I was getting used to the way people would just pass out one by one or throw up in plant pots. I was getting used to the group of boys who would always sit in the garden and smoke weed because, well, I don't really know why they did it. I was getting used to the way people got off with each other without a second thought, even if it made me feel disgusting to even watch it happen.

We walked back to the party together. It was two, maybe three in the morning.

We walked through the back garden gate and past some bodies in the grass.

She'd been so quiet that day. Quiet and sad.

We sat down on a sofa in the lounge. It was so dark inside we could barely see each other.

"What's wrong?" I said.

"Nothing," she said.

I didn't push it, but after a moment, she continued.

"I'm jealous of you," said Carys.

"What? Why?"

"How d'you just... *slide* through life like that? Friends, school, family..." She shook her head. "How d'you just slide through it all without fucking up."

I opened my mouth to say something, but nothing came out.

"You've got so much more power than you think you do," she said. "But you just waste it. You just do whatever anyone else says."

I still didn't know what she was talking about, so I just said, "You're weird for fifteen."

"Ha. You sound like an adult."

I frowned. "You're the one being patronising as *fuck*."

"You get sweary when you're drunk."

"I'm always sweary inside my head."

"Everyone's different inside their head."

"You're so..."

Suddenly we're by the fire and Aled's asleep next to Daniel in the tent and time keeps skipping. How did we get here? Is Carys actually here? In the gold light of the fire she looks demonic. "Why are you like this?" I ask her.

"I want..." She has a drink in her hand; where did that come from? This isn't really happening. This didn't really happen. "I just want somebody to listen to me."

I don't remember when she left or anything else she said apart from two minutes later when she stood up and said, "Nobody listens to me."

BLANKET BUNDLE

We were lying down on Aled's living-room carpet. The tent had been a bad idea — it was cold and we'd run out of water and none of us wanted to pee outdoors — so we stumbled inside. We must have done, I guess. I don't remember it happening. I just remember Aled muttering something about his mum being away with family for a few days, which was weird, because why wouldn't you be with your son on his birthday?

Daniel fell asleep again on the sofa and Aled and I huddled up on the floor. We had blankets on top of us and all the lights were off and all I could see of Aled was his pale eyes, all I could hear was a low synth rumble coming from the skyscraper radio. I couldn't quite believe how much I seriously loved Aled Last, even if it wasn't in the ideal way that would make it socially acceptable for us to live together until we die.

Aled rolled over so he was facing me.

"Did you hang out with Carys much?" he asked, his voice barely above a murmur. "Apart from on the train."

We hadn't talked about Carys before.

"We weren't really friends, to be honest," I lied. "We hung out when I was in Year 10, but we weren't really friends."

Aled kept on looking at me. There was a slight twitch of his eyebrows.

I wanted to ask why he never sat with his sister on the train to school. I wanted to ask whether Carys ever spoke about me during that summer when we were all fifteen. I wanted to ask what she'd said when she got home the night I kissed her, whether she was still angry, whether she'd told him how she'd screamed at me, whether she'd said she hated me now, whether she'd always hated me.

I wanted to ask whether he ever heard from her, but I couldn't, so I didn't. I wanted to tell him that it was my fault she was gone.

I wanted to tell him that I'd once had a crush on his sister, and one day I kissed her when she was sad because I thought it was the right thing to do, even though I'd been wrong.

"You know..." Aled's voice faded out and he didn't speak for half a minute. "My mum won't tell me where she is. Or how she is."

"What? Why not?"

"She doesn't want me to see her. My mum *hates* her. I mean properly *hates*. Not just parental disapproval or whatever. My mum never wants to see her again."

"That's really... messed up."

"Mm."

Sometimes I was hit by the weight of all the things I didn't know, not just about Carys but about anything, everything. What's it like to have a parent you don't like, or who doesn't like you? What's it like to run away from home? I don't know, I'll never know. I'll always feel awful about not knowing.

"I think it might have been my fault," I said.

"What was?"

"Carys running away."

Aled frowned. "What? Why would you say that?"

I needed to tell him.

I said, "I kissed her. I ruined our friendship."

Aled blinked, startled. "What— did you?"

I nodded and breathed out and felt like I'd just jumped out of the ocean.

"That's— it wasn't your fault," he said. "That wasn't…" He cleared his throat. "It's not your fault."

I hated myself. I hated myself so much I wanted to sink into the floor and fall into the Earth's core.

"I'm not friends with you because of her," I said.

"I didn't think you were."

He hugged me then. It was a bit difficult as we were both lying on the floor, but basically we went from being two separate blanket bundles to being one giant blanket bundle.

I don't know how long we stayed like that. I hadn't checked my phone for ages.

Then he said, "Do you think we'll be famous one day?"

And I said, "I don't know. I don't think I really want to be famous."

"I guess it's stressful, people trying to work out our identities all the time. The fandom… they're insane. Beautiful and passionate, but… insane."

I smiled. "It's kind of fun. Feels like we're part of some giant mystery."

He smiled back. "We *are* part of some giant mystery."

"Do you want to be famous?"

"I just… want to be special."

"You are special."

He laughed and said, "Shut up."

DARK BLUE

The next thing I remember is waking up on the carpet freezing cold in the dark – maybe it was 3am, maybe 4am – my mouth tasting like something you'd use in a chemistry lesson, everything around me dead, dust floating in the air, Aled and Daniel gone.

I desperately needed to pee so I got out of the bundle of blankets and wandered out of the room towards the bathroom, but stopped immediately when I heard voices coming from the kitchen.

They didn't see me in the doorway because it was almost completely dark. I could barely see them either – they were just slightly moonlit splotches – but I didn't really need to. They were sitting at the dining table, Aled with his head on his arm, Daniel with his chin in one hand, looking at each other. Daniel took a sip from a bottle that might have been wine, I wasn't sure.

There was a long pause before either of them said anything.

"Yeah, but it's not about people knowing," said Aled. "It's not about anyone else, I literally don't care what anyone else would think about it."

"You've quite clearly been avoiding me," said Daniel. "We've barely seen each other all summer."

"You— you were busy. You were working…"

"Yeah, but I'd make time for you if you wanted me to. You just don't seem like you want me to."

"I do want you to!"

"Then can't you just tell me what the issue is?" Daniel sounded annoyed.

Aled's voice got even quieter. "There's not an issue."

"If you don't like me, just say it. There's no point lying."

"Well, obviously I like you."

"I mean like *that*."

Aled raised his free hand and poked Daniel on the arm, but as he replied, he seemed to be talking almost entirely to himself.

"Well, why would we do this if I didn't like you like that?"

Daniel was staying quite still. "Well, exactly."

"Exactly."

I think that's when I realised what was happening. Seconds before it happened. I don't even remember feeling surprised. I don't know what I felt. Maybe a bit lonely.

Aled raised his head and lifted his arms. Daniel leaned into them and rested his head on Aled's chest and Aled hugged him tightly, rubbing a hand slowly across Daniel's back. When they drew apart, Aled sat there, waiting for it to happen. Daniel lifted a hand and ran it through Aled's hair and said, "You need a haircut," and then leaned in and kissed him. I turned around. I didn't need to see any more.

I woke up some time later on the carpet, freezing in the dark, and Aled was breathing like he was an astronaut running out of oxygen, sitting up next to me with his head bent forwards and his face completely covered by his hands. Daniel wasn't here. Aled kept breathing and breathing and holding his head and I sat up and put my hand on his shoulder and said, "Aled," but he didn't look at me, he just kept shaking and I suddenly realised that he was *crying*. I tried to move so he could look at me and I said, "Aled," again, but nothing happened, and then he made a really horrible moaning noise and it wasn't just crying, this was worse, this was the crying where you want to scratch out your eyes and smash a wall and I couldn't stand it, I can't ever stand it when other people cry, especially like this. I put my arms around him and held him and his whole body was shaking and I didn't know what else to do so I just stayed like that and said, "What's wrong?" probably a billion times, but he just kept shaking his head and I didn't know what that meant. When I managed to get him to lie down I asked it again and he just said, "I'm sorry… I'm sorry…" and minutes later he said, "I don't want to go to university," and I think he might still have been crying when I fell asleep.

The next time I woke up, Daniel was on the sofa inside a sleeping bag like he was camping under the stars.

I realised, suddenly, that Daniel was February Friday.

Of course he was. Secret romance, childhood best friend – could this get any more romantic? Not that I knew anything about that stuff. I thought I'd feel happy about finally knowing, but I didn't feel anything. I looked up at the ceiling, half-expecting to find some stars there, but there wasn't anything at all.

I needed to pee again urgently, so I sat up and glanced at Aled, who was asleep again, lying next to me on the floor, his head turned towards me, one hand curled under his cheek, and I squinted and I thought that the skin under his eyes was kind of purple, which was weird, but I suppose it might have been the light, which seemed to be stuck in a permanent state of dark blue.

2. SUMMER HOLIDAY
b)

THE WORST EPISODE

I'd woken up at sleepovers many times before, but never with someone sleeping with their arm around me, which was what Aled was doing when I woke up at 11.34am the next day with what felt like a fireworks display happening inside my brain.

I didn't remember a lot, but I did remember that Aled and Daniel were a thing, Daniel was February Friday, Aled had started crying for no reason, and we'd recorded and posted a drunk episode of *Universe City*.

I felt like something bad had happened, even though nothing had.

When I got back into the lounge with a bowl of cereal, Aled and Daniel were sitting next to each other on the floor. I wondered whether they'd had some kind of argument last night, which would explain Aled's random breakdown, but they were almost leaning on each other, watching a video on Aled's phone. It took me two seconds to realise what it was.

I sat down next to them and watched in silence.

When it had finished, Daniel said, "Well, that's embarrassing."

Aled said, "That's the worst episode we've ever made."

I said, "Look at the views."

The views, which were normally around five or six thousand for a new episode, were at 30,327.

5 WEIRD THINGS I'M OBSESSED WITH

A famous YouTuber had promoted *Universe City* on his channel. The video was called '5 WEIRD THINGS I'M OBSESSED WITH', and alongside a piggy bank shaped like a pig in a tutu, a Doge app, a game called *Can Your Pet?* and a landline phone in the shape of a burger, the YouTuber spoke about how much he loved this weird, underrated podcast called *Universe City*.

The YouTuber had over three million subscribers. His video, four hours after he posted it, was at 300,000 views, and he'd linked to the *Universe City* episode in the video description.

It took two minutes on Tumblr for me to find out that this had happened, and still sitting on the carpet, Aled, Daniel and I watched the video on Aled's phone.

"And lastly I wanted to talk about this *bizarre* channel that I'm obsessed with—" the YouTuber held up a hand and a picture of *Universe City*'s logo popped up on the screen "—*Universe City*. It's a podcast show about a student sending out SOS messages from the futuristic university they're trapped inside. What I love about the show is that nobody knows who makes it, and it has all kinds of crazy conspiracy theories about it, like whether the characters are actually real people in real life. I only just thought of adding this on to this video at the last minute because the creator of the show posted a new episode about half an hour ago – probably a few hours ago for you guys watching this video – and it's just reached a whole new level of weird. You can hardly work out what's going on at all, one minute there are just rustling sounds and shouting, the next there are people playing Never Have I Ever, then the main character Radio Silence is having a rant... it's *so* weird and I love that you just have no idea what's happening most of the time. I genuinely stayed up until 6am once just reading about all the mysteries and conspiracies in the show. If you like all my weird stories on this channel you should *definitely* go and check it out – I'll leave a link in the description!"

"This is so surreal," said Aled.

"Yeah," I said. I'd watched this particular YouTuber's videos since I was fourteen.

"I wish he'd linked to the first episode," said Aled. "I was gonna take this episode down."

I frowned. "You want to take it down?"

"Yeah," he said. "It's ridiculous. And shit." He paused. "I didn't even upload it on a Friday. I've always uploaded on Fridays."

"Well... at least it's got more people into the show. That's good!"

"Mm," he said. Then he groaned and put his head in a hand. "Why did I upload that?"

Daniel and I said nothing. I don't think we knew what to say. I thought we were supposed to be happy about this, but maybe that was wrong. Aled didn't look happy about it. He got up and said he was going to make some toast and Daniel and I gave each other a look, and then Daniel got up and walked after him and I sat very still and watched the new episode again.

??? what

Scroll down for transcript >>>

[...]

Do you remember how the rabbits glared as we drove down the road? Jealous, maybe, or scared. I was always behind her waiting for the window to drop. The Latin name for the fox is *Vulpes vulpes*. You always thought that sounded nice. I'm so angry about these ghost school problems. 'Problems' feels like an overstatement. Are you gonna go smoke your little cigarettes while you lean out of the window under the stars? You were always brave enough to get burned in the Fire. I wonder if you regret your obsession with Bukowski. I regret it and it wasn't even me who had it. At least you were careless enough to admit that you were obsessed with something. I only say horrible things because I feel guilty. I don't want anything to do with this any more, I hate people telling me what I have to do. Why should I have to go just because everyone's telling me to? My m-mother? Nobody should be able to make my decisions for me. I'm here now and I'm waiting and it's going to happen. Was there even any choice involved? Do I sound like I care about school? I don't remember it happening. I don't remember anything I've done, or why. Everything's very confused. Everything's better under the stars, I suppose. If we get another life after we die, I'll meet you there, old sport...

[...]

SLEEP NOW

Friday 16th August

(21:39) **Aled Last**
frances it's at 50,270 now
help

(23:40) **Frances Janvier**
Yeah... damn that youtuber has a lot of influence
Quite amazing really

(23:46) **Aled Last**
of all the episodes that could have gone viral...
it had to be that one didn't it
lol gr8

(23:50) **Frances Janvier**
Ah man... I'm so sorry
You could always just take it down? It's your show, you have
control

(23:52) **Aled Last**
no i can't waste this
it's already got me over 3k new subscribers

(23:53) **Frances Janvier**
Holy shit seriously!????

(23:54) **Aled Last**
yep
lots of the youtube comments said that they really liked
Toulouse

(23:55) **Frances Janvier**
Really??? I was rubbish though omg

(23:55) **Aled Last**
honestly I haven't had a reaction this positive to a sidekick
for ages
wanna be in the next one?

(23:56) **Frances Janvier**
YES are you sure???

(23:57) **Aled Last**
i wouldn't have asked if i wasn't sure haha

(23:58) **Frances Janvier**
<3 <3 <3 <3 <3 <3 <3 <3 <3 <3 <3 <3 <3 <3

Tuesday 20th August
(11:20) Aled Last
FIFTY THOUSAND SUBSCRIBERS this calls for a trip to pizza hut. you got any cash?

(11:34) Frances Janvier
MATE CONGRATULATIONS yeah I'll see you in five

Wednesday 21st August
(02:17) Aled Last
hey do you want to sing nothing left for us when we record tomorrow?
by yourself

(02:32) Frances Janvier
By myself!???!?????
You are aware that i can't sing at all, right...
I'm completely tone deaf

(02:34) Aled Last
good, that'll make it more interesting

Friday 30th August
(04:33) Aled Last
SEVENTY FIVE THOUSAND SUBSCRIBERS
HOW
WHY
WE LITERALLY JUST GOT DRUNK AND RAMBLED AT A CAMERA

(10:45) Frances Janvier
COMING ROUND YOURS RIGHT NOW
m8 you're asleep aren't you
Wake up or I will repeatedly ring the doorbell

(11:03) Aled Last
stop ringing the doorbell pls

Sunday 1ˢᵗ September
(00:34) Frances Janvier
Don't wanna go to school tomorrow
Can I come to university with you

(00:35) Aled Last
no
go 2 sleep

(00:36) Frances Janvier
You clearly don't know me

(00:37) Aled Last
4am bedtimes have to stop now summer is over

(00:37) Frances Janvier
☹

(00:38) Aled Last
do u want me to sing u a lullaby

(00:38) Frances Janvier
Yes pls

(00:39) **Aled Last**
go to sleeeeeeeeeeeeep
go to sleeeeeeeeeeeeeeeeeep
go to sleeeeeeeeeeeeeep little frances
that's all i got

(00:41) **Frances Janvier**
That was so beautiful, I'll remember this moment forever

(00:42) **Aled Last**
shut up and sleep now

3. AUTUMN TERM
a)

CONFUSED KIDS
IN OFFICE SUITS

"I can't believe I haven't seen you for like *two entire months!*" said one of my friends on the first day of autumn term. We were back at our lunch table, all Year 13s now, feeling less like confused kids in office suits and more like ageing veterans of the education system. "What've you been up to?"

I couldn't believe it either. I only realised that it'd been that long when I arrived at school on the first day back and three of them had changed their hair colours and one had a tan so extreme that she was almost the same colour as me.

"Er... not that much!" I said, without meaning to. Not that much. Understatement of the millennium.

She waited for me to add something else, but I didn't know what. What did I talk about last year when I was with my school friends? Anything? Or nothing?

"Hey, Frances," said another friend. "Weren't you hanging out with Aled Last this summer?"

"Who's Aled Last?" said the first friend.

"I think he's Daniel Jun's friend – he went to the boys' school."

"And Frances is going out with him?"

The friends looked at me and waited.

"Er, no," I said, and laughed nervously. "We're just friends."

None of them believed me. I glanced around for Raine, but she wasn't there.

"What did you do with him then?" said a friend, grinning.

Aled had told me weeks ago that nobody could know that he made *Universe City*. He said it quite forcefully, actually, with a kind of panic in his eyes – a contrast to his usual tentative air. If anyone knew it was him, he said, the entire concept, mystery and intrigue of the show would be ruined. But then he chuckled and joked that also he really didn't want his mum to find out, because that would be embarrassing and he'd feel awkward making it if she was listening.

I shrugged. "We just hung out! We live opposite each other so… yeah."

I knew it didn't sound convincing and they knew it didn't sound convincing, but they accepted it anyway. They started talking about other things and I stayed silent because I had nothing to contribute, which was nothing unusual for me around my school friends, but it felt weird, because I'd forgotten that this was how I normally behaved.

TOULOSER

"…I was so confused about how friendships worked by that point that I just accepted that I didn't have any real ones, old sport," said Aled into the microphone in his Radio voice, then glanced at me when I didn't read my line and tapped me on the hand. "It's you."

We were recording the mid–September episode on a Thursday evening a couple of weeks into term. Aled's room was dark apart from the glare of his laptop screen and the fairy lights wrapped around his bed. I hadn't been paying attention because I had been staring at my phone. I had been staring at my phone because I had just received an email notifying me that someone had sent me an anonymous Tumblr message. The anonymous Tumblr message said this:

Anonymous said:
is your real name frances janvier

I stared at it. Then Aled stared at it. Then my phone buzzed as a second email arrived.

Anonymous said:

Hey don't know if you've seen but lots of people in the Universe City tumblr tag are saying you're a girl called Frances? No pressure to say anything about it but just thought you should be aware

"Fuck," said Aled. Aled rarely swore.

"Yes," I agreed.

Without saying anything, Aled opened up an Internet tab and went straight to Tumblr. He had an account on there, but never posted anything – he just used it to lurk and spy on the fandom.

The top post in the *Universe City* Tumblr tag, with over 5,000 notes, was a long post dedicated to identifying me as the voice of Toulouse, the show's artist, and the owner of the blog **touloser**, known online only as 'Toulouse'.

Someone – someone maybe from school or the town, I don't know – had made a Tumblr post comparing a video of me presenting a speech for the parent governors at a past school event (uploaded to the school's website) to my voice in the last few episodes and some blurry screenshots of me from the ghost school episode.

Underneath the evidence, the person had written:

OMFG! Do you think Toulouse is this 'Frances Janvier' person!!? They look and sound the same lol!! XD @touloser @touloser @touloser

The 'XD' made me grind my teeth.

"They're literally one step away from finding me," said Aled. I glanced towards him and saw he was fiddling with his jumper sleeves.

"What do you want me to do?" I said, genuinely asking. "What should we do? They'd probably respect me if I asked them not to look for you."

"That's not going to stop them," he said, and rubbed his forehead.

"I could deny it..."

"They won't believe you." He groaned. "This is all because of that stupid episode... I'm such an idiot..."

I shuffled in my chair. "Well... I mean, it's not your fault, but, like, if they find out it's you... it won't be a *disaster*, will it? I mean, it's probably got to come out at some point, especially if you carry on getting subscribers—"

"*No*, it was going to be a mystery forever! That's what makes it so great!" Aled shook his head, his eyes gazing out of focus into the computer screen in front of him. "That's what makes it special – it's so— it's all contained, it's just this, kind of... ethereal thing, this special magical ball of happiness hanging in the air above everyone's heads that nobody can touch. And it's just mine and nobody gets to interfere, not the fandom, not my mum, not *anyone*."

I felt myself losing track of what he was saying so I didn't reply. I looked back at my emails and found ten new messages there.

I went ahead and made a post about it anyway.

touloser
yes, you guessed it lol

so for the past two years on tumblr you've known me as toulouse or touloser, which I'm sure you guessed was a fake name. i kept myself anonymous because no one irl knew that i did these drawings or was so embarrassingly obsessed with this beautiful youtube channel.

i guess i underestimated people's ability to put voices to faces, and there've been a lot of rumours flying around about me over the past couple of weeks.

so, yes. my real name is Frances Janvier, and i'm the artist for universe city and the voice of toulouse. i used to be just a massive fan of the show, and now suddenly i'm helping make the show, which is weird, but here we are.

no, i'm not going to tell you who radio is. please stop asking. it'd also be cool if you could not stalk me.

ok. bye.

#universe city #radio silence #universe citizens #lol can ppl stop sending me asks of the same questions now #thank u #i'll get back to drawing now

By this point, I had around 4,000 followers on Tumblr.

By the weekend, that went up to 25,000.

By the Monday after, five separate people had come up to me at school to ask me if I was the voice of Toulouse from *Universe City*, and, of course, I had to say yes.

By one week after, everybody at school knew that I, Frances Janvier, the extremely studious and boring head girl, was doing some weird YouTube thing in secret. Or not so secret any more, I guess.

ARTISTIC WAS DISAPPOINTING?

"You're probably aware of the reason I needed to speak to you, Frances."

I was sitting in Dr Afolayan's office in the third week of September in a chair that was awkwardly positioned at the side of the room so I had to turn my head to look at her. I was completely unaware of the reason why she needed to talk to me, which is probably why I'd felt especially shocked when I got a note in the register that morning calling me to her office during break.

Afolayan was a pretty good head teacher, not gonna lie. She was mostly known for her annual speech about how she got from a tiny village in Nigeria to getting a PhD from the University of Oxford. She had her PhD certificate on her office wall in an ornate wooden frame, just to remind everyone who came in here that underachievement is unacceptable.

I never really liked her, to be honest.

She crossed her legs and interlocked her fingers on her desk. She gave me a small smile which said, 'You are very disappointing to me.'

"Erm, no," I said with a vague laugh at the end as if that would make anything better.

She raised her eyebrows. "Right."

There was a pause as she leaned back in her chair and clasped her hands together over one crossed leg.

"You seem to have been involved with a viral Internet video that gives a very bad impression of what we're all about here at the Academy."

Oh.

"Oh," I said.

"Yes, it's a very entertaining video," she said with absolutely no expression. "And it contains a lot of... well, 'propaganda'."

I'm not too sure what face I was making at that point.

"It's garnered quite a lot of attention, hasn't it?" she continued. "Almost 200,000 views now? A few parents have been asking questions."

"Oh," I said. "Who— who told you about it?"

"I heard about it from a student."

"Oh," I said again.

"So I was just wondering, really, why you would post something like that? Are your views the same as—" she glanced at a Post-it note "—*Universe City*'s? Do you think we should abolish the school system and all go and live in the woods and learn to start fires? Buy food by trading chickens and grow our own vegetables? End capitalism?"

There were several reasons I disliked Dr Afolayan. She was unnecessarily rude to students and believed passionately in 'thinking tools'. But I couldn't quite remember the last time I'd disliked someone as much as I did right then. If there's one thing that makes me properly angry, it's people patronising me.

"No," I said, because if I'd tried to say anything else, I would have either started shouting or started crying.

"So why did you post it?"

I was drunk.

"I thought it was artistic," I said.

"*Right.*" She smirked. "Well then. That's… well, I've got to say, that's really very disappointing. I expected better."

Artistic was disappointing? I was zoning out of this conversation. I was trying really hard not to cry.

"Yeah," I said.

She looked at me.

"I'm going to have to remove you as head girl, Frances," she said.

"Oh," I said, but I'd seen it coming, I'd seen it coming from a mile away.

"You're just not presenting an appropriate image for the school. We need a head boy and girl who really *believe* in the school and *care* about its success, which clearly you don't."

And I'd had enough.

"I think that's a bit unfair," I said. "The video was obviously a mistake, and I'm sorry, but to be fair, the only reason you even know I was in it is because someone else has told you, it wasn't even from a YouTube account that belongs to me, and you're just assuming that I had all the same views. Plus, what I do outside of school shouldn't factor into me being head girl anyway."

Afolayan's expression changed as soon as I started to speak. Now she looked *angry.*

"If the things you do outside of school affect the school, then they affect your place as head girl," she said. "This video has gone viral around many of our students."

"What, so I'm supposed to just base my whole life and

185

everything I do around the fact that I'm head girl and someone might accidentally see what I'm doing?"

"I think you're being very immature."

I stopped speaking. There was no point trying to argue. There was no way she was going to even attempt to listen to me.

They never do, do they? They never even *try* to listen to you.

"Okay," I said.

"Not a very good start to Year 13, eh?" She raised her eyebrows again and produced a slightly pitying smile that said 'You should probably leave now before I have to ask you to.'

"Thanks," I said, but I didn't know why because I had nothing to thank her for. I got up out of my chair and walked towards the doorway.

"Oh, I'll need your head girl badge back," said Afolayan. I turned around and she was holding out her hand.

"Oh God, Frances, what's wrong? Are you all right?"

Only one of my friends – Maya – was sitting at our ILC table when I got there. I was crying, which was embarrassing – not loudly or anything, but my eyes were wet and I had to keep wiping them so my mascara didn't run.

I explained to her what had happened. Maya seemed a bit uncomfortable about the fact that I was crying. None of them had seen me cry before.

"It's okay – it's not gonna really affect anything, is it?" Maya laughed awkwardly. "I mean, at least you won't have to do any of those speeches or events any more!"

"It's messed up my UCAS application… like, an entire paragraph of my personal statement was about me being head girl, it was literally the only reason I wanted to be head girl in the first place, something I could say that I did… I don't have any other hobbies, or… Cambridge want to see you in some kind of… kind of leadership role…"

Maya just listened and made a sympathetic face and rubbed my back and tried to be helpful, but I could tell she didn't get it, so I just said I was going to the bathroom to sort out my makeup, but just ended up sitting in a cubicle and trying to calm down and hating myself for crying in front of other people and for letting other people make me cry in the first place.

RAINE

"So Frances," said a girl I knew from my history class, Jess, leaning over her chair to talk to me from a different table, "if you're Toulouse from *Universe City*, who's the voice of Radio Silence? Is it your friend Aled?"

It was the fourth week of September. A Wednesday. Aled was leaving for university in three days.

Everyone in Year 13 had been forced into the ILC during Period One to work on our personal statements for our UCAS forms, not that anyone was actually doing much work. My personal statement was pretty good, and by pretty good I mean it was the most eloquent 500 words of bullshit I've ever written, but I was still trying to work out what to put in my 'extra-curriculars' paragraph, now that I couldn't boast about being head girl any more.

"Is that why you were hanging out all summer?"

Apparently lots of people had heard about Aled and me hanging out in the summer. The only reason people found it interesting was because they thought I was some kind of schoolwork-obsessed hermit. Which was true a lot of the time, so fair enough.

I considered lying to Jess, but I panic under pressure, so I just said:

"Erm, I can't— I'm not allowed to say."

"Don't you live in the same village?" said another girl, who was sitting next to Jess.

"Well, yeah," I said.

Suddenly everyone within a five-metre radius was looking at me.

"Because, like, since you're working on the show now, you must be pretty close to the actual creator."

"Er…" I felt my palms actually starting to sweat. "Well, that's not necessarily true."

"That's what everyone on Tumblr's saying anyway."

I didn't say anything to that, because she was right. Everyone on Tumblr seemed to think that me and the Creator were BFFs.

Well, I guess they weren't too far off the truth.

"How come you're not allowed to tell us?" said Jess, grinning like this was the most fun she'd ever had. I'd never been particularly close to Jess, and she was mostly known for always having the worst fake tan streaks imaginable. In Year 10 a teacher got put on probation for calling her 'bacon legs' during a lesson.

"Because—" I caught myself before I said 'he' "—the person who it is doesn't want anyone to know." I laughed to try and ease the tension. "Like, it's all part of the mystery."

"Is he your boyfriend?"

"What— Who? Radio?"

"Aled."

"Er, no."

Jess just kept on grinning. The people listening in had started to look away again, chatting among themselves.

"Wait, are you talking about Aled Last?" someone chipped

in from the opposite end of my table. I looked over and realised that it was Raine Sengupta, tipped back in her chair against
the wall and tapping an unbreakable ruler against her table. "I
don't think it'd be him; he's like the quietest person in the
world."

She looked at me and raised her eyebrows and grinned slightly
and I suddenly became aware that she was lying.

"Also, Daniel Jun wouldn't be into that shit," she continued,
"like, all that arty stuff. I don't think he'd be best friends with a
YouTuber."

"Mm, that's true," said Jess.

Raine swung her legs, still dangerously tilted back on her chair.
"It's probs someone we don't even know."

"I just want to *know*." Jess said this too loudly and our teacher
finally realised no one was doing any work and stood up and told
everyone off.

Raine shot me a quick peace sign once Jess had turned round
and I wasn't sure whether it was the stupidest or the coolest thing
I had ever seen, and I happened to glance at the paper in front
of her, which should have been a printed-out draft of her personal
statement but was instead totally blank. When I went to talk to
her at the end of the lesson, she'd already left the room.

I didn't see her again until after school when she was walking
down the road literally three steps in front of me. I was going
that way in any case, towards the train station. Normally I'd avoid
any possibilities of running into people I only vaguely know,
but... I don't know. Maybe I was imagining that look she'd given
me in history.

"Raine!"

She turned round. I would have killed for her hair. My hair's corkscrew-curly and would look crap with an undercut, even though I tie it up every day anyway.

"Oh, hey!" she said. "You all right, mate?"

"Yeah, I'm good, thanks," I said. "You?"

"Shattered, tbh."

She looked it as well. But most of us were like that.

"So I was looking for you at lunch…"

She laughed. Her smile seemed like she knew something she shouldn't. "Oh, sorry, I have detention like every lunchtime."

"What? Why?"

"Well, you know my results were a bit shit?"

"Yeah."

"Basically they make me do work at lunch and during free periods to make up for it."

"What, even at *lunchtime*?"

"Yeah, I get ten minutes to eat and then I have to sit outside Dr Afolayan's office for forty minutes and do homework and stuff."

"That's… morally wrong."

"I know, right!? Lunchtime is a basic human right."

We turned a corner and it started to rain, the grey of the sky bleeding into the grey of the pavement. I put up my umbrella and made sure it was covering us both.

"Yeah, so, do you know Aled Last or something? It kind of looked like you were lying to Jess's face, which was hilarious, by the way."

She laughed and nodded. "Oh my God, I actually cannot stand that girl. Wait—" she snapped her head towards me, "—you're not close friends with her, are you?"

"I don't speak to her that much. All I know about her is the bacon legs incident."

"Oh my God – *bacon legs*. I heard about this. That's totally what I'm going to call her from now on." She shook her head a little, grinning. "Yeah, I just hate how she has to know, like, all the gossip all the time, she really doesn't care about other people's feelings. Classic Bacon Legs."

There was a pause. I suddenly realised that Raine was staring intently across the road. I followed her gaze to find that she was staring at a golden retriever on a walk with its owner.

I looked back at her, and her eyes snapped to mine. "Oh, sorry, I just love dogs, seriously. If I had one wish it would be for a dog. *Anyway…*"

I let out a laugh. She just said whatever she wanted whenever she wanted. Incredible.

"Aled Last…"

"Yeah."

"Daniel Jun told me about his YouTube thing."

I gaped at her. "Seriously?"

"Yep." Raine laughed. "He was proper smashed. And it's always me who looks after people when they get, like, *really* drunk, you know, when you need someone to make sure they don't choke on their own sick. We were at some party and he just started talking about it."

"Jesus… do you know if Aled knows?"

Raine shrugged. "No idea, I don't talk to him. I don't even watch the videos, so… I don't think it matters. I know he doesn't want anyone to know, so it's not like I'm gonna spread it around."

"Was this… recent?"

"Oh, yeah, like a couple of months back." Raine paused. "Daniel seemed kind of upset with Aled, or something. Gave me the impression Aled liked his YouTube channel a bit more than he liked Daniel, you know?"

I thought back to what I'd seen on results night. Aled and Daniel together, then Aled crying so hard I thought he might melt completely.

"That's pretty sad, if that's true," I said. "They're best friends."

Raine studied me. "Yeah, *best friends*."

There was a pause.

I glanced at her. "Do you... know something?"

She smiled broadly. "Do I know that Aled and Daniel are fucking on the down low? Yeah, mate."

The way she said it was so blasé that I let out a very nervous laugh. It hadn't even crossed my mind that they'd be having sex. The idea kind of freaked me out, because I'd always just assumed that mine and Aled's level of sexual experience was the same.

"Oh. I didn't know anyone else knew that."

"Just me, I think. Due to Drunk Daniel."

"Right..."

We'd reached the high street. I had to go left to the train station; she had to continue on. I didn't know where she was going.

"Anyway, thanks," I said. "You basically saved me there; I get really rambly under pressure."

"Aw, mate, that's okay." She smiled. "Anything to stop Bacon Legs being a shit-stirrer. And, like, you haven't been too chatty lately. You seem a bit zoned out."

I was surprised she'd noticed anything about me. Raine and Maya and our friends barely paid any attention to me at all.

"Oh," I said. "Erm, you know. Just stuff going on."

"All the *Universe City* stuff?"

"Yeah. It's just... it's just a lot. Online. And now people in real life know... it's stressful."

193

"Aw." She gave me a sympathetic look. "Don't worry. People will stop talking about it eventually."

I chuckled. "Yeah, *eventually*."

She walked off with a vague "See you later," and another weirdly cool peace sign before I had the chance to reply, and I felt two things. Firstly, surprised Raine knew so many things despite seeming like the shallowest person I knew. Secondly, kind of sad that I'd ever thought she'd be shallow in the first place.

LIKE THIS

On Thursday night I was at Aled's later than usual because his mum had gone away for a few days to visit other family. It was only nine thirty and I know Aled was eighteen years old, but we both still felt like tiny babies, to be honest. Neither of us could quite work out how to use his washing machine.

We were sitting at his kitchen table, waiting for some Morrisons pizzas to cook, and I was obviously talking about something completely ridiculous, and Aled was just listening quietly and contributing things here and there, and everything was normal.

Well, it wasn't.

"Is everything good?" asked Aled, once we'd come to a natural pause in conversation. "At school and stuff?"

This surprised me because Aled hardly ever asked generic questions like that.

"Yeah. Yeah." I laughed. "So tired though. I swear I don't get any sleep any more."

The oven timer bleeped and Aled clapped his hands together and went to get them out the oven and I started singing the word "pizza" repeatedly.

He was leaving for university in two days.

Once we were eating, I said, "I needed to tell you something kind of important."

Aled stopped chewing for a second.

"Yeah?"

"Do you know Raine Sengupta?"

"Only vaguely."

"She told me yesterday she knows about *Universe City*. That you're the Creator."

Aled completely stopped eating and met my eyes. Oh. I'd probably said something I shouldn't have. Again. Why did this keep happening? Why did I keep finding these things out?

"Oh." Aled ran a hand through his hair. "Jesus..."

"She said she wasn't going to tell anyone."

"Yeah, she *says*."

"She also said..."

I stopped. I'd been about to say that she knew about Aled and Daniel, but then I remembered that he didn't even know that *I* knew.

Aled was staring at me and actually looked a little scared. "Oh, God, what?"

"Erm, okay, she knows about... erm, you and Daniel."

There was a horrifying silence. Aled stayed very still.

"What about us?" Aled said slowly.

"You know..." But I couldn't finish my sentence.

"Oh," said Aled.

I shifted in my seat.

Aled let out a breath and looked down at his plate. "Did you already know?"

I had no idea why I hadn't told him already. I think I just hate bringing up things that just cause people pain and embarrassment.

"I saw you kiss on your birthday," I said, then followed up with a hurried, "Nothing else! That was it. And then a bit later on I woke up and you were just... like... sobbing."

Aled ran a hand through his hair. "Oh, yeah. I thought you might have been too drunk to remember that."

I waited for him to say more, but he didn't, so I said, "Why didn't you tell me?"

He met my eyes again and I saw how sad they were. Then he chuckled. "Honestly, same reason I didn't let you meet my mum. You're like... in a separate place to all the... difficult things going on in my life..." He laughed. "Oh my God, what a *douchey* thing to say. Sorry."

I laughed too, because it had sounded like a very douchey thing to say, but I got what he was trying to say.

It was not as simple as 'Daniel and I are in a relationship.'

Nothing was ever simple, was it?

"Why were you crying?" I asked.

Aled looked at me for a second more, and then looked back to his food, picking at a pizza crust with one hand.

"I can't remember. I was probably just really drunk." He laughed, but I could tell it was fake. "I'm an emotional drunk."

"Oh."

I didn't believe him, but he obviously didn't want to tell me.

"So is Daniel gay?" I said, because there was no way I couldn't just say it.

"Yeah," he said.

"Hm." I was still pretty shocked I hadn't guessed. "You know... I'm bisexual."

Aled's eyes widened. "What— Are you?"

"Haha, yeah. I told you I kissed Carys, didn't I?"

"Yeah, you did, but..." Aled shook his head. "I don't know. I didn't think about it very hard." He paused. "Why didn't you tell me that before?"

"I don't know," I began, but that was a lie. "I've never told anyone before."

Aled suddenly looked very sad. "Haven't you?"

"No..."

We both took a bite of pizza.

"When did you realise you were bi?" Aled said it almost so quietly I didn't hear him over the sound of my chewing.

I hadn't been expecting that question at all. I almost didn't want to answer him.

But then I sort of realised why he was asking.

"There wasn't, like, one moment," I said. "It was like... well, I found out what it was on the Internet and then it just made sense..." I'd never tried to explain this to anyone before. Not even myself, really. "Like... this sounds really stupid, but I've always been able to imagine being with a boy or a girl. I mean, obviously they're slightly different, but, like, the general feelings are the same... does that make sense? None of this makes sense..."

"No, it makes sense," he said. "Why haven't you told your school friends?"

I looked at him. "There was never really anyone worth telling."

His eyes widened a little. Maybe he realised that he was basically my only friend. I sort of hoped he didn't realise. It just made me feel sorry for myself.

I continued, "Like, it's one of the reasons that I got so into *Universe City* in the first place. Because Radio falls in love with all sorts of people, boys and girls and other genders and... like, aliens and stuff." I laughed and he smiled too.

"I think everyone's a bit bored with boy-girl romances anyway," he said. "I think the world's had enough of those, to be honest."

I wanted so badly to ask him.

But that's the one thing you can't just ask.

You've just got to wait until they tell you.

When the front door opened, both of us jumped so hard I nearly knocked the bottle of lemonade over.

Aled's mum entered the kitchen and blinked at me, a Tesco tote bag over one shoulder and her car keys in one hand.

"Oh, hello, Frances, love," she said, her eyebrows raised. "Didn't expect you to be here so late."

I glanced at the clock on the kitchen wall. It was nearly 10pm. I leapt up from my chair. "Oh, God, yeah, sorry, I'd better go home…"

She barely seemed to be listening to me, but after dumping her bag on the kitchen counter, she interrupted, "Don't be silly, you're right in the middle of your dinner!"

I didn't really know what to say, so I just slowly sat back down.

"I thought you were at Grandad's, Mum," said Aled, and his voice sounded weird. Kind of… kind of *forced*.

"Well, I was, darling, but they've got a few bits and bobs to be getting on with this weekend…" She launched into an unnecessarily long explanation of Aled's grandparents' weekend plans. I kept trying to catch Aled's eye, but he was just staring at Carol like a wild animal trying to stay still to remain undetected.

She started doing some washing-up and for the first time since she entered the room, glanced towards her son.

"Your hair's getting a bit long, isn't it, Allie? Shall I book you a haircut?"

There was an unbearably long silence.

"Erm… actually, I sort of like it like this," said Aled.

She frowned and turned the tap off. She started cleaning pans like she was trying to erode them. "What? Don't you think it looks a bit unkempt, darling? You look a bit like one of those drug addicts you always see outside the job centre."

"I like it like this," said Aled.

Carol dried her hands with a tea towel. "I could cut it for you, if you like." She looked at me. "I always used to cut his hair when he was little."

Aled didn't say anything, and then, to my absolute horror, Carol Last grabbed a pair of kitchen scissors from the counter and started walking with them towards Aled.

"No, Mum, I'm fine…"

"Look," she said, "I could just chop the ends off for you, it wouldn't take two ticks…"

"It's honestly fine, Mum."

"You'd look so much smarter, Allie."

I didn't think it was going to happen. I could see it possibly about to happen, but I didn't think there was any way it would really happen. This was real life, not some TV drama.

"No, no, no, no, Mum, *don't*—"

She literally took a chunk of Aled's hair and cut about ten centimetres off.

Aled jerked backwards and stood up so fast it was made apparent that he hadn't thought it was going to happen either. I suddenly realised I'd stood up too – when had I done that?

She'd just cut his hair.

What. The fuck.

"Mum—" Aled went to say something, but Carol cut him off.

"Oh, come on, darling, it's much too long, isn't it? You'll be a social reject if you turn up to university like that!" She turned to me again. She was clutching the chunk of hair in one hand and the open scissors in the other. "Won't he, Frances?"

But I literally couldn't say anything.

Aled had his hand over the place where a chunk of his hair used to be. Very slowly, zombie-like, he said, "Frances... has to go home now..."

Carol smiled. She smiled in a way that was either complete obliviousness or utter psychotic evil. "Ah, well, it must be nearly your bedtime!"

"Yes..." I said though my voice sounded like I was being strangled. Aled pulled me quickly to the door by one arm before I could force my legs to move by themselves. He opened the door without looking at me and sort of pushed me outside.

It was a clear night. You could see so many stars.

I turned back to face him. "What exactly... just happened?"

Aled moved his hand away from his hair and as if things couldn't get bad enough, the dark blond was stained with red. I grabbed his hand and turned it over to find a thin cut running down the middle of his palm from where he'd attempted to bat the scissors away.

He wrenched his hand back. "It's fine. She's always like this."

"Does she hurt you?" I said. "Tell me if she hurts you. Right now. I'm serious."

"*No.* I swear she doesn't." He waved his injured hand. "This was an accident."

"That's not right. She can't just— She just— What the *fuck*, I mean..."

"It's fine, just go home, I'll text you later."

"Yeah, but why would she—"

"This is what she does, she's just playing a game. I'll text you later."

"No, I want to talk about it now, Aled—"

"Well I fucking *don't.*"

Aled Last never swore, except when he really needed to.

He shut the door on me.

And I couldn't do anything about it.

At all.

UNIVERSE CITY: Ep. 132 – phone

Cyborg attack (again)

Scroll down for transcript >>>

[...]

I hid for forty-seven minutes exactly – I had my moonometer with me – in the telephone box by the power station on Tomsby Street. Nobody thinks to look for anyone there. Everyone knows the box is haunted. I don't want to talk about what I saw.

While I was hiding and waiting, I was also thinking and deciding. Was I going to let the cyborg chase me forever? Was I going to have to turn my back every two minutes to check for those marble eyes and spitting circuits? No. That's no way to live. Not even in the vicious, cruel barricades of the City of the Universe.

I can take a little beating now and then, old sport, believe me. I've been in this City for as long as I can remember, it seems. This hardly qualifies as a distress call any more – by gods, if anyone was listening, I would have heard from you by now.

I can take a little beating now and then. I'm a tough one. I'm a star. I'm steel-chested and diamond-eyed. Cyborgs live and then they break, but I'll never break. Even when my bone dust drifts over the City walls, I'll be living and I'll be flying, and I will wave and laugh.

[...]

IN THE DARK

I get an email every time someone sends me an ask on Tumblr, and I was surprised, to say the least, when I checked my email during break at school the next day and I had twenty-seven emails from Tumblr with the subject 'Someone asked a question'.

I loaded up the Tumblr app and had a look through.

Anonymous said:
are you February Friday????

This made me frown, but I continued scrolling.

Anonymous said:
Thoughts on the rumours that you're February Friday? Xx

Anonymous said:
NO BUT YOU HAVE TO TELL US WHETHER YOU'RE FEBRUARY IT'S YOUR DUTY AS FANDOM GOD

Anonymous said:

r u srsly february friday??

Anonymous said:

So ur surname is literally french for january, ur friends with the creator and ur school burned down on a february friday... COINCIDENCE? explain pls x

There were more than twenty-seven messages. Tumblr had obviously stopped bothering to send me emails at some point this morning. They were all messages about February Friday.

It took five minutes of digging to find the source of the rumours.

univers3c1ties
Potential February Friday?

Okay guys, this is all speculation but what if Frances Janvier (touloser) is February Friday? I've been doing a bit of digging (lol I'm not a stalker I swear) and I think there's a fair bit of argument for it

- Frances used to go to a school that burned down on Friday February 4th 2011 (<u>source</u>)
- She's been a fan of the show since it started – was she the first to know about it?? Did the Creator tell her about it?
- The fact that she's one of the biggest names in the fandom and now she's suddenly *working* for the show?? She clearly has some link to the Creator and the show that she's not fully telling us.
- *Her surname is literally French for January?? Coincidence??*
- Also, these tweets pretty much speak for themselves:

toulouse @touloser

I think the letters to february are my favourite part of every show, the creator is a genius!!!

13 Apr 11

toulouse @touloser

i wish there were more letters to February, they're not in the show so much anymore ;_; i miss the crazy mess of words

14 Dec 11

toulouse @touloser

Universe City has honestly saved my life <3

29 Aug 11

Idk. When will the government tell us the truth lol. All speculation obviously…

#universe city #universe citizens #radio silence #toulouse #frances janvier #touladio #february friday #letters to february

None of this was surprising to me any more. Aled and I had gone way past the comfortable realm of privacy, just us two sitting in his room and laughing into a microphone in the dark.

Anyway – none of these points were convincing at all. *Universe City* had started before I met Carys, so I hadn't even known of Aled back then. So me being February Friday was impossible.

And I already knew that February Friday was Daniel.

It was starting to get a bit annoying, really.

I decided not to show this one to Aled. It wasn't like he could do anything about it.

I thought I'd better answer at least one, or people wouldn't stop asking.

I was exhausted. I was always tired by Friday, but this time it was worse. I remember it being worse because I fell asleep on the train to school and had an actual dream. It was about two best friends who lived in an ice cave.

Aled hadn't texted me and I was worried.

I didn't know exactly what was stressing me out. It wasn't one single thing. It was more like a billion tiny things all pulling together to form one giant tidal wave of stress. It felt like I was drowning, sort of.

I checked my asks one more time before the bell went to signal the end of break. And that's when I saw this message.

YOUTUBE FAMOUS

"Do you eat the same thing for lunch every day?"

I looked up from my cheese and ham panini. Raine Sengupta sat down next to me at our usual table in the sixth-form cafeteria. She had a bright orange rucksack hanging off one arm and her phone in the opposite hand. The rest of our friends hadn't arrived yet.

"I'm very unimaginative," I said, "and I don't like change."

She gave a little nod as if this were a reasonable explanation.

"How did you know that anyway?" I asked.

"You sort of stick out, mate. Sitting here at a table by yourself for like ten minutes before the rest of us get here."

"Oh." Great. "That's completely the opposite of what I was going for."

"Not your desired lunchtime aesthetic?"

"I was going more for 'invisible girl just wants to eat her sandwich in peace'."

She laughed. "The ultimate dream for us all!"

I laughed a little too, and she lifted her bag on to the stool opposite me. It made a noise that suggested it weighed at least half of my body weight.

I'd been trying not to think about the message about Aled. I hadn't checked Tumblr since break.

Raine leaned on the table with one hand. "Just thought I'd better let you know, there's some shit happening outside the school gate involving Aled Last."

"What?"

"Yeah… I think he came to meet Daniel for lunch and he's been, like… bombarded by children."

I put down my panini.

"What?" I said.

"They're asking him *Universe City* questions. You might wanna skip over there and see what's up. Like, before they crush him."

I stood up immediately. "God, yeah, okay— Yeah."

"I didn't know you were such good mates," she said, pulling a lunchbox out of her bag. "It's surprising."

"Why's that?" I asked, but she just shrugged at me.

The Year 7–11 uniform is black and yellow so it looked a bit like Aled was being attacked by a swarm of large bees.

Around fifteen teenagers had cornered him just outside the main school gate and were firing questions at him like he was an actual and legitimate celebrity. An older boy was taking pictures of him on his phone. A group of Year 7 girls were giggling every time he said something. A Year 7 boy was shouting out questions repeatedly without stopping, such as "How d'you get YouTube famous?", "How do I get more followers on Instagram?" and "Would you follow me on Twitter?"

I stopped a few paces away from the back of the crowd.

How did they know?

How did they know he was Radio Silence?

This wasn't what we'd wanted to happen.

This wasn't what *he'd* wanted to happen.

Aled finally saw us.

He'd had a haircut. It looked kind of normal, now.

He was back in a jumper and jeans too.

He looked miserable.

"Did you do this?" he said to me, except I couldn't hear him at all, I could just see his lips move. I couldn't hear him and I felt so annoyed about it that I wanted to push into the crowd and shout at all the people and make them leave him alone.

"Did you tell them!?"

He looked *angry*.

And disappointed.

It didn't take a lot for me to believe that I was disappointing, even though I hadn't done it. I wasn't the one who'd outed his biggest secret.

"ALL RIGHT, EVERYONE."

I was shouting before I could stop myself.

The teens turned round to look at me, quietening a little.

"I don't know what you all think you're doing, but you're not allowed outside of school during lunch unless you're in the sixth form, and seeing as none of you are, I suggest you get back inside school grounds."

Everyone just sort of stared at me.

I produced a sharp look that attempted to meet every single crowd member in the eye. "Like, *now*. I might not be head girl any more, but I can still make a pretty good case to Afolayan."

And it worked. It actually worked.

I don't know if you know, but when you are a student it's a very difficult thing to get other students to obey you.

The teenagers scuttled away, leaving Aled and me standing

alone outside the gate. Aled was staring at me like he didn't even know me.

I suppose I must have hardly looked like myself, in my sixth-form suit, shouting at other students.

He started shaking his head. He looked stunned more than anything.

"*What's going on?*" Daniel's voice broke our silence, and I turned to find him walking out of the school gate towards us.

"They…" I could feel my voice breaking a little. "They found out that Aled's the Creator. Everyone."

"Was this you?" Aled asked me again, as if Daniel wasn't even here.

"*No*, Aled, I swear—"

"I don't understand," said Aled, who almost looked like he was about to start crying. "It— I needed it to be a secret. Are you sure you didn't tell them? You must have done it by accident…"

"*No*, they asked me, but I didn't— I didn't say anything, I *swear*."

Aled just shook his head again, but he didn't seem to be doing it at me.

"This is it," he said.

"What?" I said.

"This is the end. My mum's going to find out, and then she's going to make me stop."

"Wait, *what*? Why would she do that?"

"This is the end," he said, as if he hadn't heard me at all, and then his eyes misted over. "I'm going home." He turned round and walked away, Daniel in tow, and I had no idea whether he believed me or not.

LYING IS EASIER ON
THE INTERNET

Lying is easier on the Internet.

touloser
look guys… the Creator is not Aled Last. Yes Aled Last is my friend
in real life but that doesn't mean shit. the Creator is just someone
I know online. and once again – no, i'm not February Friday.
stop stalking Aled, stop posting pictures of him. stop sending the
Creator annoying messages about him. Aled is a very good friend
of mine and you're really not doing him any favours.
thank you bye
#i'm so done with these rumours #like can y'all calm down pls
#i wish you'd never found out who I was tbh #universe city
#universe citizens #radio silence #touloser

I don't know why I hadn't been able to say this to Jess, or
anyone, earlier.

I was immediately flooded with messages all claiming I was
lying.

Anonymous said:
lol we know ur lying

Anonymous said:
What even was the point of that post lmao??

Anonymous said:
NOW you decide you're a good liar.

I didn't have any idea how they knew I was lying until I messaged Aled with a link to the post.

He messaged me back almost immediately.

Aled Last
that's no good they know it was me

Frances Janvier
How??? They have no proof???

And then he sent me a link to a different Tumblr post.

universe-city-analysis-blog
Aled Last = The Creator?
There's been a lot of talk in the UC tag today about whether a teenage boy named 'Aled Last' from Kent, England, is the voice and Creator of Universe City. I thought I'd do everyone a favour by compiling what evidence we have, most of it from the UC artist Frances Janvier (touloser) and I think the conclusion is quite strongly supported.

- Those who know of Frances touloser (aka the UC artist and voice of Toulouse) have confirmed that she has grown closer to Aled Last over the summer – they have been spotted together in their hometown and are in photos together on their personal Facebooks. This is where the speculation around Aled Last began.

- When confronted in real life with the suggestion that Aled Last is the Creator, Frances reportedly responded "I'm not allowed to say" [source – obviously we have to take this person's word]. If Aled Last wasn't the Creator, where would be the harm in confirming that he wasn't?
- Similarly, Frances has not answered any questions about Aled Last on her Tumblr or her Twitter, despite people claiming to have sent her messages about it. Again – why would Frances not just confirm that Aled Last isn't the Creator?

Granted, none of this is solid proof that Aled Last is the Creator. The convincing piece of evidence comes from last month:

- On the night of the now infamous 'ghost school' episode, Frances's Twitter account, @touloser, posted a blurry picture of a pair of lime green shoes, captioned 'Radio revealed' [link]. Aled Last can be seen to be wearing these shoes in various photos on his personal Facebook:
  - [photo]
  - [photo]
  - [photo]
- These shoes are an old design of classic Vans that haven't been made for several years [source]. Aled's personal Facebook suggests that he has owned them for three or four years. They're obviously very rare shoes since most people would have thrown them away by now – very few people wear the same single pair of shoes continuously for several years.

- Also, from some screenshots of the 'ghost school' episode, you can see a blond figure with long-ish hair, which look similar to some photos of Aled:
  - [photo]
  - [screenshot]
  - [screenshot]

Feel free to make your own conclusions, of course. But in my eyes, it is almost definite that Aled Last is the Creator of Universe City.

The post had over ten thousand notes.

It was disgusting. People who knew Aled in real life had taken stuff from his *private* Facebook. They'd listened in on my conversation with Jess and *quoted* me. What was this? Who did they think I was? A celebrity?

What was worse was that it was right.

Aled Last was the Creator. They'd put the evidence together and they'd found out.

And it was entirely my fault.

Frances Janvier
Fuck... I'm so sorry aled I can't tell you how sorry I am

Aled Last
it's fine

TIME VORTEX

It was 6pm when I received a Facebook message from Raine.

(18:01) Lorraine Sengupta
Hey what happened in the end with aled?? Was everything ok??

(18:03) Frances Janvier
Everyone knows he's the creator. People on tumblr found out
:\

(18:04) Lorraine Sengupta
And he's upset about it??

(18:04) Frances Janvier
Very

(18:05) Lorraine Sengupta
Why??

Isn't he just complaining about getting a load of internet followers lol?
Kinda wanna say 'check your privilege' tbh...

(18:07) Frances Janvier
I think he really wanted it to be private though
You'd understand if you listened to the show, it's really personal to him

(18:09) Lorraine Sengupta
Yeh but there are worse things than getting internet famous lmao

I wanted to tell her that it wasn't really about that.
What had Aled said? That his mum would make him stop?
Had that just been an exaggeration? Or would that really happen?
Why would she do that?

(18:14) Lorraine Sengupta
Why you so obsessed with that white boy anyway lol

(18:15) Frances Janvier
I'm not obsessed with him haha
I just like him a lot I guess

(18:16) Lorraine Sengupta
Like you wanna bang him??

(18:16) Frances Janvier
NO omg
Can't I like a guy without wanting to get with him?

(18:17) Lorraine Sengupta
Yeh you can lol!!! I just wanted to check :D
Why dyou like him so much then??

(18:18) Frances Janvier
He just makes me feel a bit less weird I guess

(18:18) Lorraine Sengupta
Bc he's weird as well?

(18:19) Frances Janvier
Yep haha

(18:20) Lorraine Sengupta
Aw that's kinda nice
Well I think you're being a pretty good friend, anyway, so props to you
But I don't think aled has any right to be upset... he's literally upset about being famous
Not to mention he's like one of the smartest people in his school!! What uni's he going to? Like the one just below Oxbridge in the league tables? I mean, screw that!!!
He has no right to complain about anything. He's literally living the perfect life. Top uni, got a successful YouTube channel, what's he moping about?? Just because some kids want to ask him some questions? Literally the stupidest thing I've ever heard. I'd kill to be him, tbh, his life is perfect

I didn't know what to say again and honestly I just wanted this conversation to end. I wanted to fly into the sky and grab on to an aeroplane and fade away into the distance.

(18:24) Lorraine Sengupta
Your fave is problematic lmao

(18:24) Frances Janvier
Haha I guess

(18:27) Lorraine Sengupta
P.s. You going to the thing at spoons tonight??

(18:29) Frances Janvier
Thing?

(18:30) Lorraine Sengupta
Yeah, mostly people from the year above. It's the last night before most people go off to uni

(18:32) Frances Janvier
I don't really know anyone
I'd just be sitting in the corner with some crisps or something

(18:32) Lorraine Sengupta
You know me!! And aled might be there??

(18:33) Frances Janvier
Will he?

(18:33) Lorraine Sengupta
Well... maybe... but I'll definitely be there!!

I really didn't want to go. I wanted to stay home and order pizza and watch seven episodes of *Parks and Recreation* and text Aled seventy times.

219

But by this point it was too awkward to say no and I really wanted her to like me because not many people do. I'm weak and weird and lonely and an idiot.

"Oh my God, Frances, your *jacket*."

Raine was sitting in her car – a purple Ford Ka that looked dangerously close to spontaneous combustion – outside my house at 9pm, watching me walk towards her. My jacket was black denim and said 'tomboy' in white on the sleeves. I looked excellent (ridiculous). Usually when going out with my friends I tried to dress a bit more normally, but I was in a horrible mood and struggling to care about anything except what I'd done to Aled. Clothes are a window to the soul.

"Is that an 'Oh my God you look absolutely ridiculous'?" I said, getting into the passenger seat, "because that's an understandable reaction."

"No, I mean I didn't know you were so… pop punk. I thought I was gonna have to corrupt the nerdy one, but… you're not actually a nerd, are you?"

She appeared to be being genuine.

"This is real, this is me," I said.

She blinked. "Did you just quote *Camp Rock* at me? That's not very pop punk."

"I've gotta go my own way."

"Okay, firstly, that's *High School Musical*…"

We drove out of the village. Raine was wearing white platform trainers and stripy ankle socks, a grey T-shirt dress and a Harrington jacket. She always looked effortlessly cool, like an advert from some indie magazine you can only order online.

"You so didn't want to come, did you," said Raine, grinning as she spun the steering wheel. She was a surprisingly good driver.

"Haha, what else do I have to do?" I said, not mentioning the fact that I was literally sweating from how nervous I was about going to Spoons again, because there would be so many people from school there and people from the year above who I only knew a little bit and it would be really awkward and there'd be loads of groups of terrifying lads and I definitely should have worn something more boring and the only reason I was doing this, the only reason I'd want to do this all over again, was the chance that I could say sorry to Aled and we could be friends again before he went to university tomorrow and made a load of new friends and forgot about me...

"Exactly," said Raine.

We'd reached the motorway. With one hand, Raine turned the radio on, brought an iPod out of her pocket and fiddled with it. Music began to play on the car speakers – her iPod had some kind of FM transmitter attached to it.

Electronic drum and bass started to play.

"Who's this?" I asked

"Madeon," she said.

"It's cool," I said.

"It's my favourite for skuds."

"Skuds?"

"Drives. You never go for drives?"

"I can't drive. Can't afford it."

"Get a job, mate. I worked forty hours a week for the entire summer for this lump of trash." She patted the steering wheel. "My parents are proper poor, there's no way they'd get me one, and I *needed* a car, seriously. Needed to get out of my town."

"Where d'you work?"

"Hollister. They're judgemental as shit, but they do pay all right."

"Fair enough."

Raine turned the music up. "Yeah, this Madeon guy, he's the same age as me. I think that's why I like his music so much. Or I just feel like I've done nothing with my life."

"It sounds like you're in space," I said. "Or a futuristic city where everything is dark blue and you're wearing silver and there are space cruisers flying overhead."

She looked at me. "You're a proper *Universe City* fangirl, aren't you?"

I laughed. "Yep, until I die."

"I listened to a few episodes earlier. Some of the recent ones that you're in."

"Really? What did you think?"

"It's really cool." She paused for thought. "It's... it's got *something*. The stories aren't, like, amazing literature or anything, but like, the characters and the world and the language just sort of hypnotise you. Yeah. Good stuff."

"So d'you ship Radio and Toulouse?" The shipping of Radio and Toulouse had increased exponentially this month, which I felt a bit awkward about, since it was me and Aled, and lots of people thought that the characters represented people in real life. At least three people at school had asked me whether me and Radio were dating in real life. We hadn't even been trying to make Radio and Toulouse's relationship romantic.

She thought about it for a second. "Mmm. I don't know. It's not really about that, is it? Like, if they get together it'll be nice, but if they don't it won't ruin anything or change anything. The show's not really about romance."

"That's literally exactly what I think."

The music suddenly increased in volume. Raine changed gears and moved into the outside lane.

"I really like this," I said, tapping the radio display.

"What?" said Raine. The music was too loud.

I just laughed and shook my head. Raine shot me a confused grin. God, I barely knew her, but somehow here I was, having a vague hint of a good time. The motorway stretched out before us, dark blue, flashing lights. It looked like a time vortex.

Raine knew literally everyone who'd turned up to Spoons, all the people who'd left the various town schools four months ago and were getting smashed one last time before they left for university and gradually stopped speaking to each other.

It took only three awkward conversations for me to need alcohol, which Raine got for me, since I was still seventeen. She was drinking water because she was driving, but at one point she said to me, "Yeah, I stopped drinking ages ago, I used to do some really stupid stuff," and I wondered what that was all about. I should have stopped drinking, but the awkward conversations with people I didn't know would probably have destroyed me emotionally.

Spoons was packed. It was terrifying.

"Yeah, me and my girlfriend were gonna go to Disneyland last month," said some guy to me while I was waiting for my third drink. "But we decided to save our money for uni, like, neither of us could get any of the maintenance grants so I need money to keep me going while I try and get a job."

"What? I thought everyone got the maintenance grants," I said.

"The maintenance *loans*, yeah. But that doesn't cover the whole cost of your rent, unless you're living in a dive. You only get the grants if you're poor or your parents are divorced or whatever."

"Oh," I said.

"Yeah, everyone thought the boys' school head boy was gonna get into Cambridge," said a girl, half an hour later. I was drinking my fourth at a circular table, Raine talking to four different people at once. The girl was shaking her head. "He'd been the top student in the year since Year 7. But then he just didn't get in. Like, seven other people got in, but he didn't. And everyone had been like 'Oh, he's *obviously* going to get in,' for *so long*. It was horrible."

"That's really sad," I said.

"I honestly don't know what I'm doing," said another guy, who was wearing a denim jacket with a Joy Division T-shirt. He had an awkward posture, like he was embarrassed about something. "I don't know how I passed first year. I did nothing. And now I'm going into second year and it's like… I honestly don't know what I'm doing." He stared at me and he looked tired. "I wish I could go back and do things differently. I wish I could go back and change everything… I did some stupid things… I did some stupid things…"

Spoons turned into Johnny R's as it always did, and none of us noticed it happen. I don't even know how I got in there without any ID, but suddenly there I was, leaning on the far left of the Johnny R's bar with a drink that looked like water but definitely wasn't, judging by the taste.

I looked to the left and there was a girl sitting there who appeared to be doing exactly what I was doing – leaning on the bar, a drink in front of her, staring blankly at the crowd. She caught me looking at her and turned, and she was classically pretty – big eyes, wide mouth – and she also had the best hair I'd ever seen. It reached her waist and the parts that weren't dark purple were a faded grey-lilac colour. It reminded me of Aled.

"You all right?" she asked.

"Er, yeah," I said. "Yeah."

"You look a bit dazed."

"Nah, just bored."

"Haha, same."

There was a pause.

"D'you go to the Academy?" I asked.

"No, no, I'm at uni. I went to the grammars."

She'd gone to the grammars. That's what people say when they went to my old grammar school that burned down, and then had to change to the boys' grammar school.

"Oh, right."

She sipped her drink. "Hate it though. I might leave."

"Hate what?"

"Uni. I'm starting second year, but…" She trailed off. I couldn't stop myself from frowning. Why would anybody hate university?

"I think I might go home," she said.

"Aren't your friends here?"

"Yeah, but… I don't know. I don't think I'm the sort of… I don't know."

"What?"

"I used to like coming here, but I don't think…" She laughed suddenly.

"What?" I said.

"One of my old friends… she always said that I'd get tired of it eventually. Like, she'd always say no when I tried to bring her in Year 13, when we were both eighteen. She'd always be like, no, I'll hate it, and then she'd tell me I'd hate it in the end too so she was just getting the jump on me." She laughed again. "Well, she was right. As usual."

"Ah, is she here now?"

The girl looked at me. "No…"

"She sounds cool."

The girl ran a hand through her long hair. The light made the purple so beautiful she looked like a fairy. "She is." She looked past me. I couldn't see her eyes through the dark. "I can't believe she was right this whole time," she said, I think, but I couldn't really hear her because the music was too loud, and I was about to ask her "What?" again, but then she raised her eyebrows and forced a smile and said, "I'll see you later," even though I never saw her again in my life and she disappeared and I wondered whether I would stop hanging out with Aled once he was gone and one day it would just be me sat in a club with a drink, staring at other friends dancing, blank grey faces I haven't met yet, all drowning under the sound.

I downed my drink.

SORRY

"Frances, Frances, Frances, Frances, Frances..." Raine ran up to me in the middle of the third floor where they were playing a dubstep remix of 'White Sky' by Vampire Weekend.

I was drunk and had mostly no idea what I was doing or why. I was just doing it.

Raine had a plastic cup of clear liquid and for a second I genuinely believed that it was an entire plastic cup of vodka.

She saw me looking at it. "Mate, it's water!" She laughed. "I'm driving!"

'Teenage Dirtbag' started playing above our heads.

Raine raised one hand into the air and pointed at the ceiling. "Maaate! Frances, we have to dance to this."

I laughed. I kept laughing, I always did that when I was drunk. I followed her into the dancers. It was sweaty, and four guys attempted to grind on me. One guy touched my arse and I was too much of a square to do anything about it, so Raine poured her water on him and he shouted at her. I laughed. Raine laughed. I'm a really rubbish dancer anyway. Raine was a good dancer. She was pretty too. I was drunk, and I wondered if I was in love with her, and that made me laugh a lot. No. I'm not in love with anyone.

Aled kept flashing in and out of my vision, like he was teleporting around. He was magical in so many ways, but I wasn't in love with him either, even though he always looked so good in shirts and his hair was all messed up and lovely because we were all so sweaty. Later on I was dancing with Maya, to some trippy London Grammar song, and Maya was saying, "Frances, you're like an entirely different person!" and I saw Aled in the corner, talking to someone – oh, yeah, obviously it was Daniel. I needed to talk to Aled again, but I didn't want him to hate me, I so desperately wanted this to be okay, but I just didn't know how to make it okay.

Now that I knew Aled and Daniel were together, I kept noticing all the tiny things I hadn't noticed before, like the way Daniel would look at Aled while he was talking, the way Daniel would pull Aled along by the arm and Aled would follow without question, the way when they were in conversation they would lean so close together it was as if they were about to kiss. I really was an idiot.

Maya and Jess and these two guys Luke and Jamal were drunk too and they were bitching about Raine while we were dancing, multi-tasking. They said she was a slag, or something, and she made them all feel really awkward. Maya gave me a weird look while they were speaking and I realised that it was because I had frowned at them.

I was still thinking about what that girl with the purple hair had said about wanting to leave university. I was thinking about it because I didn't understand it at all, I'd never heard anyone suggest anything like that, but then again… *obviously* not everyone enjoyed university. I knew I would though. So what she'd said didn't matter. I was study machine Frances Janvier. I was going to Cambridge, and I was going to get a good job and earn lots of money, and I was going to be happy.

Wasn't I? I was. Uni, job, money, happiness. That's what you do. That's the formula. Everyone knows that. I knew that.

Thinking about it was giving me a headache. Or maybe the music was too loud.

I watched Aled and Daniel head towards the stairs so obviously I followed, not even bothering to tell Raine where I was going; she'd be fine, she talks to everyone. I didn't know what I was going to say, but I knew I had to say something, I couldn't just leave things like this, I didn't want to be left alone like this. Daniel had always been there before me, I'd been stupid to think Aled could ever consider me his best friend when he'd already had one for so long, even if he'd been the honest-to-God best and most excellent friend I'd ever had in my whole life and I might have to live my whole life without meeting another person so brilliant as him.

I almost lost them in the crowds because everyone was starting to look the same, so many skinny jeans and little dresses and undercuts and platform plimsolls and Wayfarer glasses and velvet scrunchies and denim jackets. I made it outside into the smoking area and couldn't believe how cold it was – wasn't it summer? Wait – no, it's nearly October. How did that happen? It was so quiet outside, so cold and quiet and dark…

"Oh," said Aled, when I practically collided with him. Neither of us were smoking, obviously, but it had been so hot inside I thought I was going to melt. Not that I would have complained about melting – it would have solved a lot of my problems.

Aled appeared to be on his own, a drink in one hand. He was

wearing one of his more boring short-sleeved shirts and very ordinary skinny jeans. And his *hair*... he didn't look like himself at all. I wanted to hug him, as if that would turn him back into his normal self.

It was dark and crowded outside and all the benches were taken. A remix of 'Chocolate' by The 1975 was escaping out of the doorway into Johnny R's ground floor and it almost made me roll my eyes.

"I'm so sorry," I said immediately, even though it sounded so *childish*. "Honestly, Aled, I'm just... I can't tell you how much..."

"It's fine," he said, straight-faced and obviously lying. "I was just surprised. It's fine."

He didn't look like he was just surprised.

He looked like he wanted to die.

"It's *not* fine. It's not fine. You didn't want anyone to know about it and now everyone does. And your mum, I mean... you said she might make you stop doing it, or something..."

He was standing with his legs crossed. He wasn't wearing his lime green plimsolls – instead he was wearing these very ordinary white ones that I hadn't seen before.

He shook his head slightly. "I just... I don't understand why you couldn't have just *lied*. I don't get why you couldn't have just said no when they asked you whether it was me."

"I..." I didn't know why I couldn't have lied about it either. I lied all the time. My entire personality was a lie every time I stepped inside the school building, wasn't it? Wait, no... School Frances wasn't a *lie*, she was just... I don't know... "I'm... sorry."

"Yeah, okay, I *know*," Aled snapped. He actually snapped.

I just wanted him to be okay. I just wanted us to be okay.

"Are you okay?" I asked.

He looked at me.

"I'm fine," he said.

"No," I said.

"What?" he said.

"Are you okay?" I asked again.

"I said I'm *fine*!" He raised his voice and it almost made me step backwards. "Jesus Christ, it is what it is. We can't do anything about it, stop making it a bigger deal than it already is!"

"But it is a big deal to you…"

"That doesn't matter," he said, and I felt like I was going to break into a million tiny pieces and get blown away. "It's a pathetic thing to be upset about, so it doesn't matter."

"But you *are* upset about it."

"Just stop talking about it!" His voice got louder, he sounded almost *panicked*.

"You're my most important friend," I said again.

"Don't you have your own things to worry about?" he said.

"No." I laughed again, I could have started crying. "No, my life is fine, completely boring and fine. Nothing ever happens to me. I get good grades, I have a great family, and that's it. I've got literally nothing to complain about. Am I not allowed to care about my friends' problems?"

"My life is *fine*," he said, but his voice sounded hoarse.

"Fine!" I said, or maybe I shouted it, maybe I was drunker than I thought. "Fine, fine, fine, fine, fine. Everything's fine. We're all fine."

Aled stepped back a little and he looked *hurt*, and I knew I'd done something wrong, *again*, why am I such an idiot?

"What d'you think you're trying to do?" he said, his voice louder now. "Why are you so obsessed with me?"

That hurt like a stab to the heart.

"I'm just— I'll listen to you!"

"I don't need you to listen! I don't want to talk about anything! Stop *pestering me*!"

And that was it.

He wouldn't tell me anything.

He didn't want to.

"Just— why did you do it?" he said, his hands curling into fists.

"Why did I do what!?"

"*Tell everyone I'm the Creator!*"

I started shaking my head wildly. "I— I didn't, I swear I didn't..."

"You're *lying*!"

"Wha— What..."

He walked closer to me and I actually stepped backwards. He might have been drinking, but I'd drunk a lot so I couldn't tell.

"You just— You just wanted to use me to get popular on the Internet, didn't you!"

I couldn't speak.

"Just stop pretending you care about me!" He was full-on shouting at me now. People were starting to look at us. "All you care about is *Universe City*! You're just another fangirl trying to expose me and take away the *one thing* I actually care about! I don't even know what your real personality is, you behave so differently around other people. You've literally plotted this entire thing from the start, pretending you just like hanging out with me and you don't care about Internet fame and all this shit..."

"What— N-no—" My mind was going blank. "That's not true!"

"Then what is it!? Why are you so obsessed with me?"

"Sorry," I said, but I wasn't sure whether I was making any actual sound.

"Stop saying that!" Aled's face was scrunched up and his eyes were watery. "Stop lying! You're just caught up in some stupid delusion again, just the same as you were with Carys."

I suddenly felt like I was going to vomit.

"I'm just the replacement. You're *obsessed* with me, just the same as Carys, and you've managed to fuck up the only thing I had, the only good thing I fucking have, just like you managed to fuck up Carys's. D'you fancy me as well?"

"I don't— That's— I don't fancy you…"

"Then why would you be round my house every day?" The way he said it was like someone else was speaking through him. He stepped closer again, he was so angry. "Just admit it!"

My voice was more like a shriek by this point. "I don't fancy you!"

Do you believe me? I thought. *Does anyone believe me?* I thought I might be the only person who believed me.

"So *what the fuck is it!? Why did you do this to me?*"

Tears had started to spill down my cheeks. "I— It was an accident…"

Aled stepped back. "You told me yourself that you're the reason Carys is *gone*."

He said the last word so loudly that I stepped back again and now I was crying properly and *God* I hated myself, I hated myself so much. I'm sorry, I'm sorry, I'm sorry, I'm sorry, I'm sorry…

Before I knew what was happening, Daniel was in front of me, almost shoving me backwards, saying, "Go away, Frances, leave him alone," and then Raine was in front of me facing him, saying, "Lay off, mate! What did you say to her?" and then they started shouting at each other, but I wasn't really listening until Raine was like, "He doesn't fucking *belong to you*," and then they were both gone and I was walking out of the club and sitting down on the kerb, trying to stop the tears coming out of my eyes, but they wouldn't stop…

"Frances, oh, God."

"I'm sorry, I'm sorry, I'm sorry, I'm sorry…"

"You didn't do anything, Frances!"

"I have, I've ruined everything again…"

"It wasn't you."

"It was me, everything was my fault."

"It's not important, he'll get over it, I promise."

"No— Not just that, Carys as well, Carys… it was my fault, it's my fault she's gone… and nobody knows where she is and Aled's all alone with his mum and it's all my fault…"

Suddenly I was sitting on a bench with my head on Raine's shoulder and in her hand was her phone and she was playing some music and it was like the music was coming right out of her hand, but the phone speakers were shit and the music sounded less like music and more like the dull 2am buzz of a car radio on the motorway, and the guy sang, "I can lay inside", and the music played like the darkness of the sky and it played with me, I felt drunk and blurry and I couldn't remember what I was going to say.

3. AUTUMN TERM
b)

BULLET

- The next day I texted Aled. Then I Facebook-messaged him. Then I called him. I heard nothing, and at quarter to seven in the evening I stepped out of my house with the intention of knocking on his door, but his mum's car was gone, and so was he.
- At the weekend I sent him a lengthy apology over Facebook, which felt pathetic while I was writing it, and was still pathetic when I read it back. While I was writing it, I realised there really wasn't anything I could do to make it better, and I had possibly just lost the only real friend I had ever made in my entire life.
- My behaviour throughout the rest of October was more pathetic than I even believed was possible of myself. I cried daily and couldn't sleep properly, and got very angry at myself because of both of these things. I put on some weight, but I didn't really care about that very much. Wasn't like I was skinny in the first place.
- October was full-on for schoolwork as well. I was spending most of my evenings doing homework. I had copious amounts

of art coursework to do, and we were being made to write English essays *every week*. I was trying to read some books for my Cambridge interviews, but I couldn't make myself concentrate. I forced myself to read them though. *The Canterbury Tales* and *Sons and Lovers* and *For Whom The Bell Tolls*. If I didn't get into Cambridge, everything I had tried to be throughout my school life would be a total waste.

- One evening I saw Aled walking down the road from the station lugging a suitcase – home for the weekend, I guessed. I almost ran outside to see him, but he would have replied to my messages if he'd wanted to be friends again. I wanted to know how he was finding university – he was tagged in a few Freshers' Week photos on Facebook with other freshers, smiling and drinking and sometimes in a fancy-dress costume. I didn't know whether to feel happy or sad, but looking at them made me feel horrible.

- Obviously I stopped voicing Toulouse in *Universe City* and I stopped doing the art. Aled changed the story so Toulouse was suddenly banished from the city. I felt very sad about that, as if it was me who'd been banished.

- I got a ton of messages on Tumblr asking me why this had happened. I just said that's the story – Toulouse's segment was over.

- I got a ton of messages on Tumblr asking me why my art had stopped appearing on the *Universe City* videos and why I hadn't been posting any drawings lately. I said I was struggling with school stress and needed to take some time away.

- I got a ton of messages.

- I almost bit the bullet and deleted my Tumblr entirely, but I couldn't do it, so I tried to stay away from Tumblr as much as I could.

- On the first of November, I turned eighteen. I expected to feel different but, of course, I didn't. I don't think age has much to do with adulthood.

SCHOOL FRANCES

"Frances, you look so *grumpy*," said Maya with a laugh. "What's wrong?"

Every day I spent eating lunch with my school 'friends' felt like I was walking one step closer to packing my bags, leaving town and hitchhiking to Wales.

My school friends weren't bad people. They were just friends with School Frances – quiet, studious Frances – instead of Real Frances – meme-lover, patterned-leggings fanatic, and very close to a breakdown. Because School Frances was very dull, they didn't really like talking to her, or care very much about how she was. School Frances, I started to realise, hardly even had a personality at all, so I didn't really blame everyone for laughing at her.

It was early November and I was finding it increasingly difficult to be School Frances any more.

I smiled at Maya. "Haha, I'm fine. Just stressed."

'Just stressed' was starting to take on the same meaning as 'I'm fine.'

"Oh my God, *same*," she said, and then started talking to someone else.

Raine turned to me. Raine always sat next to me at lunch and I was extremely grateful for this because she was pretty much the only person who I actually had conversations with.

"You sure you're okay?" she said in a much less patronising tone than Maya. "You look a bit ill, actually."

I laughed. "Thanks."

She grinned. "No! I mean – ugh, I just mean you haven't really been acting like yourself."

"Haha. I don't really know who that is."

"Are you still upset about Aled?"

She said it so bluntly I almost laughed again. "Partly, I guess... He just hasn't replied to any of my messages...."

Raine looked at me for a moment.

"He's an absolute cunt," she said, which made me splutter a mildly traumatised laugh.

"What? Why?"

"If he can't even think rationally enough to see that you've been his friend for all this time, what's the point in trying? He clearly doesn't care about you enough to value your relationship. You shouldn't have to care either." She shook her head. "You don't need friends like that."

I knew everything was way more complicated than that, and I knew that everything was my fault and I didn't deserve any pity whatsoever, but it still felt nice to hear Raine say those things.

"I guess so," I said.

She hugged me then, and I realised it was the first time she had done so. I hugged her back as well as I could from my seat.

"You deserve better friends," she said. "You're a sunshine angel."

I didn't know what to say or what to think. I just hugged her.

WINTER OLYMPIAN

"Frances, when're your Cambridge interviews?"

I was walking past the school hall's backstage door when Daniel spoke to me for the first time since September. He was standing next to the stage curtain with a Winter Olympian who had come to give a speech in front of Years 7, 8 and 9.

Daniel obviously had good reason to be angry with me, and since I wasn't head girl any more I had no reason to even be around him. So I hadn't been surprised when he started refusing to make eye contact with me in the school corridors.

I didn't have anywhere urgent to be, so I walked into the backstage area. He hadn't even asked his question in a particularly rude manner.

"December the tenth," I said. It was mid-November so I had a few weeks left. I hadn't read everything I'd said I'd read on my personal statement yet. I just hadn't had time to prepare for the interviews and keep up with my coursework at the same time.

"Ah," he said. "Same."

He looked slightly different from the last time I'd spoken to him. I thought he'd maybe let his hair grow a little longer, but

I couldn't really tell, since he kept it swept back into a quiff every day.

"How's it going?" I asked. "You ready? Know your stuff about… like… bacteria and… skeletons and stuff?"

"Bacteria and skeletons…"

"What? I don't know what you do in biology."

"You did it at GCSE though."

I folded my arms. "The nucleus is the powerhouse of the cell. The cell membrane – what does the cell membrane do? I hope you know what the cell membrane does. They might ask you."

"They're probably not going to ask me what the cell membrane does."

"What are they going to ask you?"

He gave me a long look. "Nothing that you would understand."

"Good thing I'm not applying to do biology then, isn't it."

"Yup."

I suddenly noticed that Raine was backstage with us. She was currently interrogating the Winter Olympian, and I felt a bit sorry for him – he could only have been a couple of years older than us and he seemed kind of nerdy and awkward for an athlete, super tall with massive glasses and jeans that were slightly too short for him. He looked a little panicked at the fact that he had to talk for twenty minutes to Years 7 to 9, and Raine was doing nothing to help. Apparently he used to go to the grammar school across town, Aled's school, and now he was here to talk about his success and achievement and stuff.

Daniel saw me looking at her, and he rolled his eyes. "She wanted to meet him."

"Oh."

"Anyway, here's the thing," Daniel continued, looking me in the eye. "I need a lift to Cambridge."

"You need a lift...?"

"Yeah. My parents are working and I don't have the money to get to Cambridge by myself."

"Can't your parents give you money for the train?"

He sort of ground his teeth like he really didn't want to say what he was about to say.

"My parents don't give me money for things," he said. "And I had to quit my job because of schoolwork."

"They won't even give you money for *Cambridge*?"

"They don't really see it as a very big deal." He shook his head slightly. "They don't even think I need to go to university. My dad— My dad just wants me to come work for him... he runs this, like, electronics shop..." His voice faded away.

I stared at him. And I suddenly felt really bloody sorry for him.

"I was gonna get the train there," I said. "My mum's working."

Daniel nodded and looked down. "Ah, okay. Yeah. That's all right."

Raine leaned over from the chair she was straddling. The Olympian guy looked sort of relieved.

"I'll drive you guys," she said. "If you want."

"What?" I said.

"What?" Daniel said.

"I'll drive you." Raine grinned broadly and rested her chin in her hand. "To Cambridge."

"You'll have school," said Daniel, very quickly.

"So?"

"So... you're just gonna skip?"

She shrugged. "I'll fake an absence note. Works every time."

Daniel looked extremely conflicted. It was still very weird to me that Daniel had drunkenly poured out his heart to a girl he has absolutely nothing in common with. Then again, maybe that was why he did it.

"Okay," he said, trying and failing to mask the irritated tone of his voice. "Yeah. That'll be great."

"Yeah, thanks," I said. "That's really kind."

There was an awkward pause for a couple of seconds, and then a teacher gestured from the other side of the stage for Daniel to come on and introduce the Olympian guy, which he did, and then the Winter Olympian walked on to the stage and Daniel walked off.

Daniel and I didn't say anything to each other while the guy was talking. To be honest, he wasn't a very good public speaker – he kept losing the point of his talk. I think he was supposed to be inspiring people to work hard in school and explain about sports-related careers and he seemed to be fairly confident in what he was saying, but he kept throwing things in like "I didn't really get along well with academia," and "I felt a bit alienated with school," and "I just think we don't all have to have our lives laid out by the grades that we get in our exams."

After the guy finished, Daniel and I smiled and thanked him for coming and all that stuff, and he asked if it was okay and we obviously said it was. He was then whisked off by a teacher, and Daniel and I started making our way back to the common room.

As we were walking through the hallways, I asked him, "Have you been seeing Aled much?"

And he looked at me and said, "You know about us, don't you?"

And I said, "Yeah."

And he said, "Well, he doesn't talk to me any more."

"Why?"

"I don't know. He just stopped texting me one day."

"For no reason?"

He paused and almost seemed to sway as he walked, as if the weight of this whole thing was about to crush him into the ground. "We had an argument on his birthday."

"About what?"

I don't know why I was surprised. People move on quicker than I can comprehend. People forget you within days, they take new pictures to put on Facebook and they don't read your messages. They keep on moving forward and shove you to the side because you make more mistakes than you should. Maybe that was fair. Who was I to judge, really?

He said, "It doesn't matter."

I said, "He doesn't talk to me either."

And neither of us said anything after that.

SPACE

"It's getting a bit late, isn't it, France?" said Mum, wandering into the lounge with a cup of tea in one hand.

I blinked up at her from my laptop. Moving gave me an immediate headache. "What's the time?"

"Half twelve." She sat down on the sofa. "You're not still doing work, are you? You've done work every night this week."

"I've just got to finish this paragraph."

"You've got to be up in six hours."

"Yeah, I'll be done in a minute."

She sipped her tea. "You keep doing this. It's no wonder you're getting stress pains."

I'd started getting weird pains in the side of my ribcage every time I sat in a particular position. It did at times feel a bit like I was having a very slow heart attack, so I was trying not to think too much about it.

"I think you should go to bed," she said.

"I can't!" I snapped, louder than I'd meant to. "I literally can't. You don't understand. This is due tomorrow, Period One, so I have to do it now."

247

Mum stayed silent for a moment.

"How about we go to the cinema this weekend?" she said. "Just a little break from all this Cambridge stuff. That space film came out a few weeks ago."

"I don't have time. Maybe after my interviews."

She nodded. "Okay." She stood up. "Okay." She left the room.

I finished the essay at 1am and went to bed. I thought about listening to the most recent *Universe City* episode because I hadn't got around to it yet, but in the end I was too tired, and I didn't feel like it, so I just lay in bed and waited to fall asleep.

HATE

I'd been avoiding checking Tumblr for a few weeks. All I was ever faced with was a ton of messages asking me why I hadn't updated for a while and the reminder that I hadn't drawn anything for over a month.

And the fandom scared me. Not gonna lie.

Now that everyone knew who Aled Last was in real life, the *Universe City* tag went through a phase of posting and reblogging every single picture of Aled they could get. To be fair, there weren't very many. A couple stolen from his personal Facebook. One stolen from the Johnny R's Facebook page. A blurry one in the street at his university. Thankfully, after a few people made posts about how this was all a disgusting invasion of the privacy of a person who clearly wanted to remain anonymous, most people stopped posting them.

Yet no one seemed to know anything about him. They didn't know how old he was, where he lived, what he was studying at university. Aled didn't confirm anything on Twitter – he just ignored everything, like nothing was happening. And gradually everyone stopped talking about him, and got back to talking about *Universe City* again. Like none of it had happened at all.

In general, I started to feel like it really wasn't as bad as we'd all thought.

Until the end of November.

That was when everything got a hundred times worse.

The first post to circulate the fandom was a new picture of Aled.

He was sitting on a stone bench in what looked like a town square. I hadn't been to Aled's university town before, but I assumed that's where it was. He had a Tesco bag in one hand and was staring at his phone. I wondered who he was texting.

His hair had grown enough again to fall into his eyes and he looked almost like the Aled I'd first met properly back in May.

There wasn't a caption with the picture and the Tumblr blog that had posted it didn't have its ask box open, so the only way for people to criticise the person who posted it was to reblog it, which is what happened, and within a couple of days the post had 20,000 notes.

The second post wasn't even from a *Universe City* blog.

troylerphandoms23756
hey so I gave 'Universe City' a go since phil recommended it recently but... does anyone else think it's like... *super* elitist? Like really really privileged? The whole thing is a giant metaphor for how crap the writer thinks the education system is, right? There are people in third world countries starving themselves so they can get an education lmao... I mean, 'Universe City' = 'university'... it's not exactly subtle is it lol

Dozens of *Universe City* blogs reblogged it with a variety of snarky comments and I almost wanted to say something myself – it was an absolutely ridiculous statement.

Then again, I guess Aled *had* said something about not wanting to go to university. Hadn't he? Or had he been joking?

And then came the third post, from the same person who had posted that sneaky picture of Aled in town.

They posted another picture of Aled. It was moderately dark and he was unlocking a door. The words 'St John's College' could clearly be read on the building's wall.

Which meant that everyone who saw it would know where Aled lived.

This time there was a caption underneath the photo:

youngadultmachine
gonna kill aled last privileged prik he doin bad things, education is a privilege and hes got No rite to make are kids question there Way in life. Hes brain washing are kids.

My stomach actually lurched while I read it.

They weren't serious, were they?

There was no way of knowing whether the person who'd written it had been the one to take the picture.

I didn't know what to make of any of this.

It was all just hate. Internet hate.

Universe City was just a story – a magical sci-fi adventure story that gave me a tiny twenty-minute period of happiness once a week. There weren't any deeper meanings. If there were, he would have told me.

Wouldn't he?

do you think this is all some sort of a joke?

Scroll down for transcript >>>

[...]

I wonder why you're even listening to this in the first place! Are you just turning your radio on each week to listen to some funny story about silly old Radio and their friends zapping a new monster and solving the mystery like we're the bloody twenty-sixth century Scooby Doo gang? I can see you now. Having a right old laugh to yourselves while we're here, slowly dying from the city fumes, being murdered in our sleep. I bet you have the power to contact us, but you just can't be bothered. Have you even been listening to anything I've been saying?

You're just the same as everyone I knew in the old world. You can't be bothered to do anything.

[...]

GUY DENNING

"Frances… I wouldn't advise putting your entire face on the desk when I've been using henna," Raine said to me during one of our art lessons in early December. I was doing an artist copy of a Guy Denning portrait using chalk and charcoal – my art coursework was on isolation. She was applying henna to a papier-mâché skeleton hand – her art coursework was on racism against Hindus in Britain.

I sat back up and touched my face. "Did I get any on me?"

Raine looked at me and made a face of concentration. "Nope, you're good."

"Phew."

"What's up?"

"Just got a headache."

"Again? Mate, you should get that checked out."

"It's just stress. And lack of sleep."

"You never know. It might be a massive brain tumour."

I grimaced. "Please don't mention brain tumours. I'm an extreme hypochondriac."

"Might be an aneurism just waiting to happen."

"Please stop talking."

"How are you ladies getting on?" Our art teacher, Miss García, appeared at our table like she'd apparated there. I jumped so hard I nearly smudged my drawing.

"Fine," I said.

She studied my drawing and then sat down on the stool next to me. "This is going well."

"Thanks!"

She tapped the paper with one finger. "You're very good at capturing likeness but keeping it in your own style. You're not just drawing things photographically – you're really interpreting it into something new. You're making it your own."

I felt sort of happy. "Thank you…"

She looked at me through her square glasses and wrapped her crocheted cardigan around her body. "What subject is it you're applying for at uni, Frances?"

"English lit."

"Oh, really?"

I laughed. "Is that surprising?"

She leaned over the table. "I didn't know you had any interest. I thought you'd do something more practical."

"Oh… like what?"

"Well, I always thought you'd do art. I could be wrong, but you really do seem to enjoy it."

"Well, yeah I do…" I paused. I'd never even considered doing an art degree. I'd always enjoyed art, but the idea of doing it as a degree… it'd just be a bit useless, wouldn't it? And what would be the point when I got such good grades in more useful subjects? I'd just be wasting my potential. "I can't choose a degree based on what I'd *enjoy* though."

Miss García raised her eyebrows. "Ah."

"I've already sent off my applications anyway. I've got my Cambridge interviews next week."

"Yes, of course."

There was an awkward pause, and then she stood up straight again and said, "Keep up the good work, ladies," before walking off.

I glanced at Raine, but she was back concentrating on the henna. She wasn't applying to uni, much to our school's irritation – she was applying for a few business apprenticeships instead. I wanted to ask her opinion, but she didn't really know the extent to which drawing was a part of my life so she probably wouldn't have been able to help.

I looked back at the artist copy I was working on. It was a smudgy face of a girl with her eyes closed. I wondered whether Guy Denning went to university, since he was one of my favourite artists of all time, and I decided to look it up when I got home.

According to Wikipedia, he'd applied to a load of art colleges and didn't get into any of them.

PRESS PLAY

It was three days before my Cambridge interviews when I realised I hadn't listened to an episode of *Universe City* in three weeks. I hadn't looked at Aled's Twitter. I hadn't checked Tumblr. I hadn't drawn anything.

It wasn't a big deal. It just made me feel weird. I thought I enjoyed all this stuff, but maybe I was an academic at heart after all. I kept peeling off layers of my personality, but I seemed to be going in circles. Every time I thought I'd worked out what I really enjoyed, I started to second-guess myself. Maybe I just didn't enjoy anything any more.

Aled and I had been good friends; there was no way he could possibly lie to himself about that. He'd decided to end it and never talk to me again, so why should I get sad about it? He was the one who was in the wrong. He didn't have any right to be angry at me. I was the one who had to go back to being School Frances, quiet, boring, stressed, tired. He was having the time of his life at university and I was sleeping five hours a night and speaking to maybe two people per day.

I loaded up an episode of *Universe City* to listen to, but couldn't bring myself to press play, because I had work to do, and that was more important.

UNIVERSE CITY: Ep. 141 – nothing day
UniverseCity

I didn't do anything today

Scroll down for transcript >>>

[...]

Every week something happens and it feels strained. The truth is, old sport, sometimes there isn't anything to report. Sometimes I might exaggerate a bit, just so I have something exciting to say. That time I told you I surfed the BOT22 down to Leftley Square? Well – that was a lie. It was only a BOT18. I lied. I really, really lied. And I am sorry.

I feel a bit like a BOT18 sometimes. Old and rusty, aching and sleepy. Wandering through the city, lost, circling, alone. No gears left in my heart, no code whirring in my brain. Just kinetic energy, being pushed gently onwards by other forces – sound, light, dust waves, the quakes. I'm as lost as ever, friends. Can you tell?

I'd like it if someone were to rescue me soon. Oh, I'd like that very much. I'd like that. I'd like that very much indeed.

[...]

WHAT ELSE WERE YOU
SUPPOSED TO DO

At 9am on the day of my Cambridge interviews, Raine rolled up outside my house in her purple Ford Ka. She texted me 'YO I'M OUTSIDE' and I texted back 'out in a sec m8', despite the fact that I absolutely did not in any way want to step out of my front door.

I had the two essays I'd submitted to the college in my bag so I could reread them in the car. I also had a bottle of water, a packet of Polos, a few *Universe City* episodes downloaded on to my iPod to calm me down, and a good luck/calm down message from my mum that she'd written underneath a printed-out picture of Beyoncé. Before Mum had left for work, she'd given me a massive hug and told me to keep her updated via Facebook messages and to call her immediately after the interviews. That had made me feel a bit better.

I was wearing what I thought was a very successful balance of I'm-a-mature-and-sophisticated-and-intelligent-young-woman and I-don't-believe-that-what-I'm-wearing-today-should-influence-your-decision, which was some plain blue skinny jeans, a very plain and normal black jumper and a green checked shirt underneath. I would never normally wear this, but I thought I looked quite intellectual yet still sort of like myself.

Basically, I was feeling extremely uncomfortable. I put it down to nerves.

Raine's eyes followed me as I walked towards her car.

"You look very boring, Frances," she said, as I got into the front seat.

"Good," I said. "I don't want to scare them."

"I was keeping my fingers crossed for colourful leggings. Or your black denim jacket."

"I don't think people wear those in Cambridge."

We both laughed heartily and drove off to Daniel's house.

Daniel lived right in the middle of town opposite a Tesco Express in a very thin terraced house that did not have a drive. It took Raine a good three minutes to park properly.

I texted Daniel – I had his number now – and when he emerged from the house, he was wearing his usual sixth-form suit.

I got out of the car so he could climb into the back. "Went for the sixth-form suit, then?"

He looked me up and down. "I thought that's what everyone wore."

"Is it?"

He shrugged. "I thought so. I might be wrong." He turned and got into the car. My anxiety about today had multiplied at least three times.

"Daniel, you're not helping, mate," said Raine with an exaggerated eye-roll. "We're all feeling very nervous as it is."

"You?" Daniel laughed as I got back into the car. "You don't even have interviews. You're just gonna sit in Costa Coffee for six hours and play *Candy Crush*."

"Excuse me, I'm extremely nervous for both you guys. And I gave up *Candy Crush* two months ago."

This made me laugh again, and for the first time since we'd agreed to do this, I was kind of glad that I wasn't going to these interviews on my own.

The drive to Cambridge was two and a half hours. Daniel sat in the back with headphones on and did not talk to us at all. I didn't blame him to be honest. Every couple of minutes my stomach would flip and I'd feel like I was about to throw up everywhere.

Raine didn't try to talk to me that much either, which I was thankful for. And she let me choose the car music from her iPod. I picked some Bon Iver remixes and then read over my essays for half an hour before staring out of the window for most of the journey. There was something calming about the motorway.

Everything I'd ever done at school had come down to this.

I found out what Oxford and Cambridge were when I was nine and I knew that was where I was clearly meant to go.

What else were you supposed to do when you got the best grades in the class, without fail, every single year?

Why would I waste an opportunity like this?

UNHELPFUL THINGS

"Well, mother of balls," said Raine as we drove through Cambridge. "It's like they built it out of caviar."

It was nearly midday. My first interview was at two, Daniel's was at two thirty. I was trying not to have an anxiety attack.

"Everything's very brown," Raine continued. "Like, there's not a lot of grey. It's like a film set."

It was a beautiful place, to be fair. It felt almost fake compared to the greyness of our town. The river in Cambridge felt like it belonged in *The Lord of the Rings*, whereas the river in our town was more like somewhere you might find some shopping trolleys or a dead body.

After a good ten minutes of randomly turning corners, we managed to find somewhere to park. Raine wasn't sure whether it was entirely legal, but decided not to worry too much about it. I worried a lot about it, but she was the driver so I couldn't really say anything about it. Daniel appeared to have entered an entirely different dimension and wasn't quite registering anything we were saying.

Some of the Cambridge colleges looked like palaces. I'd seen them in pictures, obviously, but they didn't really do the real things justice.

It didn't even feel like the real world.

We very quickly found ourselves a Starbucks.

"I take back what I said about everything being brown," said Raine, once we'd sat down. "I haven't seen a single brown person since we got here." Even she looked sort of uncomfortable, which was fair enough because she really did stick out with her undercut hair and a pastel blue bomber jacket and platform trainers.

"Preach," I said.

I sipped my coffee, but wasn't sure whether I was going to manage any of the sandwich I'd bought. Daniel had brought his own lunch and it made me think of Ron Weasley on the train to Hogwarts, sandwiches wrapped in cling film. Not that he was eating it – he was sitting entirely still except for one leg which was bouncing up and down.

Raine leaned back in her seat and stared at us for a moment. Then she said, "Well, I have a few things to say about this."

"Please don't," said Daniel immediately.

"Helpful things."

"Nothing you say will be helpful."

"Then… not-unhelpful things."

Daniel gave her a look that said, 'I want you to die.'

"Guys, I just think, like, if you two can't get into Cambridge, like, who actually can?"

Both Daniel and I looked at her.

"That's really not helpful," said Daniel.

"Seriously though." Raine held out her hands. "You two have been top of the year group since, what, like, Year 7? And I bet you were top of your primary schools as well. Like – if you two can't get into Cambridge then I don't really understand who would."

We didn't say anything.

"What if we mess up the interview though?" I said quietly.

"Yeah," said Daniel.

Raine looked a little lost for words before she said, "Well, I don't think you will. You both know lots about your subject, you're both super smart." She grinned and gestured to herself. "Like, if I tried to sit in one of these interviews, I'd probably just have to walk out. Or, like, bribe them into letting me in."

I chuckled. Even Daniel smiled a little bit.

We ate our lunch and then I set off for the college I'd applied to – I'd chosen it because it was one of the famous ones, one of the supposedly more academic ones. Raine gave me a massive hug before I went. Daniel sort of nodded at me, but even that was comforting in its own way. I messaged Mum that I was going in and she messaged back saying she believed in me. I just wished I believed in me, to be honest.

It was just because I was nervous. I felt weird because I was nervous. That's all it was.

My original plan, way back months ago, had been to listen to a *Universe City* episode to calm me down before I went inside the college. I didn't want to do that any more.

I got shown into the college by a student. He had a very wide smile, a very posh voice and was wearing a blazer voluntarily.

As I'd expected, half an hour before my interview I was given a small piece of paper with a poem on one side and a short extract from a novel on the other. I read them sitting on a sofa in the college library. They made very little sense, but I tried to look for the metaphors. The book extract was about a cave. I can't even remember what the poem was about.

And then my half an hour was up and my palms were sweating and my heart was beating. My life had built up to this; my future would be built by this. I just needed to sound intelligent, enthusiastic, original, open-minded. The ideal Cambridge student – wait, what was that again? I'd watched all of the example interviews on the Cambridge website. Did I need to shake the interviewers' hands? I couldn't remember. The girl who'd gone in before me was wearing a suit. Was everyone wearing a suit? Did I look unintelligent? Was my phone on silent? What if I messed this up? Would that be the end? What if I messed up now, after all the late nights, after reading all these books and poems for an entire year? What if I'd wasted all that time? What if all this had been for nothing?

OLD WHITE MEN

The two interviewers were both old white men. I'm sure that not all of the interviewers at the University of Cambridge are old white men, and in my second interview later that day one of them was a woman, but in my first interview, mine were old white men, and I was not surprised.

They didn't offer to shake my hand, so I didn't offer either. My interview went a little bit like this.

OLD WHITE MAN (O.W.M.) #1:   So, Frances, I see that you picked art A level alongside English, history and politics. And you did maths at AS-Level. Why such a diverse group of subjects?

FRANCES: Oh... well, you know, I've always been interested in a wide range of subjects. I just thought, at A level, you know, it'd be good to, sort of, keep that going, you know, using both sides of the brain, having a wider... broader... learning experience. I enjoy lots of different subjects, so, yeah.

O.W.M. #1:   [blinks and nods]

O.W.M. #2:   And you say in your personal statement that the book that really started your interest in the study of English literature was [glances at paper] *The Catcher in the Rye* by J.D. Salinger?

FRANCES: Yes!

O.W.M. #2:   What was it, precisely, about the book that so inspired you?

FRANCES: [completely unprepared for a question like this] Ah… yeah. Well, I think it was the themes, really, I really related to the themes of, you know, disillusionment and alienation, [laughs] you know, the typical teenage thing you go through! Erm, but yeah, there were lots of things in the book that really interested me from, like, an academic point of view, like, erm… One of the things I liked was the way Salinger sort of *got* the lingo of nineteen-forties and -fifties teenagers? It was the first time I'd read an old book – well, like, a *classic* book anyway – that, erm, you know, really felt like it had a real voice? I really felt connected to the main character, I guess… and it made me want to understand why.

O.W.M. #2:   [nods and smiles, but doesn't really seem to have heard anything I've just said]

O.W.M. #1:   So, Frances, I suppose the big question is: why do you want to study English literature?

FRANCES: [horrific pause] Well… [another horrific pause – why couldn't I think of anything to say?] Well, I- I've always loved English literature. [A third horrific pause. Come on. There are more reasons than that. It's fine. Take your time.] English literature has always been my favourite subject. [That's not true, is it?] I've been passionate about studying it at university since I was little. [What absolute bullshit. You're going to have to sound less like a robot if you want them to believe you.] I love analysing texts and learning about their— their contexts.

[I don't understand, why are you being like this? You sound like you're lying.] I think doing an English literature degree would encourage me to read a lot more than I do. [Wait, so you're saying you don't read lots already? Why are you applying to study English literature in the first place?] I think… [Why are you applying to study English literature at university?] I think I've always… [Always what? Always been lying to yourself about this? Always believed that you were passionate about something you weren't?]

O.W.M. #2:   Okay, well, let's move on.

THE ONLY SPECIAL THING

Immediately after this, I had to take an exam where I had to compare two pieces of prose. I can't remember what they were about, and I can't remember what I wrote. I was in a room with around twenty other people and we all had to sit around the same large table. I was very fidgety and by the end everyone else seemed to have written a lot more than me.

I then had my second interview, which went essentially the same as the first.

When I got back to Starbucks, Raine was reading a newspaper. She looked up as I sat down and folded the newspaper.

It struck me what a brilliant friend she was.

She'd had no reason to drive us here. She'd probably been sitting here for three hours.

"Mate, how'd it all go?"

"Er…"

It had been awful. I'd realised that I didn't want to study the subject I was applying for midway through an interview at the university I'd been aiming to go to for at least ten years. I'd lost my words and forgotten how to bullshit and I'd ruined all of my chances of getting in.

"I don't know. I think I did my best."

Raine looked at me for a moment. "Well… that's good? That's all you can do."

"Yeah, exactly." But I hadn't done my best, had I? I'd done my absolute worst. How had I not seen this coming? How had I let myself get this far into things?

"It must be useful to be smart," she said and then laughed weakly. She glanced down and suddenly looked very sad. "I'm like, constantly scared I'm going to be homeless or something. I wish our whole lives didn't have to depend on our grades."

'Useful', I thought, was a pretty good word for it.

Raine and I wandered round Cambridge for a bit while Daniel was at his second interview. Raine had already explored quite a bit of it so she took me to all the bits she thought were worth seeing, which included an old bridge going over the river and a café that sold milkshakes.

By half past six we were back at Starbucks and Daniel's interview was over, and I told Raine I was going to go and try to find him so he didn't have to walk back alone in the dark. Raine argued that this would involve me walking to his college in the dark. I suggested she come with me, but she just made a whining noise and said she didn't want to move because we'd managed to bagsy the sofas in the corner of the room.

So I went to meet Daniel by myself, still with half a cup of eggnog latte in my hand. I didn't really want to sit in Starbucks any more anyway.

King's College, the college where Daniel had applied, looked like a palace, even from where I was staring at it in the dark. It was giant, white and gothic, and nothing like the cottage-like college I'd applied to. It really was exactly where Daniel belonged.

Daniel was sitting alone on a low brick wall outside, his face illuminated by his phone and his body wrapped up in a thick Puffa jacket. You could still see his suit and tie underneath and he honestly looked like he belonged here. I really could imagine him at age twenty-one walking to a cathedral for his graduation in a fancy gown, or laughing with a lanky guy named Tim as they walked to the debating society where Stephen Fry was giving a speech on NHS privatisation.

He looked up as I approached. I gave him an awkward closed-mouth smile, which is a classic Frances thing to do.

"Hey," I said, sitting down next to him. He tried to smile at me, but wasn't quite successful. "You okay?"

I couldn't tell entirely whether he'd been crying.

I felt like it was a strong possibility.

"Yeah," he said, breathing out, but he wasn't.

He leaned forward suddenly, his elbows on his legs and his head in his hands.

Anyone could see he wasn't okay.

"I just... really need to get in," he said. "It's the only thing... I just..."

He sat up again, not quite looking at me.

"When I was thirteen, I got this award at school... I got the highest CAT test scores out of anyone who'd ever taken them at our school..." One of his legs was bobbing up and down. He shook his head and laughed. "And I was so... I thought I was so *smart*. I thought I was the smartest person in the whole world."

He shook his head.

"But now... I'm just... when you get to this age, you realise that you're not anyone special after all."

He was right. I wasn't special.

"It's... all I've got," he said. "This is the only special thing about me."

He cared about his subject, I knew that much. I didn't care about mine.

He glanced at me. He looked tired, and his hair was messy, and his knee was bobbing up and down. "Why are you here?"

"Thought you might need some moral support," I said, then felt like that was a dickish thing to say, so I followed up with, "Also, it's dangerous for a young man to be walking around in the dark by himself."

Daniel snorted.

We sat in silence for a moment, staring at the dark street and the empty shops opposite us.

"Do you want some eggnog latte?" I held out my cup to him. "It tastes a bit like dirt."

He looked at it as if suspicious, but then took it and sipped. "Thanks."

"No problem."

"What shall we do now?"

"Go home, I guess. I'm literally freezing."

"Sounds good."

There was another silence.

"Was your interview really that bad?" I asked.

Daniel chuckled. I hadn't seen him do that sober before. "Do we have to talk about it?"

"Oh. No. Sorry."

He took in a breath. "It wasn't bad. It just wasn't perfect." He shook his head. "It should have been perfect."

"I think you're being too hard on yourself."

"No, I'm being realistic." He ran a hand through his hair.

"Cambridge are only gonna take the best. So I have to be the best."

"Did Aled tell you good luck at least?"

He laughed. "Aled... wow. You just say whatever you want, don't you."

"Only to you." I shook my head. "Sorry, that sounded creepy."

"Ha. Well, no, he didn't. I told you we weren't talking, right?"

"Yeah."

"You two still not talking either?"

"No."

"Oh. I thought you might have made up by now."

He sounded almost bitter.

"I think he'd make up with you before me—" I began, but he laughed, interrupting me.

"Do you really?" he said, shaking his head. "Wow. You are stupider than I thought."

I fidgeted nervously. "What d'you mean?"

He turned to me and stared in disbelief. "You're better than me in every possible way, Frances. You *really* think he cares more about me than he does about you?"

"What—" I stammered. "You—You're his boyfriend. And best friend."

"No, I'm not," he said. "I'm just someone he kisses sometimes."

CHILDISH KISSES

It started to spit rain, and the streets looked much less posh in the dark. Daniel was holding the half-empty Starbucks cup and tapping it against his knee.

He laughed and glanced at me again like he couldn't be bothered to be mean to me any more. "Am I going to do the 'reveal my entire life story' thing now?"

"Not if you don't want to…"

"But you want to know, don't you? You want to know about us."

I did.

"Kind of," I said.

Daniel sipped the latte.

"And I want to understand Aled better," I said.

He raised his eyebrows. "Why's that?"

I shrugged. "I don't really understand any of the things that he does… or the decisions he makes. It's… it's sort of interesting." I crossed my legs. "And I do care about him, still. Even though I wish I didn't."

He nods. "That's understandable. You were friends."

"When did you become friends?"

"When we were born. Our mums used to work together, and then they were pregnant only a couple of months apart."

"And you've been best friends since then?"

"Yeah. We went to the same primary school, then both went to the boys' grammar school, obviously until I moved to the Academy for sixth form. We'd hang out every day – I used to live in your village, did you know that? Until I was eleven."

I shook my head.

"Yeah, we'd hang out every day, play football in the fields or make secret bases or ride our bikes or play video games. Just… best friend stuff. We were best friends."

He didn't say anything after that, but he did take a large gulp of latte.

"And… so…" I didn't quite know how I was going to broach the topic. "When did you start, erm, going out? If you don't mind me asking…"

Daniel was silent for a moment.

"There wasn't really a beginning to that," he said. "It wasn't— I don't even know whether we were going out."

I almost asked him what he meant, but then thought I should just let him explain in his own time. He seemed nervous and was stumbling over his words; his eyes were cast downwards at the pavement.

"He knew I was gay for ages," he said, his voice soft. "We both did. Since we were, like, ten or eleven, maybe. As soon as we understood what gay was, we knew that's what I was. We…"

He ran a hand through his hair.

"We used to kiss sometimes, when we were kids. When we were alone. Just little childish kisses, little pecks on the lips because we thought it was fun. We were always… really affectionate with each other. We'd cuddle and… we were kind to each other, rather than nasty like most children. I think we were so caught up in each other that we just… missed all the heteronormative propaganda that's thrust at you when you're that age."

It sounded like the sweetest thing in the world, but Daniel's voice shook like he was talking about a dead person.

"We didn't really realise it was weird until— yeah, until we were ten or eleven. But that didn't really stop us. I guess… I guess I always felt like it was more romantic than Aled did. Aled always just treated it like it was something that friends did rather than boyfriends. Aled… he's always been weird. He doesn't care what people think. He doesn't even, like, register the social norms… he's just caught up in his own little world."

A pair of students walked past us, laughing, and Daniel paused until they were gone.

"And I guess… you know… when we were teenagers, it all got a bit— a bit more serious. It wasn't just pecks on the lips any more, you know?" He chuckled awkwardly. "When we were around fourteen, I think, I was— I made the first proper move. We were just playing a video game in his room and I just… I just asked him if I could kiss him properly. He was a bit surprised, but he was like, 'Yeah, okay,' so I did."

I was holding my breath and Daniel laughed at the look on my face.

"Why am I even telling you all this? Jesus. Yeah, so… we sort of went from there… kissing more, and… doing other stuff as well. I always asked him, you know… he's not— He's never been very clear about what he wants… he's so quiet and— and he's a massive pushover as well… so whatever we did, I always asked him first, I always said he could say no if he didn't want to do something… But he always said yes."

Daniel paused then, like he was living it, like he was reliving all of it. This was a life I could barely imagine. I could barely imagine sharing so much of yourself with someone else, for so long.

"It was really… just something for *us*. We didn't want to be 'in a relationship', or be couple-y around other people we knew. It was all just for us in private, like we had to protect it, because we didn't want the rest of the world to ruin it. I don't really know why… I guess it didn't feel like we were in a relationship at all. Because we were best friends, first and foremost. So we never knew how we'd explain it to people."

Daniel took a breath.

"We were so important to each other. We'd tell each other everything and anything. We were each other's first everything. First and only everything. He's— he's an angel."

I didn't think I'd ever heard anyone speak about someone else like this before.

"But the thing was, Aled— he didn't want to come out because… he doesn't think he's gay, like, he says he doesn't really feel attracted to anyone except me."

"There are lots of other things he could be," I said, quickly.

"Well, whatever he is, he doesn't know," said Daniel. "And I didn't really want to come out at an all-boys' school. That's just asking for abuse. I mean, there were people who'd done it… there was this guy in the year above I really admired, one of Aled's friends… but… I was too scared of what people would say. I thought I'd wait until I got to the Academy for sixth form and come out there, but then… I never really made any close friends, and… the topic never really came up with anyone I spoke to…"

He shook his head and took another long sip of latte.

"But the past year or so, since Carys left… he's changed. I've changed as well. We hang out less… and I feel like when we do, he's just coming to me to escape from his problems, it's not like he really wants to see me at all. You know about his mum, yeah?"

"Yeah."

"Well… before you two were friends, he used to come to my house a lot so he didn't have to be around her. And then you arrived and… he didn't really need me any more, I guess."

"That's— But you've been friends since you were *born*. You've been together for years."

"If he cared, he'd talk to me more." He took a breath, like this was the first time he was admitting it to himself. "I don't even think he likes me that much, in that way. I only think he does that because he's used to it, because he's comfortable around me and… because he feels sorry for me. I don't think he's really… into it… or anything."

He paused and I noticed his eyes were tearing up. He shook his head again and wiped one of them.

"It's usually me who initiates it."

"Then why…" My voice was near a whisper, even though we were the only people on the street. "Why don't you just… end it? If neither of you are that into each other any more?"

"I never said *I* wasn't into *him*. I care about him *so badly*." A tear dripped down Daniel's cheek, and he huffed out a laugh. "Sorry. This is lame."

"It's not lame." I raised my arms and pulled him into a hug. We stayed like that for a moment before I let him go again.

"I tried to talk to him about it on his birthday," he continued, "but he wasn't having any of it. He just kept trying to reassure me that he likes me. And that just made me angry, because I could tell he was lying. He even lied in that Never Have I Ever game… pretending he'd never lied when he said 'I love you', to me. I can tell. I can tell when he lies to me! Why would he avoid me so much if he fucking *loved me*? He doesn't even want to admit what his sexuality is. Not even to *me*."

He wiped an eye again.

"And… that night… he kept saying that he wanted to, you know, get with me, but I didn't think he was telling the truth, so I said no, and then he got angry as well." Daniel shook his head. "He's just used to me and he doesn't want to upset me because he knows— he knows I'm in love with him. He doesn't like me in that way any more."

"How do you know that for sure?"

He glanced at me. "You're pathetically optimistic."

"No, I mean…" I bit my lip. "But… what if… I know he finds it hard to say what he's really thinking… and like, I know *I* find it hard to tell what he's thinking, but… what if he does… erm… love you? How can you know for sure if he hasn't said he doesn't?"

Daniel laughed. It sounded like he'd given up entirely.

"Everyone wants the gay couple to get the happy ending, don't they," he said.

I felt so sad that I wanted to leave.

"My worst nightmare is making him do something he doesn't want to do… without knowing…" More tears fell from his eyes. "A-and… I guess people change and we have to move on, but…" He leaned forward and put his head in his hands. "He could have at least— at least broken up with me officially, instead of just leaving me like this…" His voice was shaking badly through his tears and I felt so sorry for him that I almost thought I was going to cry too. "It's okay if he doesn't like me in that way any more… it's okay… but I just want my best friend back… I just want to understand what he's actually feeling. I don't know why he avoids me. Every time I decide he just doesn't like me any more, I start to doubt myself because he hasn't *told* me *anything*. I just want him to tell me the truth. When— when he lies to me because he thinks it'll make me feel better, it *hurts*."

He let out a sob and I hugged him again and I wished there was something I could do for him – *anything*.

"Sometimes I think he only cares about his YouTube channel… It's all him, his Universe City. It's just his soul in audio form. Radio and February Friday and being trapped in a grey world… it's just his life. A… dumb science-fiction analogy."

At the mention of February Friday I felt my heart lurch a little. I wondered whether he even knew that it was him.

"He's my only real friend," he said. "And he just left me here. I just miss him… not even getting with him, just… being with him… him sleeping round my house… playing video games… I just want to hear his voice… I want him to tell me the truth…"

I held him for a few minutes as he cried and it struck me how we were both in the exact same situation though it was a hundred times worse for Daniel. I wanted Aled to come back too. Why wasn't he answering our messages? Did he really dislike us *that much*?

It had been me, hadn't it?

I'd betrayed his trust. I'd driven him away. And he wasn't coming back.

We didn't know whether we'd ever hear his voice in the real world again.

Once Daniel had calmed down a bit and sat up properly again, he said, "You know what? The first time I kissed him properly… he flinched."

EXTREMELY TIRED

On the drive home, Daniel and I didn't really say anything to each other, though there was the vague sense that we were friends now. After around half an hour of silence, Raine said:

"Guys... like... if you don't get in, I mean, it's not a *disaster*, is it?"

We both felt that it would be a disaster, but I very quickly said, "No. It's fine."

I think Raine could tell I was lying. She didn't try to talk to us for the rest of the journey.

Back home I re-enacted with maybe a little exaggeration the exact expressions the interviewers had made as I'd rambled through my interviews. Mum laughed and called them all a variety of names. Then we ordered pizza and watched *Scott Pilgrim vs. the World*.

I was pretty relieved it was over, to be honest.

I'd been stressed about it for almost a year.

Even if, maybe, I didn't actually want to do English literature any more, it didn't matter. The decision had been made. What was going to happen was going to happen.

I decided to give myself a night off homework. I collapsed into bed at around twelve and tucked myself in with my laptop on my lap. I thought about doing some drawing – I hadn't done any for weeks now – but for some reason I didn't really want to; I couldn't think of anything to draw. I scrolled through Tumblr for a while before the feeling that I should really stop wasting my time crept in and I closed the tab to stop myself continually refreshing the page.

I considered trying to catch up on some of the recent *Universe City* episodes – how many episodes had I missed now? Four? Five? I hadn't ever missed so many in a row before.

That was… that was pretty weird, wasn't it?

For someone who prides herself as one of the top fans in the fandom.

For someone who knows the Creator so well.

I didn't even check Aled's Twitter any more. I didn't check the *Universe City* Tumblr tag. I'd turned off my ask box on Tumblr ages ago so people stopped asking me questions about Aled and the Creator. I wasn't on the show any more and I wasn't making art for the show; I wasn't even connected to the show any more. I hadn't posted any drawings on my blog for over a month.

I suddenly felt extremely tired. I turned off my laptop – there wasn't really anything interesting I could do on it – and turned off my fairy lights. I put some earphones in, downloaded the latest episode of *Universe City* on to my iPod and started to listen.

hi

[...]

I don't know... I'm getting a bit tired...

[10 sec pause]

So I was walking yesterday evening down Brockenborne Street and I saw this— this phosphorescent...

Hm.

You know, it doesn't matter.

I was thinking, actually— I mean, I had a thought... I was thinking... what if— what if we were to end this?

Haha, no, sorry, that's a— that's not—

Ah.

I do wish February Friday was here. I haven't seen them in... in, well, years upon years.

[...]

HOURS AND HOURS

It was abysmal.

It was a terrible episode.

Radio barely spoke any full sentences. There was no discernible plot. No characters appeared. It was just Radio rambling on for twenty minutes about things nobody but Aled could possibly understand.

And that February Friday mention at the end?

What was *that*?

Hadn't seen them for years?

Wasn't February Friday Daniel? Aled had seen Daniel only a few months ago. Was he just exaggerating? Surely he was just exaggerating.

Daniel had said that Aled was writing about his life in *Universe City*, which sounded ridiculous at the time, but after hearing this…

I mean, February Friday was a real person. Aled had essentially confirmed that.

Maybe the rest of it was real too.

I sat up. I wasn't tired.

February Friday was Daniel.

Or – I don't know.

If Aled had been literal in saying they hadn't seen each other for years…

I decided to re-listen to the episode to see if there were any more clues in there, but all that ended up doing was reminding me of how *tired* Aled's voice sounded, how much he stumbled over his words and didn't seem to know where he was going. He hadn't bothered to pitch-change his voice – it was just him, here, putting on that silly old-time radio accent. Even that slipped a few times.

This wasn't like him. If there was one thing Aled cared about, one thing he never allowed to be half-hearted, it was *Universe City*.

Something was wrong.

I tried to sleep, but it took me hours and hours.

4. CHRISTMAS HOLIDAY

AN INTERNET MYSTERY

Aled's Twitter account, @UniverseCity, was something that I used to have open on a tab on my browser at all times.

Here are some examples of Aled's tweets from @UniverseCity:

RADIO @UniverseCity
THE SOUNDS ARE LOUDER IN THE DARK -!

RADIO @UniverseCity
i know what ur dreams did last summer,,, yes im talking 2 u, romy. u cant hide anymore

RADIO @UniverseCity
universe city fashion update: gravel is in, hobgoblins are out, make sure u have a holepunch with you always (u have been !!! WARNED !!!)

RADIO @UniverseCity
@NightValeRadio we are listening "" always listening

These usually made absolutely no sense to me and that's what I loved about them. Needless to say, I always retweeted them.

But after I got to know the person behind the Twitter account, I began to read into Radio's – Aled's – tweets far more than I probably should have done.

He tweeted this after his English literature exam:

RADIO @UniverseCity
\the alphabet has been compromised, only seven letters remain..,
!! SAVE THEM !!

He tweeted this one September night at 4am, several hours after he told me he'd argued with his mum:

RADIO @UniverseCity
*** IMPORTANT: the stars are always on ur side. ***

But now that he was at university, Aled's tweets were becoming darker and darker.

RADIO @UniverseCity
how many miserable young people does it take to change a light bulb. please , i am serious , i have been sitting in the dark for 2 weeks

RADIO @UniverseCity
career options: metallic dust, the cold vacuum of outer space, supermarket cashier

RADIO @UniverseCity
Does anyone have any tips for avoiding sinking into the concrete?

I supposed he must have been doing it deliberately. *Universe City* was taking a bit of a darker turn anyway. I didn't worry too much about it.

Instead, I spent most of our three-week Christmas holiday re-listening to every single *Universe City* episode in an attempt to work out who February Friday was.

But I still had no idea.

Aled had actually mentioned several times before that he hadn't seen February Friday for "years upon years". So it couldn't be Daniel, really. I'd been wrong.

Which was annoying. I hated being wrong.

And you know what? When it comes down to it, there's nothing I hate more than an Internet mystery.

GALAXY CEILING

It was the afternoon of December 21st and Mum was psyching me up to go and knock on Aled's door.

I was doing a little jog on the spot in our porch and Mum looked down at me, her arms folded.

"If Carol answers the door," said Mum, "don't bring up the following: politics, school dinners laws, alcohol, and the old lady who works at the post office."

"What does she have against the old lady who works at the post office?"

"She overcharged her once by accident and Carol never forgives, Carol never forgets."

"Of course."

"And if it's Aled..." Mum sighed. "Don't blather on saying *sorry* over and over. I think he knows you're sorry since you've said it a billion times already."

"Thank you, Mother, that's very sensitive of you to say."

"Going into the marsh, gotta be harsh."

"Great."

Mum patted me on the shoulder. "It'll be fine. Don't worry.

Talking always makes things a little better, I promise, especially in person. I still don't trust you young people and your... what is it? 'Tumble'?"

"Tumblr, Mum."

"Yes, well, it all sounds a bit dodgy to me. Talking in person is the easiest way forward."

"Okay."

She opened the door and pointed out of it. "Go!"

When Carol Last opened the door to her house, it was the first time I had seen her since the hair-cutting incident, which I genuinely still thought about at least once a day.

She looked exactly the same. Cropped hair, plump physique and wide, blank expression.

"Frances!" she said, clearly a little surprised to see me. "Everything all right, love?"

"Hi, yes, I'm really good, thanks," I said, speaking too fast. "How are you?"

"Oh, I'm getting along, you know." She smiled and looked into the air above my head. "Got a few bits and bobs going on. Being kept busy, bustling about!"

"Ah," I said, trying to sound interested but not so interested that she would embark on a conversation. "Well, I was just wondering whether Aled was in."

Her smile dropped. "I see." She studied me as if deciding whether she was going to start shouting at me. "No, my love. Sorry. He's still at university."

"O-oh." I shoved my hands into my pockets. "Is he— is he coming back for Christmas at all?"

"You should probably ask him yourself," she said, her mouth a thin line.

I was terrified by this point, but decided to press on.

"It's just— he hasn't been answering my texts. I was just... erm... a bit worried about him. I wanted to see if he was okay."

"Oh, *darling*." She laughed pityingly. "He's just fine, I promise you. He's just a bit busy with all his university work. They really do work him hard up there – as they should! He stayed behind during the holiday because he missed a few deadlines." She shook her head. "Silly boy. He was probably out partying instead of doing his work like he should have been."

Partying was the least likely thing for Aled to be doing, but I didn't want to accuse his mum of lying.

"And you know," she continued, "he's always had some problems with his work ethic, that boy. He's got such potential – he could do a PhD if he put his mind to it. But he's always distracted by his silly little projects and whatnot. Useless stuff. Did you know he used to spend all his time writing some ridiculous story and *reading it out* on his computer? I don't know where in God's name he got his hands on a *microphone*."

I laughed, even though it wasn't funny.

She continued, "So silly! This is such a vital stage of your life, you know. You should be one hundred per cent focused on your studies, otherwise you could ruin your entire life!"

"Yes," I said, forcing the word out.

"I've always been very supportive of our Aled, but... I do worry sometimes he doesn't have the right attitude, you know? He's an *exceptionally* bright boy, but he just doesn't *utilise* that. And I've tried so hard to help him, ever since he was a toddler, but he just doesn't listen. He was never as bad as his sister, of course." She laughed bitterly. "Hateful child."

I started to feel very awkward, but she met my eyes with a new excitement.

"I've been working on a little something since he telephoned me a few weeks back actually. He was complaining he was feeling unmotivated about his degree, and... well... I really do think it's to do with the mindset he puts himself in. So I've been moving a few things around in his bedroom."

I did not like the sound of this.

"You've really got to be in the right place to stay motivated, haven't you? And I really do think his bedroom was one of the main problems. *So* messy all the time – you remember, don't you?"

"Er, I guess so..."

"Well, I've had a little rearrange and I think he'll do *much* better with things like this." She stepped back suddenly. "Why don't you come and take a look, darling?"

I was starting to feel a little ill.

"O-okay," I said, and followed her inside and upstairs towards Aled's bedroom.

"It's just a few little rearrangements here and there. I'm sure he'll appreciate a change."

She opened the door.

The first thing that took me aback was how white everything was. Aled's multicoloured duvet and cityscape blanket were gone and had been replaced by plain white and cream striped sheets. The same thing had happened to the curtains. The carpet was the same, but it now had a white rug on it. The fairy lights were tangled up in a cardboard box at the side of the room. All of his stickers had been scraped off his chest of drawers and there was not a single poster, postcard, ticket, leaflet, flyer or piece of paper on any of the walls – there were a few of these crumpled up in the same box that the fairy lights were in, but there definitely wasn't everything in there. The houseplants were still there, but they were all dead. The walls were a plain white and I honestly didn't know if they'd always been like that or if Carol had painted them.

To my horror, the galaxy ceiling *had* been painted over.

"Feels very *fresh*, don't you think? A cleaner, emptier space makes a cleaner, sharper mind."

I forced out a "yes", but I'm pretty sure it sounded like I was choking.

Aled was going to cry when he saw this.

She had taken his private space – his home – and destroyed it.

She took everything he loved and ruined it.

3.54AM

I probably worried my mum quite a bit when I got back to my house with the cardboard box under one arm and the cityscape blanket under the other, blabbering about room decorations.

Once I'd finished explaining the situation properly, Mum was making a face of absolute, unabashed disgust.

"She should be ashamed of herself," said Mum.

"I bet that's why he's still at uni – I bet he thinks he can't come home, he's trapped there, he doesn't have anyone to look after him..." I started blabbering again and Mum made me sit down on the sofa to calm down. She went into the kitchen, made me a hot chocolate and then sat down next to me.

"I'm *sure* he has friends at uni," she said. "And there are so many support systems at universities – pastoral tutors and counsellors and anonymous services. I'm sure he's not alone."

"But what if he is," I whispered, trying not to cry for the billionth time. "What if he's... suffering..."

"Is there really no way you can contact him?"

I shook my head. "He doesn't answer my texts or messages or calls. He lives six hours away. I don't even know his address."

Mum took a deep breath. "Then… I know you're worried, but… there's not a lot you can do. This isn't your fault, I promise."

But it felt like my fault, just because I knew about it and couldn't do anything to help.

It was taking me roughly three to four hours to actually fall asleep each night by this point, but that night was particularly bad. I didn't want to turn my laptop off because I felt too alone in my bedroom and I didn't want to turn the lights off because I hated the dark.

I couldn't stop thinking. I couldn't turn my brain off. I felt like I was panicking.

I was. I was panicking.

The last time I failed to help someone in trouble, they ran away and weren't ever heard from again.

I couldn't make the same mistake this time.

I had to pay attention to what was happening and do something about it.

I was scrolling through my Tumblr, looking at all the art I had drawn. I imagined someone deleting it all, smashing up my laptop – even thinking about it made me angry. I loved my art more than anything, I enjoyed it more than anything. What if someone took that away from me, like Aled's mum had taken his world away, his tiny little safe place…

I scrolled through my phone while huddled up in bed and found Aled's name. The last time I'd called him was in October.

One more time couldn't hurt.

I clicked on the phone symbol next to his name.

The dial tone sounded.

And then it didn't.

A: ...Hello?

His voice was exactly as I remembered. Soft, a little hoarse, a little nervous-sounding.

F: A-Aled, oh, Jesus Christ, I— I didn't think you'd pick up...
A: ...Oh. Sorry.
F: No, don't apologise, I'm— I'm just— It's so, *so* good to hear your voice.
A: Ah...

What was I going to say? This might be the only chance I had.

F: So... how are you doing? How's university?
A: It's... fine.
F: Good... that's good.
A: It's quite a lot of work.

He chuckled. I wondered how much he was still keeping from me.

F: But, you're doing okay?
A: Er...

There was a long pause and I could hear my own heartbeat.

A: You know. It's... tough. I'm finding it a bit hard.
F: Yeah?
A: I think lots of people are too though.

There was something weird about his voice.

F: Aled... you can tell me if you're not feeling too great. I know we don't really talk any more, but I still... I still really... like... care about you... I know you might still hate me, and I don't know what you really think about me... and I know you don't want me to just keep saying sorry. But I do... I do care about you. That was why I called you in the first place.

A: Haha, yeah, I thought you said you were scared of calling people on the phone.

F: I was never scared of calling *you* on the phone.

He didn't say anything to that.

F: I went to your house today to see if you were there.

A: Did you? Why?

F: I... wanted to talk to you. You haven't been answering my messages.

A: Sorry... I've just... I've been finding it a bit... difficult to, erm...

His voice faded out into nothing and I had no idea what he was trying to say.

F: Well, your mum... I spoke to your mum. She's... she's rearranged your bedroom. She's painted over the ceiling and stuff.

A: ... Has she...?

F: Yeah... but I saved a load of your stuff, I convinced her I'd use it all instead of it getting thrown out...

There was a silence.

F: Aled? You still there?

A: Wait — s-so, she just… threw out everything…?

F: Yeah, but I saved loads of it! I mean, I don't know if I got all of it, but I did save some of it…

A:

F: Why— Why would she *do* something like that — without your permission…?

A: That's…

F:

A: Haha. Don't worry.

I had no idea what to say.

A: Mum's always been like this. It doesn't surprise me any more. It doesn't surprise me at all.

F: Are you… going to come home for Christmas?

A: …I don't know.

F: You could stay at my house, if you like?

I was almost certain he would say no, but then, he didn't.

A: Aren't you… Would your family mind?

F: No, not at all! You know my mum, and my grandparents and aunts and uncles and cousins are all very loud and friendly. And we'll just tell them you're my boyfriend.

A: Okay… that'd— Yeah, that'd be really good. Thank you.

F: That's okay…

He'd forgiven me. He didn't hate me. He *didn't hate me.*

F: What are you doing awake at this time anyway?

A: Er... I'm just... trying to write an essay... I had to get my deadline extended...

There was a long pause.

F: Ah... That sounds dull.

A: Yeah...

I suddenly heard him breathe in quite hard. I wondered whether he had a cold.

F: It's quite late to be writing an essay...

A: (pause) Yeah...

Another excruciatingly long pause.

F: Is it... going okay?

A: Erm... well... not really...

When he next spoke, his voice was wobbling, and that's when I realised he was crying.

A: I just... really— I don't... I don't want to write it. I've just been staring at the screen like— like all day...

F:

A: I don't want to... do this any more...

F: Aled, it's way too late to be writing an essay, just go to sleep and write it in the morning.

A: I can't, it's— My deadline's at ten am tomorrow.

F: Aled... this is why you don't save essays for the night before...

He didn't say anything to that at first. I heard him take in another shaky breath.

    A: Yeah.
    F:
    A: Yeah, sorry. Sorry, I shouldn't have… yeah.
    F: It's okay.
    A: I'll see you later.

He hung up before I could stop him.
    I looked at my phone. The time was 3.54am.

BURNING

"Holy shit, your *hair.*"

Aled got off the train on the evening of December 23rd with a suitcase in one hand and a rucksack on his back.

His hair was shoulder-length. It was also pastel pink at the ends.

He was wearing black skinny jeans, a beige corduroy coat with fleece lining and lime green plimsolls with purple laces and he had earphones in his ears. I was wearing my giant Topman coat, grid-print leggings and *Star Wars* Vans.

He smiled at me. It was a little awkward, but it was a smile.

"D'you think it looks okay?"

"It looks *rad as hell.*"

I stood in front of him for a few seconds, just gazing at him, before he took his earphones out. I could hear what he'd been listening to – 'Innocence' by Nero. I'd introduced him to Nero.

"You're playing your music too loud," I said, before he could say anything else.

He blinked, and then smiled a little. "I know."

★

We walked back into the village and chatted about trivial things – his train journey, Christmas, the weather. I didn't mind. I knew we couldn't immediately go back to the way things were before.

I was just thankful to have him here.

We got to my house and Mum welcomed him in with the offer of a cup of tea, but Aled shook his head.

"I'm gonna go and talk to my mum," he said. "Explain to her I'm staying here for Christmas."

I blinked. "I assumed she knew already."

"No, I think this is something I have to explain in person."

He dropped his rucksack on to the floor in the hallway and leaned his suitcase against the wall.

"I'll probably only be ten minutes or so," he said.

I didn't believe him.

After he'd been gone for half an hour, I was starting to panic. So was Mum.

"Do you think I should go over there?" asked Mum. We were standing at the lounge window watching Aled's house, waiting for any sign of movement. "Maybe it would help if I spoke to her. Most adults prefer listening to other adults."

And then we heard Aled scream.

It wasn't really a scream. It was more of a long wail. I'd never heard anyone sound like that in real life before.

I pelted to our front door and opened it, just as Aled opened his and stumbled out of it. I ran to meet him and he was staggering and for a minute I thought he was injured, but I couldn't see anything physically wrong with him except the fact that his face was contorted because he was sobbing uncontrollably, and I caught him in my arms just as he sank to the ground on the kerb, making the most painful noises I'd ever heard, like he'd been shot, like he was dying…

Then he started to cry out, "No, no, no, no, no, no, no…" the tears falling continuously from his eyes, and I started to ask him frantically what it was, what had happened, what had she done, but he just shook his head over and over and choked like he couldn't form any words even if he wanted to, and then I heard it…

"Sh-she killed him— Sh-she killed him."

I felt like I was going to be sick.

"Who? What happened, tell me…"

"My… my dog… my dog Brian…" And then he started to sob again, so loudly, like he'd never cried before in his whole life.

I stayed very still.

"She… killed… your dog…?"

"She s-said… she couldn't look after him… because I was gone, and he— He was getting old, s-so She— She just— She went and… had him *put down*."

"No…"

He let out another wail and pressed his face into my jumper.

I didn't want to believe anyone was capable of doing something like that.

But we were sitting under the streetlamps and Aled was shaking in my arms and this was real, this was happening. She was taking everything Aled had and burning it. She was burning him, slowly, until he died.

RUSTY NORTHERN HANDS

"I'll call the police on her," said Mum for the fourth time. We'd been sitting in the lounge for over half an hour. "At least let me go and shout at her."

"It won't do anything," said Aled. He sounded like he wanted to die.

"What can we do?" I asked. "There must be something…"

"No." He stood up from the sofa. "I'm going back to uni."

"What?" I stood up too and followed him out of the door. "Wait, you can't spend Christmas up there alone!"

"I don't want to be near her."

We were all silent for a moment.

"You know…" he continued, "when me and Carys were ten… our mum burned a load of clothes Carys bought from a charity shop. Carys was really, really excited about these trousers she'd bought when she went out with her friends… they were made out of this galaxy-pattern fabric… but our mum said they were trashy and she just took them and burned them in the garden while Carys was just screaming and crying. Carys tried to get them out of the fire and burned her hands and Mum didn't even comfort her." His eyes were vacant, like there was nothing there. "I had to… I had to hold her hands under the… the cold tap…"

"Jesus Christ," I said.

Aled looked down and his voice quietened. "She could have just thrown them away, but she chose to *burn* them…"

Me and Mum spent another fifteen minutes trying to persuade him to change his mind about leaving, but he wouldn't.

He was leaving.

Again.

It was almost 9pm when Aled and I made it back to the station, and though I'd only met him two hours earlier, it felt like days ago.

We sat on a bench together. The countryside stretched out opposite us, the winter sky black and bleak.

Aled lifted up his legs so his knees were bent and his feet tucked up on the bench. He started fiddling with his hands.

"It's really cold up north," he said, and then he held out his hands in front of me. The skin of his knuckles was all dry. "Look."

"Rusty northern hands," I said.

"What?"

"That's what my mum calls it." I stroked the dry skin of his knuckles with one finger. "When the skin on your hands gets all dry. Rusty northern hands."

Aled smiled. "I think I need to buy some gloves. I'd wear them all the time."

"Like Radio." In Universe City, Radio never takes their gloves off. No one knows why.

"Yeah." He took his hand back and wrapped his arms around his knees. "Sometimes I think I *am* Radio."

"D'you want my gloves?" I said, suddenly, taking mine off. They were navy and had a Fair Isle pattern on the back. I held them out to him. "I've got loads of gloves."

He looked at me. "I can't steal yours!"

"These are really old anyway." This was true.

"Frances, if I take those, I'll feel really bad about wearing them."

He really wasn't going to take them. I shrugged and said, "Fine," and put them back on.

We sat in silence for a minute, before he said, "Sorry I didn't reply to any of your messages."

"It's fine, you had the right to be angry at me."

There was another pause. I wanted to know everything that he'd done at uni. I wanted to ask him to tell me everything I didn't know about *Universe City*. I wanted to tell him how shitty school was these days, how I was so sleep-deprived that I'd started getting headaches every single day.

"How are you?" he said.

I looked at him. "I'm fine."

And he knew I wasn't. And he wasn't either. But I didn't know what else to say.

"How's school?" he asked.

"Just can't wait to get out," I said. "But also… I'm trying to enjoy it."

"You're not one of those people who's determined to lose their virginity before they go to uni, are you?"

I frowned. "Is anyone actually like that?"

He shrugged. "Not that I've ever seen."

I laughed.

"So you're keeping on top of your work okay?" he asked.

I couldn't lie to him. "Not really. A lot of sleepless nights, I guess."

He smiled and looked away. "Sometimes I think we're the same person... but we just got accidentally split into two before we were born."

"Why?"

"Because you're literally me, but with all of the trash cleared away."

I snorted. "Under the trash... There's just more trash. We're trash to the bone."

"Ah," he said. "The title of my debut rap album."

We both laughed at that. Our laughs echoed around the station. And then a voice sounded above our heads.

"The next train to arrive at — Platform One — will be the — 21.07 — to — London St Pancras."

"Oh," said Aled. He didn't show any sign of moving.

I leaned over and hugged him. Hugged him properly, arms tight around his neck, my chin tucked over his shoulder. He hugged me back too. And I think we were okay.

"Are there people up there you can spend Christmas with?" I said.

"Er..." He paused. "Yeah, erm... I think there are some international students staying..."

And then his train arrived, and he stood up and took hold of his suitcase and opened the door and stepped on to the train. He turned back and waved and I said, "Bon voyage!" and he smiled sadly and said, "Frances, you really are..." But he didn't seem to be able to finish his sentence and I had no idea what he was attempting to say. He put his earphones in and the door shut and he walked away from the window and I couldn't see him any more.

When the train started to roll away again, I thought about jumping up from the bench and running along and waving at him through the window like people do in movies. Then I thought about how stupid that would look, and how pointless that would be, so instead I just sat there on the bench and waited until the train had gone, and then it was just me and the countryside again, me and the fields and the grey.

MY FRIEND

I'd kissed Carys Last the day before she ran away and she'd hated it and hated me and then she'd left and it was my fault.

It happened on GCSE results day – my Year 10 one, her Year 11 one. She came round my house that evening to celebrate, or in her case, commiserate, because she had failed everything.

She had failed every single exam she'd taken.

I sat on one sofa with bags of unopened crisps and bottles of fizzy drinks – unused celebratory food and drink – and watched her rant about it on the other sofa.

"You know what? I don't even care any more. I literally do not care. So what, what's gonna happen? I'll just have to repeat Year 11. No one can do anything about it. And if I fail again – then so what! I'll get a job. Somewhere that doesn't care about grades. I might be stupid, but there are loads of things I can do. My mum's such a *bitch*, I just— I mean, what does she expect? Like, I'm not my brother! I'm not the fucking golden child! What did she expect!?"

She went on like this for a while. When she started crying I moved over to the sofa where she was sat and put my arm round her.

"I'm not useless, I can do stuff! Grades – they're just letters. So what if I can't remember trigonometry and stuff about Hitler and photosynthesis and shit." She looked at me, her mascara just black smears under her eyes. "I'm not useless, am I!?"

"No," I said, barely more than a whisper.

Then I leaned in and kissed her.

To be honest, I don't really want to talk about it.

I cringe just thinking about it.

She stood up almost immediately.

There was a moment of unbearable silence, like neither of us could quite believe it had happened.

And then she started screaming at me.

"I thought you were my friend," came up several times. "Nobody cares about me," too. "You were just pretending this whole time," was probably the thing that hurt the most.

I hadn't been pretending. She was my friend and I cared about her and I hadn't been pretending about any of that.

She ran away from home the next day. Within a day, she'd blocked me on Facebook and deleted her Twitter. Within a week, she changed her phone number. Within a month, I thought I might be over it, but in reality, I've never been over it. I might not have a crush on her any more, but that doesn't mean it never happened, and it will always be my fault that Carys Last ran away.

SKULL

"Do you want me to leave the room?" asked Mum. "I can leave. If that'd make you feel better."

"Nothing is going to make me feel better," I said.

It was January. It was The Day. We were standing on opposite sides of our kitchen counter and I had an envelope in my hands and inside the envelope was a letter that would inform me whether I'd got into the University of Cambridge.

"Okay, I'm going in the other room," I said, changing my mind.

I walked into the living room with the letter and sat down on the sofa.

My heart was pounding and my hands were shaking and I was sweating everywhere.

I was trying not to think about the fact that if I hadn't got in, I had wasted a strong percentage of my life. Almost everything that I'd done at school had been done with Oxbridge in mind. I'd chosen my A level subjects for Oxbridge. I'd become head girl for Oxbridge. I'd continuously got amazing grades for Oxbridge.

I opened the envelope and read the first paragraph.

It took one sentence for me to start crying.

It took two for me to make a sort of screeching sound in the back of my throat.

I didn't read any more than that. I didn't need to.

I hadn't got in.

Mum came and held me while I cried. I wanted to punch myself. I wanted to punch myself until my skull cracked.

"It's okay, sh, you'll be okay," Mum kept saying, rocking me slightly like I was a baby again, but it wasn't going to be okay, I wasn't going to be okay.

When I told her this, or sobbed it, she said, "Okay, well, you're allowed to be upset about it. You're allowed to cry about it today."

Which I did.

"They don't know what they're doing," Mum muttered after a little while, stroking my hair. "You're the cleverest person in the school. You're the best person in the world."

FUCK YOU ALL

To say that I was extremely upset about it is a major understatement. I'd known that my interviews were awful, but some small part of me had still hoped that I'd get in. This was the first lot of shock and disappointment, and then by the time Mum and I had ordered pizza and watched *Back To The Future*, I was angry at myself for expecting to get in, which was the second. By the time I was lying awake at 3am, I hated myself for being a privileged twat. Who cried because they didn't get into *one* university out of the *five* they applied to? Some people cried from *happiness* because they got into one university.

The numerous "Omg I got a place at Cambridge/Oxford University!!! :D" Facebook statuses that popped up throughout the day were not helping, particularly when they were from people who always did worse than me in exams.

Though when I saw that Daniel Jun had posted one, I did feel a *slight* bit of joy that he'd got in. He deserved it.

He'd worked himself to death. It wasn't like he had anyone cheering him on. He honestly deserved this. And I liked him, I guess. I really did like him now.

But would you let me have a really selfish moment?

I just…

I'd done literally everything. I'd read an outrageous amount of books. I'd been preparing for this for an entire year. I was the cleverest girl in the class, I had been since I knew what it meant to be clever, and Cambridge was where clever people went.

And I still hadn't got in.

Everything had been for nothing.

I'm sure you think I was complaining about nothing. You probably think I'm a whiny teenager. And yeah, it was all in my head, probably. That doesn't mean it wasn't real. So fuck you all.

5. SPRING TERM
a)

WHITE NOISE

Throughout the rest of January I tried not to think too much about anything. I did my schoolwork without thinking about it. I didn't talk to anyone about Cambridge, but everyone knew that I hadn't got in. I'd texted Aled several times to check how he was, but he hadn't replied.

I had a lot of coursework due at the end of the month. I had to stay up very late to finish it every night. I actually didn't go to sleep at all the night before it was due, I just stayed up the whole night and went to school in the morning without any sleep. I had to call Mum and ask her to pick me up at break because I thought I was going to pass out.

And alongside all of this, I continued listening to *Universe City*. The episodes in December and January were pretty bland. Aled didn't seem to know what he was doing. He forgot almost entirely about several ongoing subplots. The new characters were uninteresting and didn't appear in the story very often.

And on the final Friday of January, Aled posted the episode that would destroy the *Universe City* fandom.

The episode was titled 'Goodbye' and it was twenty minutes of white noise.

YOU MUST HAVE
COME FROM A STAR

The fandom pretty much collapsed in collective despair. The Tumblr tag was overflowing with lengthy obituaries, miserable text posts and emotional fan art. It was all very sad so I didn't look at it for too long.

Aled tweeted his final tweet on the same day:

RADIO @UniverseCity
i'm sorry. i need some time. you may be very small but you are all very important in the universe. goodbye <3
31 Jan 14

And people flooded my inbox with questions, even though I was nothing to do with *Universe City* any more.

Anonymous asked:
You haven't been consistently active on Tumblr for a few months now. You are the only person apart from the Creator who has ever had any involvement in the show. You recently turned your

ask box back on so I hope you won't mind me sending this message. Do you have any insight into Universe City's 'Goodbye' episode that was posted two weeks ago (assuming you've listened to it)?

touloser answered:
i don't really know what to say except i'm as sad as you are that the creator decided to do this but they're obviously going through some personal things right now. nobody except the creator knows whether universe city will ever return so i suggest everyone starts trying to move on. things like this happen. it's just unfortunate that it's happened to something that's so important to so many people.
i knew the creator. universe city was very very important to them. in fact, that's an understatement. universe city really was the only thing they had. universe city was the only thing i had for a long time too. i don't really know what to do with myself any more. i don't know what the creator is going to do either. i don't know what to say.

I didn't know why he'd decided to end it. Maybe his mum had made him. Maybe he hadn't had enough time to make it. Or maybe he just didn't want to make it any more.

It still confused me, because it was clearly important to him. He cared about it more than anything.

He hadn't even revealed who February Friday was yet.

On the night of the white noise episode, I sat in the lounge with my laptop and thought, for the first time in at least a month, about who February Friday might be.

It came to me almost instantly.

What Aled had said about Carys the night he'd come back to

the village had been rattling around my mind for weeks, and then suddenly I realised why.

Fire.

The bonfire of clothes.

She'd burned her hands in the fire.

It was such a random story for him to tell us. Of everything he could have said about Carys's relationship with their mum, he chose that particular event.

I loaded up Aled's *Universe City* transcription blog and ran a CTRL-F Find for the word 'fire' in each of the first twenty episodes. I then copied and pasted relevant quotes into a Word document.

- And after the fire, that was it, you were gone
- I see you in every fire that lights
- In the end I wish it had been me who'd fallen into the Fire, though maybe that's a selfish thing to say
- The Fire that touched you must have come from a star
- You were always brave enough to get burned in the Fire

There wasn't any doubt in my mind after that.

Carys Last was February Friday.

FAILURE

It had all been a cry for help.

Universe City. The entire thing.

It had been a cry for help from a brother to a sister.

It took me that weekend to work out what I needed to do.

I needed to get Carys to help Aled.

At this point, she was the only person who could help him.

The Letters to February had been there since the beginning. Aled had been writing about Carys for years. He missed her. He wanted to talk to her. And he had no idea where she was.

If she was anywhere at all.

It was Aled's mum who was keeping Carys's location from him – I didn't know how and I didn't know why. But I couldn't stop thinking about it and worrying. I'd had my chance to help Carys and I'd missed it by 10,000 miles.

Well, that was exactly it, wasn't it?

I'd had my chance to help before and I failed.

And I've never liked failure.

SILVER-HAIRED GIRL

"Yo, small blonde person, swap seats with me."

I looked up from my history worksheet on the Monday after to see a silver-haired girl jostling the boy in the seat next to me out of his seat and then sitting in it herself. She made herself comfortable, put her elbow on the table and her chin in her hand, and gazed at me. The silver-haired girl was Raine Sengupta.

She'd recently dyed her previously black hair bright silver and her side-undercut was so extreme that she'd basically just shaved the right side bare. Hair is a window to the soul.

"Frances, my pal, you are not doing so great, are you?" she said with a solemn nod.

I still hung out at school with Raine and Maya and all of that lot and I still spoke to Raine fairly often, but they didn't know anything about what had gone down with Aled or *Universe City*.

I laughed. "What d'you mean?"

"I mean you've been moping around like a damp biscuit, mate." She sighed. "Are you still in mourning for Cambridge?"

I felt like I was about to explode with how much I was

panicking about Aled, about Carys, about helping them, about doing something good for once in my absolute failure of a life, but instead I said:

"*No*, no, I'm fine. I promise."

"Well, that's good."

"Yes."

She continued to stare at me. Then she looked down at what I was doing, which was doodling on a worksheet instead of filling in the answers.

"Hey, these are good! These are like your drawings for *Universe City*."

I nodded. "Thanks…"

"You should screw uni and just go to art college or something," she said. "Miss García would love you." She'd meant it as a joke, but for a very brief second I took the idea completely seriously, and it startled me, and I tried not to think about it after that.

"So what's been going on?" she continued.

I wanted to tell her and I didn't. I wanted to tell *someone*, but I wasn't sure if Raine was the right person. Was there a right person to vent to about all the stuff that's been happening?

I did it anyway.

From my involvement with *Universe City* to what Aled did to Daniel to what I did to Aled to what his mum did to Aled to Carys being February Friday and the 'Goodbye' episode. All of it.

All of it, except the one thing I still couldn't admit to anyone except Aled – about me and Carys. I still couldn't quite find the words to tell that bit.

"That's a lot of stuff," she said. "What's your plan?"

"What d'you mean?"

"You're just going to let everything end like this?" She folded her arms. "Aled's all alone and trapped at university. Carys is out there in the world and has no idea what's going on with her brother. *Universe City* ended with absolutely no explanation. And nobody's going to do anything about any of this. Except maybe you."

I stared down at my worksheet. "Well... I want to find Carys so she can help Aled, but... it's probably impossible."

"Aren't you Aled's friend?"

"Yeah, of course."

"So don't you want to help?"

"Well..." Of course I wanted to help. Why was I still hesitating about this? "I don't know."

Raine tucked the longer side of her hair behind her ear. "It's like – okay, this is going to sound really silly, but, my mum, she always says this thing about – when you've got a lot going on, you have to look at the bigger picture. Just take a step back and look at the big picture and think about what's really important at this moment in time."

I sat up straight. "My mum says literally the exact same thing."

"What? No way!"

"Yeah, she calls it The Big Scheme of Things!"

"Mate! That's literally what I'm talking about!"

We both grinned.

Raine really was trying to help me.

"You know what I think would help in The Big Scheme of Things?" said Raine. She crossed one leg over the other and looked me in the eye. "Finding Carys Last."

FILOFAX

The reasons why I was scared about finding Carys Last were as follows:

- The last time I had seen and spoken to Carys Last had been eighteen months ago.
- The last time I had seen and spoken to Carys Last, I had kissed her without asking, and she had not been happy about it, and it had made her run away from home, and I had been embarrassed and guilty about it every day since.
- The effort it would take to locate Carys Last when the only person who knew her location was a terrifying dog-murderer would probably make me even more stressed than I already was (if that was possible).

Despite all of this, the idea of doing something helpful for once in my absolutely useless life was what kept me going.

That was the thing, I guess.

I'd been rejected from Cambridge and I felt like my entire life had been a waste.

Which is silly and pathetic, I know. Believe me, I understand.

Raine came round my house after school the next day to discuss her 'Find Carys' plan.

Because Raine was still severely underachieving in all three of her A levels, she was still being forced to sit outside Dr Afolayan's office every lunchtime and free period to do homework.

This also meant that Raine saw a lot of people pass in and out of the office, which, by the way, was more of a large conference room – air-conditioned, plasma TV on the wall, several potted plants and comfy armchairs.

One of these people was parent governor Carol Last.

According to Raine, Carol carried a pink Filofax with her whenever she came into school for a meeting.

Also according to Raine, if Carol had any record of Carys's address, it would be inside the Filofax.

I had no idea how we were supposed to steal Carol's Filofax from under her nose, and to be honest I didn't really want to. It's not like I'd stolen anything before or wanted to become a thief. The idea of getting caught by her was enough to make me feel a bit ill.

"Don't worry about it," she said. We were sitting at my breakfast bar eating Bourbon biscuits out of the packet. "I have way less morals. I've stolen stuff before."

"You've *stolen* stuff?"

"Well… sort of. I stole Thomas Lister's shoes because he threw a sandwich at me on the bus." She grinned and looked up. "He had to get off the bus and walk in his socks in the snow. Beautiful."

The plan was that Raine would walk directly into Carol as she exited Afolayan's office and drop a load of books everywhere. Theoretically, Carol would then drop her Filofax and Raine could grab it without her noticing.

I thought this was a terrible plan because it relied on a) the Filofax being in Carol's hand and not her bag, b) Raine dropping her books in such a way that she could pick up the Filofax without Carol seeing, and c) Carol immediately forgetting she had been holding the Filofax after dropping it.

In other words, I couldn't see any way this was going to work.

We didn't even know for sure whether Carys's address would be in there.

Mum happened to be in the kitchen at the time, and as Raine finished speaking, she said this:

"I'm not too sure this is going to work, girls."

Raine and I turned to her.

Mum smiled and tied up her long hair. "Let me deal with this."

We knew for sure that Carol would be in school at 2pm on Thursday 13th February for a meeting of all the parent governors. I wondered what jobs these parents did that allowed them to be free at 2pm on a Thursday. I wondered why Carol was a parent governor of a school that neither of her children went to.

Mum had taken a day off work. She said she never used up all of her holiday time anyway.

I think Mum was very excited to be part of this plan, actually.

She'd scheduled an appointment to see Dr Afolayan at 3pm. She said she was going to talk to Carol as she left the parent governor meeting. She didn't say how she was going to get Carys's address. Raine and I would be in a history lesson while this was happening so we had no idea what was going to happen.

"Leave it all to me," Mum had said with a wicked grin.

Raine came back home with me on the train after school that day. Mum was waiting for us at the kitchen table. She was wearing the only trouser suit she owned and her hair was pinned up with a hair claw. She looked like the most stereotypical mum I had ever seen.

She was holding up the pink Filofax.

"*Jesus Christ!*" I shrieked, kicking my shoes off into a corner and hurling myself on to a barstool. Raine quickly joined me, with an expression of absolute awe. "How the hell did you do it?"

"Asked her if I could borrow it," she said, with a nonchalant shrug.

I coughed out a laugh. "*What?*"

Mum leaned on the table. "I asked her if she had the contact address of our local MP because I wanted to write a strongly-worded letter about the honestly *weak* amount of homework you lazy students are being set and how the local schools are letting you down and making you all slackers." She held out the Filofax to us. "But of course, I had to hurry into a meeting, so I didn't have time to stop and copy the address down. So I asked if I could borrow it and said I'd drop it through her letterbox after the meeting, so you two had better be quick."

"She must seriously like you," I said, shaking my head and taking the Filofax.

Mum shrugged and said, "She always tries to talk to me at the post office."

★

It only took Raine and me ten minutes to look through the entire address book section and to discover that there was no entry for Carys Last.

We then looked through the notes section, but only found a variety of shopping lists, to-do lists, work-related notes (I still had no idea what she actually did), and Mum's notes from her meeting, which consisted of the words 'blah blah blah', a smiley face and a small drawing of a dinosaur. I made sure to tear that page out.

"I don't think it's here," I said, feeling my stomach drop a little. I had honestly believed we might find something. Surely Carol had a record of her daughter's address *somewhere*.

If she even *had* an address.

Raine groaned. "What are we going to do now? It's already February, Aled's been gone for nearly two months…"

"February," I said, suddenly.

"What?"

February.

"February." I pulled the Filofax towards me. "Let me just have one more look."

I turned each page of the address book very slowly. And then I stopped, cried, "YES!" and stabbed a finger on to the page.

"Oh my God," Raine whispered.

In the 'F' section of the address book, there were only four entries. The top one was for a person who apparently didn't even have a surname. There was only one word on the 'Name:' dotted line:

'February.'

LONDON'S BURNING

I took the train to London that Friday. Mum made me promise to carry a rape whistle at all times and text her every hour.

I was going to do this.

I was going to find Carys. She was going to help Aled.

I found myself at a fairly clean-looking townhouse in a residential area. It was a lot fancier than I'd expected. Obviously it wasn't one of those posh white townhouses that everyone thinks of when they imagine London living, but Carys wasn't living in a hovel. I'd been expecting something with crumbling walls and boarded-up windows.

I walked up the steps to the door and rang the doorbell. It rang in the tune of 'London's Burning'.

A young black woman with vibrant pink hair opened the door. It took a moment for me to say anything because she'd nestled daisies into her explosion of curls and it really was the best hair I had ever seen.

"You all right, mate?" she asked in a typically London voice. She sounded a bit like Raine, actually.

"Er, yeah, I was looking for Carys Last?" I cleared my

throat because my voice was a bit wobbly. "Apparently she lives here?"

The woman made a sympathetic face. "Sorry mate, nah, there's no Carys here."

"Ah…" My heart sank.

And then I had a thought.

"Wait – what about someone called February?" I asked.

The woman looked a little surprised. "Oh! Yeah, that's Feb! You an old friend or…?"

"Er… yeah, sort of."

She grinned and leaned on the doorframe. "Man. I knew she'd changed her name, but… *Carys*. Bloody hell, that's so *Welsh*."

I laughed too. "So… is she in?"

"Nah, mate, she's at work. You could probs go find her there if you've got the time? Or you can chill here for a bit?"

"Oh, right. Is she far away?"

"Nah, she's just down on South Bank. She works at the National Theatre, she's, like, a tour guide and she runs, like, workshops for kids and stuff. 'Bout ten minutes on the tube."

As I had been half-expecting Carys to be struggling along with some sort of horrible minimum wage job, this was an extreme surprise to me.

"Would she mind? Would I be interrupting her or something?"

The woman checked her watch, which was chunky and yellow. "Nope, it's gone six so she'll have finished her workshops. You'll probs find her in the gift shop, she usually helps out there till she finishes at eight."

"Okay." I paused on the step. This was it. I was going to see Carys.

Or – no. Wait. I had to check. Just to be sure.

"So, Carys—" I corrected myself – "*February*... erm... just to check, she's— She's got blonde hair—"

"Dyed blonde hair, blue eyes, big tits and a straight-face like she could rip out your throat?" The woman chuckled. "Is that her?"

I smiled nervously. "Erm, yeah."

It only took me another twenty minutes to get to the National Theatre. South Bank – a riverside area filled with cafés and stalls and restaurants and buskers – was heaving with people out for dinner and going to the theatre and it was pretty dark already. Someone was playing a Radiohead song on an acoustic guitar. I'd only been here once before – I'd been with school to see a production of *War Horse*.

As I walked towards the theatre using Google Maps as a guide, I checked what I was wearing – a stripy pinafore dress over a T-shirt that had speech bubbles all over it, thick grey tights and a Fair Isle cardigan. I felt like myself, and that really did make me feel a bit more confident about the situation.

Right before I stepped into the National Theatre I genuinely had a moment when I was about to turn round and go home. I texted my mum the crying face emoji and she texted back a thumbs-up, several salsa-dancing girls and a four-leaf clover.

I entered the building – a huge, grey block that looked nothing like your typical London theatre – and immediately located the gift shop near the entrance. I walked in.

It took me a minute to spot Carys, though it really shouldn't have, because she still stood out just as well as she always had.

She was sorting through some books on a shelf, rearranging and adding some in from a cardboard box she had under one arm. I walked over to her.

"Carys," I said, and hearing that name she immediately frowned and whipped her head around to face me, like I'd frightened her somehow.

It took her a moment. And then she recognised me.

"Frances Janvier," she said with an absolutely expressionless face.

GOLDEN CHILD

Lots of things were freaking me out. Her hair, for one. The blonde was peroxide now, almost white, and her fringe only reached halfway down her forehead – her eyes looked so much *bigger*, you could actually see her *looking* at you. Jesus Christ, her winged eyeliner must have taken, like, half an hour to do.

She was wearing red lipstick, a nautical striped crop top and a calf-length beige skirt with platform pastel pink Mary Janes. She had a National Theatre lanyard round her neck. She looked approximately twenty-four years old.

The only thing that was the same was the leather jacket. I couldn't remember whether it was the same one she'd worn all the time back then, but it produced the same effect.

She looked like she could probably murder me, or sue me. Perhaps both.

And then she started to laugh to herself.

"I knew it," she said, and there it was, that slightly posh, *Made in Chelsea* voice, soft like Aled's, like she belonged on the TV. "I knew someone would find me eventually." She looked down at me and it really was her, but I didn't feel like I was talking to someone I had even met before. "I just didn't think it'd be you."

I chuckled awkwardly. "Surprise!"

"Hm." She raised her eyebrows, and then turned away and shouted towards the woman at the till, "Hey, Kate! Can I leave early?"

The woman shouted back that she could, and then she went and got her bag and we left together.

Carys took me to the theatre bar, which didn't surprise me at all. She'd liked drinking when she was sixteen, and she still liked drinking now.

She also insisted on buying me a drink. I tried to stop her, but before I knew it she was ordering us two daiquiri cocktails, which probably cost twenty pounds each, knowing London. I took my jacket off and put it on my stool and willed myself to stop sweating quite so profusely.

"So what called for this?" she asked, sipping on her cocktail through two tiny straws and looking me dead in the eye. "How'd you find me?"

Thinking about the Filofax fiasco made me laugh out loud. "My mum stole your mum's address book."

Carys frowned. "My mum shouldn't have my address." She looked away. "Oh, shit. I bet she read my letter to Aled."

"You— You sent Aled a letter?"

"Yeah, last year when I moved in with my housemates. Just telling him everything was okay and what my new address was. I'd even signed it February so he'd know I was using that name."

"Aled…" I shook my head slightly. "Aled hasn't heard anything from you. He told me."

Carys almost didn't seem to have heard me. "My mother. Christ.

I don't know why I'm surprised." She let out a breath, and then raised her eyebrows and looked at me.

I wondered where I was supposed to start. There were so many things I needed to tell her, I needed to *ask*.

She got there first with, "You look different. Your clothes are more *you*. And your hair is down."

"Er, thanks, I—"

"So how are you?"

Carys continued to bombard me with questions for several minutes, preventing me from bringing up anything I actually wanted to talk about such as 1) your twin brother has been displaying worrying behaviour for around seven months, 2) I'm extremely sorry for being a crap friend, 3) how do you have your life so *together*, you are literally eighteen years old, 4) please explain why your name is now February.

She was still the most intimidating person I'd ever met. *More* intimidating now. Everything about her bloody terrified me.

"Did you get into Cambridge in the end?" she asked.

"No," I said.

"Ah. So what's the plan?"

"Erm… I don't know. It doesn't matter. I didn't come here to talk about that."

Carys gazed at me, but said nothing.

"I came to find you because of Aled," I said.

She glanced at me, eyebrows raised. The stony expression I knew was back. "Oh, right?"

I started from the beginning. I explained how Aled and I had become friends, how we'd found each other and our weird *Universe City* coincidence. I explained about how I'd accidentally outed him as the Creator and how he'd stopped texting me and how his mum was out to destroy everything he had.

Carys listened, taking small sips as I spoke, but I could tell that she was getting more and more concerned. I was fiddling with my glass, passing it from one hand to the other.

"This is..." she said, once I'd finished. "God. I never thought— I *never* thought she'd start with him too."

I almost didn't want to ask. "Start what?"

Carys thought about it for a moment, crossing one leg over the other and swishing her hair. "Our mother doesn't believe that there is any way to have a fulfilling life unless you are academically successful." She put down her glass and held up one hand, pointing to each finger as she spoke. She still had those tiny burn scars covering her skin. "This means that you need brilliant grades all of the time, only academic GCSE and A level subject choices, and an academic top quality university degree." She put down the hand. "She believes in this so strongly that she would actually rather we died than didn't do all of that."

"Fuck," I said.

"Yes." Carys laughed. "Unfortunately for me, as you well know, I was one of those people who— No matter how hard I tried, I just couldn't get good grades. At anything. But Mum thought she could just *force* me to become magically clever. Tutors, extra homework, summer camps, etc. Which was ridiculous, obviously."

She took another sip. She was telling this story with the sort of nonchalance a person might have when talking about their summer holiday.

"Aled was the clever one. He was the dream child. The favouritism was obvious even before our dad left when we were eight. Mum absolutely despised me because I couldn't solve maths problems – I was the fat, dumb child – and she made my life a literal hell."

I didn't want to ask, but I did anyway. "What did she do?"

"She just slowly took away anything that brought me any joy in my life." Carys shrugged. "It was like – you don't get an A on this test, fine, you can't see your friends this weekend. You don't get ten out of ten on this worksheet, okay, I'm taking your laptop away for two weeks. And it got gradually nastier, you know? It turned into, like – you don't get an A in your mock GCSE, I'm locking you in your room for the weekend. You fail your exam, you're not getting any birthday presents."

"God…"

"She's literally a monster." Carys held up a finger. "But she's *cunning*, as well. She doesn't do anything illegal, or anything that sounds abusive. That's how she gets away with it."

"And… d'you think… she's doing this stuff to Aled now?"

"From what you've just told me… I mean, it sounds like it. I never thought she'd actually turn on him. He was the *golden child*. I never would have… I mean, if I'd known… if he'd seen my letter and replied and *told me*…" She shook her head, abandoning her sentence. "I couldn't even defend myself against her, let alone him. I guess if I wasn't there… she just needed someone else to destroy."

I didn't know what to say.

"And I can't believe she had the dog *put down*," she continued. "That's just… horrific."

"Aled was devastated."

"Yeah, he loved that dog to bits."

There was a pause then and I took a long sip of my drink, which was very strong.

"Honestly though, I hated him at the time."

This was a shock. "You *hated* him? Why?"

"Because I got all the torment from our mum. Because he was the golden child and I was the stupid one. Because he never stood up for me, ever, even when he could see how badly she was treating me. I blamed him entirely." She saw my look of disdain and raised her eyebrows. "Oh, don't worry, I don't think like that any more. I don't blame him at all any more, it's all that woman's fault. If he'd have tried to stand up for me, she just would have made *both* our lives unbearable."

The whole thing *was* desperately sad and I knew that I *had* to get them talking again, even if it was literally the last thing I ever did.

"Anyway, one day I just had to get out." She finished her drink and put the glass down. "If I stayed there, I would have been miserable for the rest of my life. She'd have made me do A levels, probably repeat a year when I inevitably failed them, and then I'd struggle to get a job that matched up to my mum's expectations." She shrugged. "So I just left. Tracked down my grandparents – my dad's parents – and lived with them for a while. My dad's a goner, but my grandparents always stayed in touch. Then I got involved with the National Youth Theatre, managed to get funding for one of their acting courses I'd auditioned for. Then applied for a job here." She flipped her hair like a film star, making me laugh. "And now my life's great! Living with friends, a fun job doing something I enjoy. Life isn't all textbooks and grades."

I felt a glow at the knowledge that she was happy.

I had expected to learn a lot of things about Carys Last when I found her, but that was not one of them.

"But…" She leaned back in her seat. "I am sorry that Aled's having a rough time."

"I've been really worried about him since he stopped making *Universe City.*"

Carys tilted her head. Her white-blonde hair shimmered a little under the LED lights of the bar. "Making… university?"

And then I realised.

Carys had no idea what *Universe City* was about.

"You-you don't know the story of *Universe City*." I brought my hand up to my forehead. "Oh my God."

She stared at me, baffled.

And then I told her everything that had happened in *Universe City*. Including about February Friday.

Her icy expression melted as I spoke. Her eyes widened. She shook her head several times.

"I assumed you knew," I said, once I'd finished. "I mean… you're twins."

She snorted. "We don't have a psychic connection."

"No, I thought he would have told you."

"Aled doesn't *say anything*." She was frowning again, deep in thought. "He doesn't bloody *say anything*."

"I thought that might have been why you chose the name February—"

"February is my *middle name*."

There was a piercing silence.

"And it was all for me, was it?" she asked.

"Well… it was mostly for him, really. But he wanted you to listen. He wanted to talk to you."

Eventually she sighed. "I always thought you two were similar." I spun the straw round my glass. "Why?"

"You never say what you're actually thinking."

FAMILY

We stayed there for a while longer, talking about our lives. She was only three months older than me, but she was ten times as adult. She'd done job interviews, she paid bills and taxes and drank red wine. I couldn't even make a doctor's appointment by myself.

When it got to nine thirty I said I'd better leave, so she paid for our drinks (despite my protests) and we left to walk back to Waterloo station.

I still hadn't managed to ask her to help Aled somehow, and this was the only chance I was going to get.

After we'd hugged to say goodbye in the middle of the station, I asked her.

"Is there any chance you'd-you'd get in touch with Aled?" I said in a quiet voice.

She seemed unsurprised. Her face resumed her classic expressionless mask. "That's the main reason you came to find me, right?"

"Well... yeah."

"Hm. You must really like him."

"He's... the best friend... I've ever had." I immediately felt a bit pathetic for saying it.

"That's cute," she said. "But— I don't think I can talk to him again."

My stomach dropped. "What— Why?"

"I've just—" She fidgeted awkwardly. "I've put that life behind me. I've moved on. It's not any of my business any more."

"But... he's your brother. He's your family."

"Family means nothing," she said, and I knew she believed it. "You have no obligation to love your family. It wasn't your choice to be born."

"But— Aled's *good*, he's— I think he needs help and he won't talk to me—"

"It's just not my business any more!" she said, raising her voice slightly. No one noticed – people were rushing about around us, their voices echoing around the station. "I can't go back, Frances. I made my decision to leave and not look back. Aled will be fine at university, it's where he's always been destined for. Honestly, trust me, I grew up with him. If anyone was supposed to be at university doing some sort of difficult academic degree, it'd be him. He's probably having the time of his life."

And I realised then that I didn't believe her.

He'd told me he didn't want to go. Back in the summer. He'd said he didn't want to go to university and nobody listened. And now there he was. When I'd called him in December, he'd sounded like he wanted to die.

"He wrote the Letters to February to you," I said. "For you. Even when you were still at home, he was making *Universe City* and hoping you'd find out and talk to him."

She said nothing.

"Do you care?"

"Obviously, but—"

"Please," I said. "Please. I'm scared."

She shook her head slightly. "Scared of what?"

"That he's going to disappear," I said. "Just like you did."

She froze, and then looked down.

I almost *wanted* her to feel guilty about it.

I wanted her to feel how I'd felt for two years.

She chuckled.

"You're guilt-tripping me, Frances," she said, grinning. "I think I liked you more when you were a massive pushover."

I shrugged. "I'm just telling the truth this time."

"Well, there's power in truth, or something."

"Are you going to help him?"

She drew in a deep breath, narrowed her eyes, and put her hands in her pockets.

"Yes," she said.

THE 'INCIDENT'

We went to Carys's house for her to pick up some clothes, then to St Pancras to get the train back to mine. It was too late to get a train all the way up north to Aled's university, so we decided to sleep at mine and head off in the morning. I'd texted my mum about it and she'd said that was fine.

We spoke only a little on the train. It felt almost surreal to be with her like this again – sitting on opposite sides of a table, staring out of the window into the dark. So many things were different, but the way she leaned on her hand and the way her eyes flickered were exactly the same.

We reached my house and she stepped inside and took off her shoes. "Wow. Nothing's changed."

I laughed. "We're not big into DIY."

Mum entered the hallway from the kitchen. "Carys! Cor, I like your hair. I had a fringe like that once. Looked terrible on me."

Carys laughed too. "Thanks! I can actually see these days."

Carys made small-talk with my mum for a few minutes and then we headed up to bed – it was going on midnight. It was dark outside, but the streetlamps shone in a little, a dim orange glow amid the dark blue.

"D'you remember when I slept over your house that time?" she asked me, after I'd changed into my pyjamas in the bathroom.

"Oh, yeah," I said, as if I'd only just remembered. I hadn't forgotten. It had been two days before the 'incident'. We'd crashed here after Carys had dragged me to another house party I didn't really want to go to. "You were drunk, haha."

"Yeah."

She went to clean her teeth and change into pyjamas and I tried to ignore how awkward I felt and the way Carys kept looking at me.

We both got into my double bed. I turned the ceiling lights off and put my fairy lights on, then Carys rolled her head towards me and said, "What's it like to be clever?"

I huffed out a laugh, but couldn't really look at her. I looked at the fairy lights on the ceiling instead. "Why do you think I'm clever?"

"I mean, grades. You get good grades. What's that like?"

"It's... not that special. It's useful, I guess. Useful."

"Yeah, that makes sense." She rolled her head away and looked up at the ceiling too. "Would have been useful. My mum kept trying to make me get good grades. Wouldn't work. I'm just not clever."

"You're clever in more important ways though."

She looked at me again and grinned. "Aw. That's cute."

I glanced at her and couldn't resist a smile. "What? It's true."

"You're cute."

"I'm not cute."

"You are." She brought up a hand to brush my hair. "Your hair looks cute like this." She stroked my cheek gently with one finger. "I forgot you have freckles. Cute."

"Stop saying 'cute'," I said, with a snort of laughter.

She just kept on stroking my cheek with her fingertips. After a while I rolled my head to face her, only to find we were just centimetres apart. Her skin flashed blue from the fairy lights, then softly changed to pink, then green, then blue again.

"I'm sorry—" My voice cracked before I could get the words out. "—I'm sorry I wasn't a better friend."

"You mean you're sorry you kissed me," she said.

"Yeah," I whispered.

"Hm." She dropped her hand, and then I realised what she was about to do and I couldn't think of a way to say no in time, so I just let her lean forward and press her lips to mine.

I let it happen for a couple of minutes. It was fine. Somewhere in the time that it was happening, I realised that I was not attracted to her any more, and I did not want this to be happening at all.

Also in that time, she rolled over so her elbow was on the other side of my head and she was almost leaning on top of me, a leg pressed against me, and she kissed slowly, like she was trying to make up for shouting at me two years ago. I got the impression that she'd kissed quite a lot of people in between then and now.

After I'd finished processing what was happening, I broke away by turning my head to one side.

"I don't... want that," I said.

She stayed very still for a moment. And then she moved off me and laid back on the bed.

"Okay," she said. "That's fine."

There was a pause.

"You don't secretly have a crush on me, do you?" I asked.

She smiled to herself.

"No," she said. "I just wanted to say sorry. An apology kiss."

"Apology for what?"

"I literally screamed at you for a good ten minutes just because you kissed me."

We both laughed.

I felt relieved.

I felt relieved mostly because I definitely did not have a crush on Carys any more.

"Has Aled got a girlfriend?" she asked.

"Oh… you don't know that either…"

"What?"

"Aled, erm… d'you remember his friend Daniel?"

"They're a *thing*?" Carys let out a witch cackle. "That's brilliant. That is brilliant. I hope it pisses Mum right off."

I laughed because I didn't know what to say.

She tucked her hands underneath her cheek.

"Can we listen to *Universe City*?" she asked.

"You want to listen to an episode?"

"Yeah. I'm curious."

I rolled over so I was facing her again and rummaged under my pillow for my phone. I loaded up the first episode – might as well start at the beginning – and pressed play.

As Aled's voice started to sound across the room, Carys moved again so she was lying on her back. She listened to Aled's voice and stared up at the ceiling. She didn't make any comments or even show much of a reaction, though she did smile at a few of the funny lines. After a few minutes, I started to zone out too, feeling like I was about to fall asleep, and then all I knew was Aled's voice, speaking to us from the air above our heads, speaking to us as if he were here in the room. When the episode finished, the final chords of 'Nothing Left For Us' fading away into nothing, the room felt painfully empty and so quiet. Silent.

I glanced over at Carys and was surprised to find her still in the same position, blinking slowly as if in deep thought. And then a tear dripped down from the corner of her eye.

"That was sad," she murmured. "That was really sad."

I didn't say anything.

"He was doing this all that time. Even before I left... he was calling."

She closed her eyes.

"I wish I could be as subtle and beautiful. All I know how to do is scream..."

I rolled over to face her. "Why didn't you want to help him?"

"I'm scared," she whispered.

"Of what?"

"That if I see him, I won't be able to leave him again."

She fell asleep almost immediately after that and I decided to text Aled. I doubted he would reply. Maybe he wouldn't even see it. But I wanted to do it all the same.

Frances Janvier

Hey Aled, hope you're okay pal. Just wanted you to know that I found Carys, and we're coming to see you tomorrow at your university. We're really worried about you and love you and miss you xxx

In Distress. Stuck in Universe City. Send Help.

Scroll down for transcript >>>

[…]

I am not in love with you, but you, my friend, I want to tell you *everything*. Long ago I was afflicted with a terrible predisposition to never say a word, and I honestly cannot understand why or how that happened. C'est la vie.

But there is something about you which makes me wish I could speak like you do – I've watched you from afar and you really are the best person that I have met in my whole life. You possess the ability to make people listen to you without question, even if you don't often use it. I almost want to *be* you. Does that make any sense? I bet it doesn't. I'm just rambling on. I'm sorry.

Anyway. I hope, when one day we meet again, you will listen to me, and pay attention. I do not have anyone else to whom I could say these things. You might not even be listening now. Then again, you do not have to listen if you do not want to. Who am I to make you do anything? I'm not, I'm nothing. But you – oh, *you* – why, I'd listen to you for hours.

[…]

5. SPRING TERM
b)

ART REFLECTS LIFE

"Btw, I'm broke," Raine said through the open window of her tiny Ford Ka. "So I hope you guys have cash on you."

I'd called Raine the next morning, praying she would be up for the 'rescue Aled from university' plan, which, of course, she was.

"I'll pay petrol," said Carys as she climbed into the back seat. Raine watched her with amazement.

"I'm Carys," said Carys.

"Yeah," said Raine. "Wow." She realised she was staring and cleared her throat. "I'm Raine. You don't look much like Aled."

"Well, we are twins, but we're not actually the same person."

I moved the seat back up and sat down. "You sure you're okay to drive us all the way up north?"

Raine shrugged. "Beats going to school."

Carys chuckled. "Very true."

Just as Raine started the engine, I had a sudden thought.

"D'you think we should see if Daniel wants to come?"

Raine and Carys turned to look at me.

"I think if he knew about all this, he'd... he'd want to come," I said.

"You are literally the most thoughtful person on this Earth," said Raine.

Carys shrugged. "The more the merrier."

I took out my phone and called Daniel. I told him everything.

"All okay?" said Raine.

"Yep. We need to pick him up."

Carys was staring out of the window.

Raine looked at her in the rear-view mirror and said, "You all right, mate? What are you looking at?"

"Don't worry. Let's go."

We drove to his house to pick him up. He was sat waiting on the low brick wall outside his house, wearing a burgundy jumper under his school suit. He looked slightly like he was about to have an anxiety attack.

I got out of the car to let him climb in next to Carys. He sat down and they exchanged a long look.

"Jesus fucking Christ," he said. "You're back."

"I'm back," she said. "And it's good to see you too."

It was a six-hour drive. It started off fairly tense – Raine seemed to be a bit wary of Carys in the same way that I used to be, mainly because Carys was extremely intimidating. Daniel kept passing his phone from hand to hand and asking me to repeat exactly what had happened to Aled over Christmas.

Around two hours into the drive we stopped at a service station so Raine could fuel up on coffee and we could all go to the loo. As we were heading back to the car, wind blowing around the car park, Raine asked Carys, "So where'd you disappear off to, then?"

"London," said Carys. "I work for the National Theatre, I run workshops and stuff. Pays pretty well."

"Mate! I know the National. I saw *War Horse* there a few years ago." Raine stared at Carys intently. "Didn't you need any qualifications for that?"

"No," said Carys. "They didn't even ask."

Daniel frowned at this, and Raine didn't say anything in response, but her mouth stretched into a grin, and as Carys was climbing back into the car, Raine murmured to me, "I like her."

Things in the car eased up a bit after that. Raine let me take control of her iPod so I put Madeon on, but Daniel grumbled that it was too loud, so I gave up and put on Radio 1. Carys stared through her sunglasses out of the window like she was Audrey Hepburn.

I was feeling extremely on edge. Aled had not texted me back. Chances are Aled would just be in his uni room or at a lecture or something, but I still couldn't stop thinking about him doing something… more serious.

Things like that happened, didn't they?

And Aled didn't have anyone any more.

"You okay, Frances?" asked Daniel. We were sitting next to each other in the back seat now. The question appeared to be sincere and he was gazing at me with dark eyes.

"He just… hasn't got anyone. Aled hasn't got anyone any more."

"Oh, that's bullshit," Daniel sat back with a sneer. "There are four of us in this car. I skipped a chemistry lesson for this."

There was something calming about the motorway. I'd always thought that. I put my earphones in and listened to an episode of *Universe City* and watched the blur of grey and green outside.

Daniel was next to me, leaning his head on the window, both hands gripping his phone. Carys was sipping a bottle of water. Raine was moving her mouth along to the words of whatever song was playing on the radio, but I had my earphones in, so I couldn't quite make out what the song was. In my ears, Aled said, or Radio said, "I wished I had as many stories as her," and although we were all panicking about the same thing, I momentarily felt like we were at peace. I felt the least stressed I had been in a long time. I closed my eyes, the hum of the car and the buzz of the radio and the murmur of Aled's voice all mixing into one glorious sound.

When we were half an hour away, I said, "I feel like we're in Universe City."

Raine laughed. "In what way?"

"Radio's trapped in Universe City. And someone's finally heard him. Someone is going to rescue him."

"Art reflects life," said Carys. "Or... maybe it's the other way round."

A COMPUTER WITH A SAD FACE

Before we knew it, much quicker than I'd expected, we reached Aled's university town.

In many ways, it was extremely similar to our own hometown. Tall Dickensian buildings and cobbled streets, a small market square with an array of high-street shops, a river running through the whole thing. It was gone 9pm now – everywhere was busy and there were students all over the place, walking around town or hanging around pubs.

It took a good twenty minutes of driving to find St John's College. Raine parked outside on double yellow lines. It looked tiny, just like a terraced house, and I didn't really understand how a building so small could be an entire university college. Once we were inside, however, we found that the college stretched into many of the surrounding buildings.

We stood awkwardly in the college foyer. There was a large staircase to our right, and also two corridors up ahead.

"Now what?" I said.

"Does Aled know we're coming?" asked Daniel.

"Yeah, I texted him."

"Did he reply?"

"No."

Daniel turned to me. "So... we've just turned up uninvited."

Everyone was silent.

"To be fair, mate, we were in a bit of a panic," said Raine. "It sounded like Aled was about to kill himself or some shit."

She'd said the words that nobody had dared to say yet, and it sent us all back into silence.

"Does anyone even know where his room is?" asked Carys.

"Maybe we should ask at reception," I said.

"I'll ask," said Carys with absolutely no hesitation, and she walked towards the reception desk where an elderly man was sitting. She talked with him for a moment, and then walked back. "He's not allowed to tell us, apparently."

Daniel groaned.

"We could ask a few students?" Raine suggested. "See if they know him?"

Carys nodded in agreement.

"What if no one even *knows* Aled though?" I asked.

Raine was about to say something when a completely different voice sounded from the staircase.

"Sorry – did you guys say 'Aled'?"

We all turned around in unison to find ourselves faced with a guy wearing a university rowing polo shirt.

"Yes?" I said.

"Are you friends from home?"

"Yes, I'm his sister," said Carys, sounding ten years older than she was.

"Oh, thank god," said the student.

"Why thank god?" Daniel snapped.

"Er – well, he's just been acting a bit strangely. I live opposite him and he— Well, he doesn't leave his room hardly ever, for starters. He doesn't come to college meals any more. Stuff like that."

"Whereabouts is his room?" said Carys.

The student gave us directions.

"I'm so glad he's got friends from home," said the student, just before he left. "I mean, he seems so *isolated*."

It was decided that I would go alone to Aled's room.

I was kind of glad, in a way.

I seemed to have been walking for ages, down blue-carpeted halls with cream, chipped walls and shiny doors, when I found the room.

I knocked.

"Hello?"

There wasn't a reply, so I knocked again. "Aled?"

Nothing.

I tried the handle – it was unlocked, so I went inside. The room was dark – the curtains were closed – so I turned the lights on.

It was a demolition site.

The room itself was a typically miniscule uni room. Smaller than my room at home. It had space for a single bed, then a couple of square metres of floor, a dingy-looking wardrobe, an equally dingy desk. The curtains were so thin that you could see the streetlights through them.

But it was the contents of the room that worried me. It was way beyond normal mess, and Aled had never been very messy in the first place. There was a huge pile of clothes on his desk chair and more on the floor, pretty much covering up every bit of carpet. His wardrobe was almost empty and his bed was unmade and it didn't look like the sheets had been changed in months. There were at least twelve empty bottles of water on his bedside table, along with a laptop, its *on* light flashing gently. The walls were the only clean part of the room. He hadn't put up any posters or pictures at all – they were just dull, mint green breezeblocks. It was freezing – he'd left his window open.

The desk was covered in miscellaneous sheets of paper, tickets, leaflets, food packets and fizzy drink cans. I picked up a piece of paper from the desk. It was mostly blank apart from a few lines.

Poetry 14/1 – George Herbert: Form and Voice lecture
- 1630s
- Paratext – Gerard genette. The textual form on a poem takes – what it looks like on the page
- Dialogue – trochaic
- John wesley's christ 1744 1844?????

The rest of the page was covered in swirly lines.

I continued searching through the papers on the desk, not entirely sure what I was looking for. I came across a lot of lecture notes with only one or two bullet points on them. There were also several letters from Student Finance reminding him that he had to reapply if he wanted funding next year.

Then I found the first handwritten note.

Honestly how fucking dare you take away a show that's so precious to so many people? You think that you control everything about it but the show's gone way beyond that *now – you wouldn't even be in this position if it wasn't for us. Bring back Universe City or you'll regret it.*

Then I found a second.

FUCK YOU ALED LAST!!! YOU HAVE RUINED THE HAPPINESS OF SO MANY PEOPLE ACROSS THE WORLD. HOPE YOU ARE HAPPY

And then a third.

Lol why bother staying alive if you're not making Universe City? You have ripped out the hearts of thousands of people. JUST KILL YOURSELF

Then a fourth. Then a fifth.

I found nineteen of them, scattered across his desk.

I was confused and terrified and then I remembered that photo of Aled from months ago showing him walking into the college. All these people had to do was write a letter, put his name on the envelope and address it to the college, and the result was Aled getting bombarded with hate mail.

Then I came across a letter that had the YouTube logo on the header, along with a variety of other logos I didn't recognise. I quickly skimmed it.

Dear Mr Last,

As you have failed to respond to our emails, we hope you do not mind us contacting you via mail – we at Live!Video would like to invite you to take part in our summer convention, Live!Video London. As your YouTube channel Universe City has risen to great popularity within the last year, we wondered whether you would be interested in putting on a live version of the show. We have never staged a live version of a storytelling channel such as yours before and it would be a great honour for us to have you as the first.

There were several other follow-up letters confirming that Aled hadn't responded to any of them, which made me feel suddenly very sad.

Underneath the pile of papers, I found Aled's phone. It was turned off, so I turned it on, since I knew his passcode, and immediately he received eight new messages. Most of them were from me, dating back from early January.

He hadn't turned his phone on since January.

"What the fuck?" said a voice from behind me.

I turned round, and Aled was standing in the doorway.

He was wearing a white T-shirt that had a computer with a sad face on it, with pale blue ripped jeans. His hair was below his shoulders now and it was the sort of green-grey of someone who'd dyed their hair multiple times different colours and then left it for a while. In one hand he was holding a toothbrush and a tube of toothpaste.

The most notable thing, however, was that he had lost a rather extreme amount of weight since the last time I'd seen him at Christmas. Aled hadn't been particularly skinny during the time I'd known him, and now his face had lost its roundness, his eyes looked sunken and his T-shirt hung off him like a tent.

His mouth was open in shock. He tried to say something else. And then he bolted.

LISTEN

I pelted after him, but I quickly lost him and found myself outside in the dark. I was pretty sure he'd run out of the building, but I couldn't see which way he'd gone and in this weather he was probably freezing his arse off in just his T-shirt and jeans. I fumbled for my phone and found his name in my contacts and called him, but obviously he didn't answer, but then remembered that his phone was back in his room, and he hadn't used it for weeks.

I didn't know what to do. Would he turn up if I just waited for him inside? Or would he do something dangerous?

He clearly wasn't thinking rationally.

I turned round and looked at the college door.

I couldn't go in.

I started to run down the street and into the town centre.

I spotted him almost instantly. He stood out in just his white T-shirt among all the students in big coats and jumpers, laughing and chatting and looking like they were having the time of their lives. They probably all were.

I called out for him and he turned and saw me, and started running again.

Why was he *running*?

Did he not want to see me *that badly*?

I followed him down some steps in the street and round a corner and on to a bridge. He turned right again and disappeared down some more steps and I followed, realising suddenly where he was going.

He disappeared into the door of a nightclub.

Music was blaring out of the club. There wasn't a queue, but I could see it was already packed inside.

"All right, lass?" said the bouncer in a strong Geordie accent. "You got any ID for me, love?"

"Er…" I didn't. I didn't drive and it wasn't like I carried my passport with me. "No, it's just…"

"I can't let you in without any ID, love."

I grimaced. Arguing with a six-foot-five bald Geordie man was probably not the best idea. But I didn't have any choice.

"Please, my friend just ran into here, he's really upset, I just need to talk to him and I'll leave as soon as I found him, I *swear*…"

The bouncer gave me a sympathetic look. He checked his watch and sighed.

"Go on then, lass, it's only ten o'clock."

I gasped out a thank-you and then ran inside.

It was worse than Johnny R's. The floor was sticky and dirty, the walls were dripping with condensation, and you could hardly see anything through the dark or hear anything other than the blare of classic pop tunes. I barged through the crowds of students jumping up and down – oddly, most of them seemed to be in jeans and T-shirts, nothing like the dressed-up sixth-form crowd at Johnny R's back at home. I searched and searched, ignoring the students giving me disapproving looks when I barged past them, then went upstairs and did it again, and then...

There. White T-shirt, leaning against a wall. His hair looked grass-green against the flashing lights.

I grabbed him by the upper arms before he saw me coming and he jumped so hard I could feel his bones move.

"ALED!" I shouted though there wasn't much point. Even I couldn't hear any sound come out.

The music was so loud that everything was vibrating: the floor, my skin, my blood.

He was gazing at me like he'd never seen a real human being before. His eyes had deep purple shadows underneath them. He hadn't washed his hair for at least several days. His skin flashed blue, red, pink, orange...

"What are you doing?" I shouted, but neither of us could hear it. "The music's too loud!"

He opened his mouth and said something, but I couldn't hear and I couldn't lip-read either, even though I was trying to listen harder than I had ever listened before. Then he bit his lip and stayed very still.

"I missed you so much," I said, the only true thing I could think of saying, and I think he might have been able to lip-read it because his eyes filled with tears and he mouthed "Me too," and I'd never wanted to hear his voice so badly in all the time that I'd ever spent with him.

I didn't know what else to do so I just wrapped my arms round his waist and put my head on his shoulder and held him.

At first he didn't do anything. Then he raised his arms, slowly, and placed them round my shoulders, and then he rested his head against mine. After a minute or so, I could feel him shaking. After another minute, I realised I was crying as well.

It felt so real. It didn't feel like I was trying to be someone I'm not, like I was putting on an act.

I cared about him. And he cared about me.

That was all it was.

NO ONE

We went to the town square. We didn't even say anything while we were walking there. We held hands because it felt like the right thing to do.

We sat down on a stone bench. I realised several minutes later that this was the exact spot where Aled had been in that stalker photo posted on Tumblr several months ago.

The thing I hate most when I'm in a bad mood is other people being very pitying and sympathetic with me. And I knew this wasn't just any old 'bad mood', but I decided I'd take a different approach.

"So you've been feeling a bit shit, then?" I asked. We were still holding hands.

Aled's eyes crinkled a little – the hint of a smile. He nodded, but didn't say anything.

"What's been doing that, then? If it's a specific person, I can one hundred per cent beat them up."

He smiled again. "You couldn't beat a *fly* up."

The sound of his voice in the air – in the real world – nearly made me start crying again.

I thought about it. "That's probably true, actually. They're too fast. I'm very slow in most areas of life."

He laughed. It was magic.

"So what seems to be the trouble?" I said, in what I imagined was a doctor voice.

Aled tapped my hand with his fingers. "Just… everything."

I waited.

"I hate being at university," he said.

"Yeah?"

"Yeah." His eyes welled up again. "I hate it. I hate everything about it. I'm going insane." A tear fell and I squeezed his hand.

"Why don't you quit?" I whispered.

"I can't go home. I hate it there too. So… I've got nowhere to go," he said, his voice croaky. "Nowhere to go. No one to help me."

"I'm here," I said. "I can help you."

He laughed again, though it died away almost instantly.

"Why did you stop talking to me?" I said, because even now I still didn't understand. "And Daniel?"

"I—" His voice caught. "I— I was scared."

"Scared of what?"

"I— I just run away from all the difficult things in my life," he said, and then laughed exasperatedly. "If something's hard, if I have to talk to someone about something difficult, I just avoid it and ignore them, as if that'll make it go away."

"What… so… with us, you—"

"I couldn't face the idea of you two… I don't know… rejecting me forever. I thought it'd be better if I just ignored you."

"But— But why would we do that?"

He wiped his eyes with his free hand. "Well… okay, so, me and Dan… we argued about lots of things. Mainly about the fact that he doesn't believe me when I say I like him. Like, he thinks I'm lying to him, or something ridiculous, he thinks I'm just *pretending* to be attracted to him because I feel sorry for him and because we've been friends for so long." He glanced at me, seeing the expression on my face. "Oh, you don't think that as well, do you?"

"Daniel sounded pretty convinced…"

Aled groaned. "This is so stupid. Just because I— I don't shout about my feelings all the time…"

"Why would ignoring him solve that?"

He shook his head. "It wouldn't. I know it wouldn't. I was just scared of talking about it. Facing the possibility that he— He might just end our relationship because I seem like I'm not into it. I've been doing it since before the summer because I'm— I'm a fucking *idiot*. And now we've grown apart and… I don't know if we'll ever go back to the way we were…"

I squeezed his hand.

"What about me?" I said.

"I tried," he said immediately, looking me in the eyes. "I tried. I wrote so many replies to your texts, but I just… I couldn't send them. I thought they'd make you hate me. And as time went on, it just got worse and worse, and I got more and more convinced that you hated me and anything I said to you would just make you forget me forever." His eyes welled up again. "I thought it'd be better if I just said nothing. At least then… there was still the possibility that I had something good in my life… now that *Universe City* has… has gone…"

"I don't hate you," I said. "Far from it, actually."

He sniffed.

"I'm really sorry," he said. "I know I've been an idiot. Everything would be fine if I could have just… said all this earlier…"

I knew that this was true.

"It's okay," I said. "I get it."

Sometimes you can't say the things you're thinking. Sometimes it's too hard.

"Why did you end *Universe City*?" I asked.

"My mum kept calling me whenever I made an episode. Telling me to stop doing it or she'd— She'd stop sending me money, or she'd call the university, or stuff like that. I didn't listen to her at first, but it got to the point where I was dreading every single episode and I ran out of ideas and I just hated doing it." His face crumpled and more tears fell. "I *knew* she would ruin this for me. I knew she would take the one last thing I have and *ruin it*."

I dropped his hand and hugged him again.

We fell into silence for a moment and though nothing was fixed, it was a relief to hear him say exactly what he felt for once.

"We all just want you to be okay," I said, dropping my arms. "All of us."

"All— You and Daniel?"

I shook my head. "Carys is here."

Aled froze.

"Carys?" he whispered, like he hadn't said the name in years.

"Yeah," I said, almost whispering too. "She's here to see you. She came with me to see you."

Aled started to cry like I'd turned on a tap. Tears just started to pour out of his eyes.

It made me laugh, which was probably very insensitive, but I couldn't help feeling happy in some weird way. I hugged him again, because I had no idea what to say, and realised that he was laughing too, sort of, through his tears.

WE HOPED

Carys, Daniel and Raine were still sitting in the foyer when we got back to college. When we entered through the door and Aled saw Carys, he stopped in his tracks and stared.

Carys stood up from her seat and gazed at him from across the room. They'd once been similar – blue eyes and blonde hair – but they really looked nothing alike any more. Carys was taller and rounder and everything about her was clean, bold, block colours. Aled was small and pointy and looked ruffled and shadowed, his skin a little blotchy, his clothes crinkled, his hair several different shades of green, purple and grey.

I walked away from Aled as Carys approached. As Carys moved in for a hug, I heard her whisper, "I'm sorry for leaving you alone with her."

Daniel and Raine were staring without reserve from their armchairs, Daniel looking a little unnerved at how physically different Aled was, Raine looking on with heart-eyes as if this were some sort of touching family drama documentary.

I put my hands on each of their heads and gently turned them so they were facing away.

"How is he?" whispered Daniel as I sat down.

There was no point lying. "Absolutely terrible," I said. "But at least he's not dead."

I'd meant it half-jokingly, but Daniel nodded in agreement.

We'd done it.

We'd found him. We'd helped him. We'd rescued him – we hoped.

That's what we thought until the college door exploded open and in walked a plump woman with cropped hair and a tote bag over one shoulder.

I jumped out of my seat faster than I had ever moved in my life. Upon seeing her, Carys sort of pulled Aled farther away from the door towards us, and in the moments before he turned and saw her, I could see the confusion in Aled's eyes.

"Allie, darling," said Carol.

ON YOUR OWN

Everybody was on their feet. I wasn't entirely sure what a stand-off was, but I felt like this might be one of them.

Carol blinked. "Carys. What exactly are *you* doing here?"

"I came to see Aled."

"I wasn't aware you still cared for any member of your family."

"Only the good ones," said Carys through gritted teeth.

Carol raised an eyebrow. "Well, it is how it is. I'm not here to see you and, frankly, I don't want to. I want to talk to my *real* child."

"I don't think you deserve to," said Carys, and I could feel the inaudible gasps of everyone in the room.

"Ex*cuse* me?" said the woman, her voice raising. "You have *no* say in how I interact with my son."

Carys cackled. It echoed around the foyer. "Ha! Oh, believe me, I do; I do when you've been torturing him like he's a fucking *doll*."

"How *dare* you…"

"How dare *I*? How dare *you*. You killed the dog, Carol? You killed the dog? Aled loved that dog, we *grew up* with that dog…"

"That dog was a burden and a nuisance and its life was miserable."

"Let me talk to her," Aled interrupted, sending everyone into silence despite his voice still being almost at a whisper. He stepped out of Carys's grip and walked towards his mum. "Come on, we'll just talk outside for a minute."

"You don't have to do this on your own," said Carys, though she didn't move from where she stood.

"Yes, I do," said Aled, and he followed his mum out of the college door.

We waited for ten minutes. Then another ten. Raine kept jogging up to the door and listening through it to check that they were still there. Students kept walking past us and giving us funny looks.

Carys was chatting softly to Daniel, whose knee was bouncing frantically up and down. I was sitting in a chair, contemplating what was happening and what Carol could possibly be saying to him.

"He'll be all right, won't he?" said Raine, coming to sit down next to me for the sixth time. "He'll be all right, in the end."

"I don't know," I said, because I honestly didn't. Aled's fate rested entirely on what he decided to do tonight.

"How did she even know we were here?" I asked, because there was no way anyone believed that Carol just happened to be here on the same day four of us had driven six hours up the country to rescue him.

"She saw us leave," said Carys abruptly. "I saw her looking out the window."

"She didn't know where we were going though!" said Raine.

Carys laughed. "Aled's long-lost sister sets off with his best

378

friend in the same car, with bags of food for a long journey? Not that hard to guess, is it."

Raine was about to say something else when we heard a car door slam. She bolted from her seat and swung open the door and shrieked "*NO!*" and we ran to join her just in time to see Aled and his mother driving away in a taxi.

UNIVERSITY

"I didn't think this could get any worse," said Daniel, "but it literally just did. Great."

We were standing in the middle of the road watching the taxi drive away.

"They'll be going to the station," said Carys. "She'll be wanting to take him home."

"Well, we obviously can't let that happen," I said.

Raine was already walking towards her car, which was still innocently parked on the double yellow lines by the college building. "Everyone get in the car."

It took us a moment to react, and a cry from Raine of "GET IN THE FUCKING CAR!" and then we all got into the car and Raine tore off after them.

She broke the speed limit and got us there in three minutes, Daniel shouting, "Slow down, we're all going to die," most of the way. We piled out of the car and into the station and checked the departures board and there was a train to King's Cross leaving in three minutes on Platform One. We ran towards Platform One without speaking to each other, and then there he was, standing by a bench with his mum, and I shouted out to him – we couldn't get any closer because we couldn't get through the ticket barrier – and he turned, his eyes wide as if he thought maybe he'd been imagining us this whole time.

"Don't go home with her!" I shouted. The station was lit up orange and gold against the darkness. "Please, Aled!"

He made to move towards us, but his mum grasped his arm and he stopped in his tracks. He opened his mouth to say something, but nothing came out.

"We'll help you!" I tried to think about what I was saying before I said it, but my heart was pounding and I couldn't think properly about anything, anything except that if Aled got on that train we might never get him back. "Please, you don't have to stay with her!"

Carol tutted at me and turned away as if she couldn't hear me, but Aled continued to stare. The train was almost at the station.

"It's my only option," he replied, although I could barely hear him. The train pulled in with a huge screeching noise. "I can't stay here, I have nowhere else to go—"

"You can stay with me instead!"

"Yeah, or me!" Carys shouted. "In London!"

"You're not meant to be there!" I continued. "She'll just make you go back to university! You were never meant to be at university…"

Carol started trying to pull him towards the train door. He moved slowly with her, but he was still looking at me.

"You made the wrong decision… you— You thought you had to go to university even though you didn't want to, or— Or you thought you wanted to go, but you really didn't… just because we were told that's our only option." I was leaning most of my body weight over the ticket gate, as if I could snap it in two. "I promise it's not! I understand... I think— I think I made that mistake as well, or— or I haven't made it yet, but— I'm going to change it..."

Aled stumbled on to the train, but remained standing in the doorway, looking at me.

"*Please, please, Aled...*" I was shaking my head wildly at him and I felt myself start to cry, not from sadness but from *fear*.

I felt someone nudge me in the side and when I looked Raine had linked her fingers together and was holding them by my leg as a foothold. I realised what she was doing as she winked at me and said, "Go before the ticket gate guy notices."

I put my foot in her hands and Raine practically threw me over the ticket gate. I heard the ticket gate man shouting at me, but I ran towards the train door and stopped right in front of Aled. His mum was trying to pull him farther on to the train, but Aled wasn't moving. He was just standing there, watching me.

I held out my hand to him.

"Please don't go with her... you have other options... you are not trapped." I could hear my voice shaking, the panic and the desperation.

"What if I don't?" he whispered. "What if I... can't get a job, and... I'll never be able to leave home... and—"

"You can live with me and we'll get joint shifts at the village post office and we'll make *Universe City* together," I said, "and we'll be happy."

He blinked away tears. "I—" He looked down, fixed on some point on the ground, and he didn't say anything else, but I *saw* him decide...

"Aled!" Carol's voice sounded from somewhere behind him, sharp and demanding.

Aled wrenched his arm out of her grip, and took my hand.

I mumbled, "Thank God," and saw he was wearing his lime green plimsolls with purple laces.

And then he stepped off the train.

5. SPRING TERM
c)

UNIVERSE CITY

We all stayed the night. It was too late to drive back home. Aled had a spare duvet for us to lie on and the four of us didn't think we'd get much sleep, but Raine fell asleep only ten minutes after she exclaimed, "I haven't been to a sleepover in *months*," and Carys quickly followed, covering herself with her leather jacket.

Daniel was asleep within the next fifteen minutes, wearing a pair of Aled's pyjama shorts and a T-shirt instead of his school suit and tucked slightly under Aled's desk because there definitely wasn't room for five people to sleep in here. Then only Aled and I were awake, sitting on his bed against the wall.

"What did you mean about you, like, making a mistake about uni?" he whispered, rolling his head towards me. "Are you—What's your plan now?"

"Well… the thing is… I don't actually think I care about English literature. I don't want to do it at university."

Aled looked startled. "Don't you?"

"I'm not sure I really want to go at all."

"But… that was— That was what you cared about more than anything."

"Only because I thought I had to," I said. "And because I was good at it. I thought that was the only way I was going to have a good life. But... that's wrong."

I paused.

"I love making *Universe City* with you," I said. "I don't feel like that when I'm studying."

He stared at me. "What d'you mean?"

"I feel like myself when I'm with you. And... that version of me... doesn't want to study books for three more years just because other people are and school told me that I should... That version of me doesn't want to get a desk job just for the money. That version of me wants to do what I want."

He let out a small laugh. "What do you want to do?"

I shrugged and smiled. "I don't have any plans. I just... I might need to think about it all a bit more carefully. Before I make any decisions I regret."

"Like I did," said Aled, but he was smiling.

"Well, yeah," I said and we both laughed. "I could do anything, though. I could get a septum piercing."

We both laughed again.

"What about art?" Aled said.

"Hm?"

"You like art a lot, don't you? You could go to art college. You're really good at it. And you love it."

I thought about the idea. Really thought about it. It definitely wasn't the first time someone had suggested that to me. And I didn't have any doubts that I would enjoy it.

For a moment there it actually felt sort of brilliant.

All I remember from the rest of that night was waking up briefly and hearing Daniel and Aled talking to each other, whispering so quietly that they were barely making any sound at all. Aled was still next to me on the bed. Daniel was, as far as I could tell, looking up at him from the floor. I quickly shut my eyes again before they noticed I was awake and thought I'd been eavesdropping.

"Wait, I don't understand," said Daniel. "I thought that meant someone who doesn't like having sex at all."

"I think that's the case for some people..." said Aled. He sounded a little nervous. "But asexuality means... erm... someone who doesn't feel, like, sexually *attracted* to anyone."

"Right. Okay."

"And some people just feel like they're... like... *partly* asexual, so... they only feel sexually attracted to people who they know really, *really* well. People they have, like, an emotional connection with."

"Okay. And that's you."

"Yeah."

"And you are attracted to me. Because you know me really well."

"Yes."

"And that's why you never have a crush on anyone."

"Yeah." There was a pause. "Some people call that 'demisexual' but, erm... it doesn't really matter what the word is—"

"Demisexual?" Daniel chuckled. "Haven't even heard of that one."

"Yeah, it doesn't matter what the word is, to be honest... I'm just trying to explain what I actually... like... feel. It's the feeling that's the important thing."

"It's fine. It's just a bit complicated." There was a rustling sound which might have been Daniel rolling over. "Where did you find out about all this?"

"The Internet."

"You should have told me about it."

"I thought you might... think it was silly, or something."

"Who am I to judge anyone's sexuality? I'm massively gay."

They both laughed softly.

Aled continued, "I just wanted you to understand, like, why I don't want to come out or anything. It's definitely not because I don't like you in that way—"

"No, I get it. I get it."

"And I was just scared... I didn't know how to explain it to you and make you believe me. And I just slowly started avoiding you... which made you think I don't like you... and I was scared you'd just break up with me as soon as I spoke to you. I'm so sorry, I've been so horrible to you—"

"Yeah, you've been an absolute bloody arse." I could hear that Daniel was smiling, and they both stifled a laugh. "It's okay. I'm sorry too."

Aled moved his arm off the bed. I wondered whether they were holding hands.

"So can we just go back to the way things were?" whispered Aled. "Can we just be us again?"

Daniel took a moment to reply.

"Yeah, we can," he said.

In the morning, Aled and I walked to Boots to get some toothbrushes for everyone, because Carys said she was not going anywhere until she'd brushed her teeth. While we were there, Aled wandered off to look at hair dye, and once I joined him, I asked him if he wanted me to dye his hair for him when we got back to his room, and he said yes.

Aled sat on his desk chair, his hair freshly washed, and I

stood behind him with a pair of scissors we'd picked up in WHSmith.

"Frances…" The nervousness in his voice was unmistakable. "If you give me a bad haircut, I'm probably going to run away to Wales and live there until my hair grows back."

"It's fine!" I snipped the scissors in the air. "I'm arty. I got an A in my art AS."

Raine laughed from where she was sitting on Aled's bed. "But you didn't do hairdressing A level, did you?"

I turned round and pointed the scissors at her. "But I would have if they'd offered it."

I cut Aled's hair a few centimetres shorter – it was still past his ears, but not so long that it was flat and heavy – and I attempted to cut in a few layers so he didn't look like a medieval squire. Overall it turned out pretty well, in my opinion, and Aled said it was better than anything he'd ever asked for at the hairdressers.

Then we bleached his hair, which took ages and turned it a kind of yellowy-orange, which I thought was hilarious, and I took many photos on my phone.

Once we'd done that, we dyed his hair pastel pink after he showed me a gif of some band member in a heavy denim jacket – longish, just longer than his chin, and a soft, muted pink. After it was finished, I realised it was exactly how Radio's hair is described in *Universe City*.

We had been driving for five minutes when Raine's car broke down.

She pulled over to the side of the road and sat very still for a moment, before asking, quite politely, "Is this an absolute joke?"

"What do you do when you break down really far away from home?" I asked.

"Isn't there some breakdown company we can call?" asked Daniel.

"I don't know," said Raine. "I've never broken down before." We all got out of the car.

"Who do you call?" I asked, and looked at Carys.

"Don't look at me. I may know how to pay my income tax, but I know nothing about cars. I live in London."

Daniel didn't drive either, and obviously Aled and I didn't. So we all just stood there.

Carys sighed and reached into her pocket for her phone. "Let me Google it. Hang on."

"I need to get home," said Daniel. "I've already missed three chemistry lessons and that shit is difficult to catch up on."

"We could always get the train," I said.

"It's like ninety pounds to get to Kent. I checked."

"I'll pay," said Aled. We all looked at him. "I haven't really been spending any money much recently. My student loan came in a few weeks ago."

"But what about my *car*?" Raine flopped dramatically over the bonnet and stroked it with one hand. "I can't just *leave* her here."

"And Aled's stuff is in there," Daniel pointed out.

Carys sighed. "I'll stay with you, Raine, and we'll sort out your car. You three go home on the train."

"What?" I said. "Are you sure?"

"Yeah." Carys smiled. "I want to talk to this one, anyway." She pointed towards Raine, who was making cooing noises and stroking the car bonnet.

"About what?"

"University alternatives for people who aren't good at maths problems." She shrugged. "Stuff they forget to tell you at school."

★

Despite saying he was going to revise on the train, Daniel fell asleep almost immediately. Aled and I sat opposite each other with a table between us and eventually we got on to the topic of *Universe City*.

"I don't want it to end," I said.

He drew in a breath and said, "Neither do I."

"I think— I think you should start it back up again."

"Well... I want to."

"So you're going to?"

And he said, "Maybe," but after that, we almost immediately started planning a new episode. Toulouse was in it, making a dramatic comeback from her sudden disappearance at the Gate of the Dead, and we started planning out some of the longer subplots as well – the Dark Blue Building, February Friday and Universe City itself. We started whispering lines of script to each other and Aled jotted them down in his phone, but we ended up waking Daniel anyway, and he rolled his eyes when he realised what we were doing, but he was smiling too. He tried to go back to sleep but couldn't, so he just listened to us.

"You're doing the washing-up for at least three weeks," said Mum. We were still on the train, about halfway home, and I was talking to her on the phone. I'd walked down the aisle to stand by the door, in between two carriages, because both Aled and Daniel had fallen asleep. "Also, I get to choose what Saturday night movie we watch for the next month. I can't just fork out ninety pounds whenever I want. Believe me. I would if I could. I was at the garden centre the other day and they had a fountain shaped like a dog having a wee. Eighty quid. I mean, these are essential purchases we're talking about here, Frances, *essential purchases* I'm sacrificing just so you can catch a train—"

"Okay, okay, that's fine." I grinned. "You can choose the movie on Saturday. As long as it's not *Shrek*."

"What about *Shrek 2*?"

"*Shrek 2* is allowed."

Mum laughed and I rested my head on the train door. We were passing a town. I didn't know what town. I didn't know where we were exactly.

"Mum," I said.

"What's up, sweetheart?"

"I don't think I want to do English lit at university any more." I paused. "I don't think I want to go to university."

"Oh, Frances." She didn't sound disappointed. "That's okay."

"Is it okay?" I asked, because I wasn't sure.

"Yes," she said. "It's okay."

SUMMER

A NEW VOICE

Aled's event was one of the headliners. 4pm in the biggest arena. I was passing some time watching one of the other YouTubers while Aled was getting ready and rehearsing the show with some of the backstage crew. The girl on at the moment was a musical comedian. She talked about Tumblr a lot, and interviewed a couple of actors who were making appearances, and then sang a few songs about *Supernatural*.

As I was watching, I found myself standing next to someone who I felt like I had met before.

Her hair was a weird black, or maybe very dark brown, I couldn't quite tell, and she had a thick, full fringe concealing her eyebrows. She looked kind of tired, like she wasn't quite aware of where exactly she was.

After I'd been staring at her for going on a full ten seconds, she returned the stare.

"I think I've seen you before," she said, before I could. "Did you go to Higgs?"

"Yeah, years ago. I moved to the Academy though…" My voice trailed away.

She looked me up and down. "Did you dress up as Doctor Who once? For a party?"

I laughed out of surprise. "Yeah!"

There was a pause.

"How's the Academy?" she said. "I heard it's pretty academic now. Like my school was."

"Yeah… yeah. You know. It's school."

We both chuckled knowingly.

The girl turned towards the stage. "God, school nearly killed me. So glad it's over."

"Same," I said with a grin.

I went backstage. I had to run to avoid being late because I hadn't been keeping an eye on the time.

A woman wearing all black clothes and a head-microphone tried to call me over as I stormed down a backstage corridor, but I quickly said, "I'm with Radio," and waved the pass I was wearing round my neck, and she left me alone. I guess I looked a bit like a fan – I was wearing my Teenage Mutant Ninja Turtles leggings and an oversized band sweatshirt. I walked. Doors upon blank doors. At the end, a sign pointing left. STAGE.

I turned left. Climbed some steps. I passed through the door that said 'STAGE' on it and found myself in the dark shadows of the backstage area. There were strange pulleys and ropes and wires everywhere, flashing lights and technical equipment, duct tape randomly plastered all over the place. Men and women all dressed in black hurried around, trapping me in a sort of hurricane of bodies, until one guy stopped and asked me, "Are you here with the Creator?" And I replied in the affirmative.

He grinned freakishly. Fairly large, bearded, an iPad in his hands. He must have been at least thirty.

"Oh my God. You must know who he is then? Oh my God. I haven't seen him yet. All I've heard is that his name is Aled, but I have no idea what he looks like. Vicky said she saw him, but I haven't seen him yet. He should be waiting over on stage-right. Oh my God, I'm just *so excited*."

I didn't really know what to say to this, so I let him scuttle away and then made my way round the back of the stage, a narrow corridor between the back curtain and a black brick wall bordered by lights, as if we were aeroplanes that needed guiding in to land.

Stage-right was practically empty compared to stage-left. There were three figures up near the front, two of them sort of fussing over the third.

And then I saw him.

I stopped for a moment.

I couldn't quite believe this was happening at all.

No – I could believe it. And it was amazing. It was spectacular.

The three figures eventually noticed me and turned, stepping into the light. Aled and two of the backstage crew, a man and a woman. The man, early twenties, had blue hair. The woman, forties, had dreadlocks.

Aled walked towards me. He looked amazing in the weirdest way imaginable. He looked me in the eye, nervously, for only a few seconds, before turning his head away with a shy smile. He fiddled with his gloves. I grinned and looked him up and down. Yes. Radio. His hair that stupid pastel colour, and that stupid length, all tucked behind his ears. Three-piece suit, tie, gloves. There was a whole fresh wave of fan art on its way. They were going to love him.

"You look so cool," I said, and I meant it – he looked so cool, he looked like he could rise from the ground and float among the clouds and become the new sun, he looked like he could kill someone with a smile, he looked like the best person in the world.

I had my art college acceptance letter in my pocket. Aled didn't know about it yet. I'd never been more excited about anything, but I wasn't going to tell him now. I was going to surprise him later.

Today really was a wonderful day.

"I—" He went to speak, but sort of swallowed instead.

The whole hall blacked out, sending the audience wild with screams. Backstage, we could only see each other by a tiny desk lamp attached to a pipe on my right.

"Twenty seconds," said Dreadlocks.

"It's going to be all right, isn't it?" Aled said, his voice shaking. "The script... it was— It was okay, wasn't it?"

"Yes, it was brilliant, as usual," I said. "But it doesn't matter what I think. This is your show."

Aled laughed. A rare and beautiful thing. "I wouldn't be here without you, you giant idiot."

"Stop making me cry!"

"Ten seconds," said Blue Hair.

"AND NOW, INTRODUCING A NEW VOICE TO THE EAST CONCERT HALL..."

And he went white. I swear to god. Even in the thin light I could see it, his smile dropped and he just temporarily died.

"A YOUTUBE PHENOMENON WHO HAS RECENTLY PASSED 700,000 SUBSCRIBERS..."

"What if people don't like it?" he said, his voice only just audible. "They're all expecting something brilliant from me."

"It doesn't matter," I said. "It's your show. If you like it, then it *is* brilliant."

"THE MYSTERIOUS STUDENT WHO HAS HIDDEN BEHIND A BLANK SCREEN FOR THE PAST THREE YEARS…"

The stage exploded into colour, flashing lights soaring around the concert hall. The bass introduction to 'Nothing Left For Us' began to play and Aled picked up his guitar and hung it over his head.

"Oh my God," I said. "Oh my God, oh my God…"

"Five seconds."

"THE ELUSIVE…"

"Four."

"THE ALL-POWERFUL…"

"Three."

"THE DEATH-DEFYING…"

"Two."

"THE GOVERNMENT-OVERTHROWING…"

"One."

"RADIO… SILENCE."

I could only see the back of his head, with the back of his neck just visible above his suit jacket as he stepped into the light of the stage, his steps happening so slowly, as heart-stopping music erupted into the air. I stopped breathing and saw everything. I saw the audience rise to their feet, just so wonderfully happy to finally see him in person, and it amazed me how many people Aled had made smile just by taking two steps on to a lit stage.

I saw the backstage crew gather at the curtains on stage-left, clambering over each other to get a look at the Anonymous Creator. I saw Aled raise a gloved hand. I could see every face in the crowd. Every face smiling, wearing gloves and suits like Radio, some dressed as Chester or Atlas or the new characters from this year: Marine, Jupiter, Atom. I saw a girl near the front dressed as Toulouse, and it made my heart hurt.

I watched Aled, or Radio, or whoever that guy was, grasp the microphone and open his mouth, and I whispered the words into the air while he roared them into the crowd.

"Hello. I hope somebody is listening…"

Universe City Live At Live!Video London 2014

Published on 16 Sep:
Radio's first ever live appearance at Live!Video London 2014 in the East Concert Hall on Saturday 22nd August. After revealing what they truly look like, Radio describes the outcome of their search for their Lost Brother and the latest developments in their quest to find an escape route from Universe City. They also discuss the future of Universe City and its sister cities across the country.

Info:
Radio is the creator of internationally-celebrated web podcast series 'Universe City', whose podcasts have reached over ten million views on YouTube since March 2011. Each podcast runs for 20–25 minutes, and the series follows students of Universe City as they discover the City's secrets, faults and hypocrisies, as narrated by the one student who does not want to be there – the enigmatic Radio Silence.

[TRANSCRIPT UNAVAILABLE]

ACKNOWLEDGEMENTS

Thank you to everyone who supported me during the writing of my second book. It took a long time, but here we are!

Thanks to the most important people in my career – my agent Claire and my editors Lizzie, Sam and Jocelyn. You keep me believing that what I'm doing is great and not terrible and everything is fine. I wouldn't be anywhere without you.

Thanks to my parents and brother, as always, for being the best family ever.

Thanks to my beautiful friends from home, whom I can always rely on for laughs and hugs and sing-a-long car rides. Thanks to my beautiful housemates from university, who genuinely keep me sane. Thanks to my very important friend, Lauren James – you kept me believing in this book every step of the way.

Thanks to *Welcome to Night Vale*, a major inspiration for *Universe City* and a genuinely excellent podcast.

And thanks to you, reader. Whether you're new, or whether you knew me back when I was posting on Tumblr in 2010 about how desperately I wanted to be an author. Whoever you are and however you found this book – I wrote it for all of us.

'The Catcher in the Rye for the digital age' – The Times

This is **not** a love story.

Solitaire

Alice Oseman

My name is Tori Spring. I like to sleep and I like to blog. Last year I had friends. Things were very different, I guess, but that's all over now.

Now there's Solitaire. And Michael Holden.

I don't know what Solitaire are trying to do. And I don't care about Michael Holden. I really don't.

"*The Catcher in the Rye* for the digital age" – *The Times*

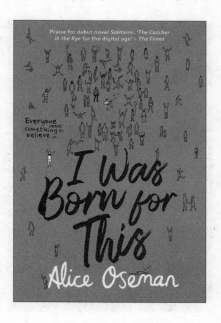

Everyone needs something to believe in...

I Was Born for This

Alice Oseman

For Angel, life is about one thing: The Ark – a pop-rock trio of teenage boys taking the world by storm. Being part of The Ark's fandom has given her everything she loves – her friend Juliet, her dreams, her place in the world.

Jimmy owes everything to The Ark. He's their frontman – and playing in a band with his mates is all he ever dreamed of doing.

But dreams don't always turn out the way you think and when Jimmy and Angel are unexpectedly thrust together they find out how strange and surprising facing up to reality can be.

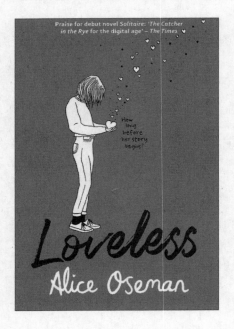

Georgia has never been in love, never kissed anyone, never even had a crush. As she starts university, Georgia makes a plan to find love. But when her actions wreak havoc among her friends she questions why romance seems so easy for other people yet not for her. With new terms thrown at her – asexual, aromantic – Georgia is more uncertain about her feelings than ever. Is she destined to remain loveless? Or has she been looking for the wrong thing all along?

Read the Heartstopper novellas...

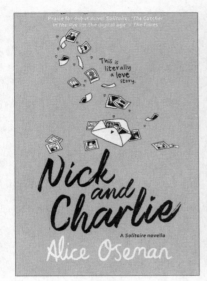

Read Alice's graphic novel series...